Make It Without You

Healing in Cincy
Book 2

Elleese Black

Contents

Make It Without You

Healing in Cincy Book 2
A single dad, age gap, and second chance at love book

Disclaimer

While I intended each book in this series to hold on its own, it's important to note that each book in this series is interconnected. Before diving into Emily's book, I highly recommend reading The Night We Met to avoid any spoilers or confusion as storylines overlap.

This book contains parental abandonment/neglect, the death of three characters (not overly descriptive), cancer, and grief. Emily's book is not short on the emotional factor or the spice.

She will heal.

But it takes her a couple of years.

*There is talk of custody and court hearings and while I'm not a lawyer I did my best to adhere to Ohio law.

Content Warnings

Death of three characters
Grief
Cancer
Parental Abandonment/Neglect

Playlist

Perfect Day by Hoku
Saturn by Sleeping At Last
Dark Blue by Jack's Mannequin
Cruel World by Lana Del Rey
Video Games by Lana Del Rey
Violin Concerto No. 5 in A Major, K. 219 "Turkish": I.
Allegro aperto by Wolfgang Amadeus Mozart
If Tonight Is My Last by Laura Izibor
Save You by Matthew Perryman Jones
I and Love and You by The Avett Brothers
Make It Without You by Andrew Belle
Feels Like Letting Go by Matthew Perryman Jones
Some Streets Lead Nowhere by Matthew Ryan
Quiet In My Town by Civil Twilight
If I Should Go Before You by City and Colour
Mmm... by Laura Izibor
Watch The Wind Blow By by Tim McGraw
Never Let Me Go by Florence & The Machine
Spectrum by Zedd, Matthew Koma
Where's My Love - Alternate Version by SYML

Lemonworld by The National
Wicked Games by The Weeknd
Feels Like I'm Home by Ross Copperman
Ave Maria (Violin Solo) by Franz Schubert
Hunger by Ross Copperman
When I Was Younger by Liz Lawrence
Cherry Wine - Live by Hozier
Bitch, Don't Kill My Vibe by Kendrick Lamar
Drive by Miley Cyrus
Slow Show by The National

make it

WITHOUT YOU

HEALING IN CINCY

ELLEESE BLACK

*To those who sat in the hands of grief as the world moved
around them in a chaotic web
of music and color.*

This one's for you.

Emily
2007

The First Meeting

"**E**mily, sweetie! You're going to be late for your first day!" My mom's muffled calls out from downstairs and travels through my closed bedroom door.

I blow out a nervous breath as I stand in front of my floor-length mirror Mia Thermopolis style. My chameleon persona has me dressed in simple clothing. A dark navy cotton dress that hits right below my knees with cap sleeves and white Keds. My thick hair falls down my back and is pushed back with a navy-striped headband.

It's my first day of high school with a new backpack, a fresh packet of ink pens, and never-used erasers on mechanical pencils. Really. It should be what dreams are made of.

Not my dreams.

I've been a loner in school for as long as I can remember. Add being in a new environment and my nerves shoot through the roof.

When I was in middle school I could handle it. Only

three grades were in that school and I excelled amazingly well. I had the same kids in each of my classes, so I was able to get used to the familiarity of seeing them every day. But, high school? Where everyone has known each other since grade school? And I have to warm up to different kids in each of my classes. The thought that I'll be alone until graduation has me considering begging my mom to have me home-schooled.

It's not easy being a little fish in a big pond. But my parents always told me that people can smell fear. Like sharks in the ocean when they can smell blood.

Here goes nothing.

I grab my backpack from the back of my desk chair and pick up my violin case that's right next to it. See, loner. Nerd. Music geek. But as long as I have a book or my violin with me, I don't consider myself to ever be alone.

With one last longing glance at my room, which provided me with solitude for the majority of the summer, I heave an exaggerated sigh as I walk downstairs into the kitchen where my parents await. Should I join the drama department?

"Oh, honey. I can't believe we have a high schooler among us. Can you believe that Mark?" My mom gushes when she sees me.

My Dad looks up from his newspaper and gives me a wink. "It was bound to happen sometime, Christie. Next thing you know, she'll be off to college and married with kids."

"Mark!?" My mom says with mock shock. "None of that. I just want her to stay my baby forever. Can you do that sweetie?" She asks with a little smile on her face.

"Does that mean I get to stay in my room forever?" I counter-offer.

She shakes her head and her smile vanishes. "No. Now eat some breakfast, you don't want to be late for the bus."

Gloria, our housekeeper, places some toast and bacon in front of me.

"Thank you."

"You're welcome, sweet girl."

Gloria has been with my family since before I was born. While my parents were getting their careers started in New York, she was with them. When I was born and got older, my parents decided they wanted to raise me in a more home-like environment and Gloria came with them. She taught me a lot when Mom and Dad were too busy building up their portfolios to get ahead in their jobs. They work as lawyers with the public relations teams for celebrities in New York. I don't begrudge them for it because I was able to build a pretty solid relationship with her.

Once I finish breakfast, with my stomach in knots, my family walks me to the front door to see me off. Mom was way more emotional than I expected her to be. And I understand as I'm an only child about to start high school as the new kid. But I know Dad and Gloria will reassure her that I'll be fine at school.

I'm walking towards the bus stop when I see a lone figure there. My nerves come alive again.

My hands start to sweat.

It's too early to talk to new people.

Is he a freshman? Does he even go to school? Maybe I should keep a safe distance from him just in case.

"Hi," the lone figure says to me when I come to a stop a foot away from him.

I give him a half-wave. "Hi."

"I'm James," he volunteers when I say nothing else. "What's your name?"

After a pause, I respond, "Emily."

"Are you a freshman?"

"Yes. Are you?" My conversation skills are lacking. But it's hard to talk with kids my age when I grew up being treated like an adult.

He shakes his head. "No. I'm a sophomore."

Disappointment ensues. Wait, why am I disappointed? "Oh."

"I think we're neighbors," James observes.

"We are?" I perk up at that.

"Yep. My family's house is right next door to yours." He points down the street towards the direction of our houses.

"Oh..." I'm sure my parents would have mentioned kids my age living in the neighborhood.

"We were out of town for most of the summer. So that's probably why you didn't know." He says matter-of-factly with a shrug of his shoulders.

"I was out of town too," I say, wondering why he keeps talking to me and questioning why I can't string a full sentence together.

The roar of the bus turning down our street has my heart rate kicking into overdrive. My hands begin to sweat again and I have to adjust my hold on the handle of my violin case.

"Did you want to sit next to me on the bus?" His offer is so kind it makes me want to cry. Right here on the sidewalk.

I should say no. My loner status and all. But maybe, just maybe, it wouldn't be so bad to have one friend at this school.

I find my head nodding in quick motion. "Okay."

The bus pulls up, and James lets me on first. I pick a seat that's not in the middle of the bus, but not in the front and slide in. My violin rests against the bus frame while my backpack comes to rest on my lap. James slides onto the seat next to me and puts his backpack on the bus floor. The jolt of the bus pulling forward to pick up more kids is terrifying, but also what a normal school experience should be like.

I never experienced this in New York. We lived a street over from my school so I either walked or my parents had a car drop me off and pick me up. A little part of me was envious of the kids who got to experience an early bus ride to school and a boisterous ride home at the end of the day.

The bus makes five more stops, filling up fairly quickly with the rest of the kids. At that, my knee starts bobbing up and down. It's a nervous habit that I've had forever.

"Nervous?" James asks from next to me.

My gaze collides with James's and my voice comes out soft, as it always does when I'm in an unfamiliar setting. "A little."

"Don't be," he tells me like it's that simple.

James does his best to make conversation with me. But my nerves have taken over my brain so conversation is short at best. And sooner than I hoped, we're pulling up to the school.

"Where's your first class?" He asks me when we're both off the bus.

I unzip my backpack and pull out my class schedule, handing it to him wordlessly.

"Oh, that's right down the hall from my class," he exclaims. "I'll show you where it's at."

"Don't you have friends to get to?" I'm grateful but also confused as to why he's helping me out.

He hands me back my schedule and I tuck it back into the front pocket of my backpack. "I don't have a lot of friends. Well, two friends. Which I guess is all you need."

He admits with a shrug of his shoulders and I instantly feel bad.

"Oh. Sorry."

"Don't be. They're plenty of friends for me."

"But don't you play sports?" He looks like the kind of boy who plays sports.

"Yep!"

"Oh." My observation of him is correct. Because he'll have his jock friends and I'll have no one. Despite my loner status, the thought of having one friend made me happy.

I'm such a contradiction it's annoying.

James walks me to where my class is supposed to be. I finally get a better look at him. He's cute for a boy, tall, if not a little too leggy, his pants are a teensy bit too big and short on him, and he's still got his baby fat on his face. His blond hair is overdue for a trim and his brown eyes are bright and alive. It's as if he glows sunshine even on the cloudiest of days.

"Well, hopefully, we can have lunch together," James tells me with a hopeful lilt to his voice as we stop in front of my classroom. "We can sit together and I'll introduce you to my friends."

"Yeah. That sounds good," I say even though I'm absolutely terrified to meet more new people.

The bell rings signaling for students to get to class.

"Gotta get going. I'll see you later, Emily." He parts with a wave.

"Yeah. See ya." I say with a small wave as I watch him become absorbed by the other students in the hallway until I can no longer see him.

Emily

I'm still blown away by how different middle and high school are. In middle school, we had six classes a day for forty-five minutes each. In high school, we have four classes that are an hour and fifteen minutes each. So staying awake and focusing on one subject for an extended time is draining.

I wished I could say I cliqued with the kids in my classes. Their childhood bond was easy to spot when they took their seats. A few kind girls tried to include me in their conversation but I stared at them blankly as I still have no idea how to talk to kids my age.

Am I destined to not make friends the instant I walk into a classroom? Possibly. I shouldn't have anything to worry about. It's the first day.

Until lunch rolls around and the panic sets in. Who do I sit with at lunch? Do I go to the library? Do I hide and eat in the bathroom?

But the panic recedes when I spot James pacing outside of the cafeteria. The relief I feel at seeing him is evident.

Although I love being a loner I'd rather be a loner with him by my side.

"Hey," he greets me when I'm a few steps away.

"Hi."

"How's your first day going?"

We walk toward one of the eight lunch lines that are already filled with students ready to get some fuel to finish the rest of the day. "It's okay. Kind of scary, I guess."

"That's high school. Some days I'm still scared to walk into the school. I hope you don't mind, but I told my two friends, Liam and Kamryn, that they could join us for lunch."

I swallow down my nerves and nod. "Yeah. That's okay."

Once we get our food and settle in at a table, a boy with a tan earned from spending time outside and a girl with a caramel complexion and curly hair, plop down in seats at our table.

"First day blows," the boy says with defeat in his tone.

"Emily, this is Liam and Kamryn," James introduces the newcomers to me.

"Hi," I shyly wave to them in greeting.

"He's only saying that because he has to retake a class," the girl, Kamryn, says. Her brown eyes are a shade lighter than her hair and I instantly take comfort in the calm vibe she exudes.

"What?" James says shocked. "Coach will flip if he finds out."

Kamryn turns her attention to me when she sees my confusion. "They both play football...and baseball. Junior varsity. But sports nonetheless."

I nod my head as if I understand. "Gotcha."

"So you're a freshman?" She asks while the boys continue with whatever they're talking about.

"Yeah," I'm sure my response is barely audible over the volume in the cafeteria. But she nods like she heard me.

"I have a sister who's a couple years younger than me. Liam does too. So you all should be in high school together." The light in her expression as she talks about her younger sister is why I always wished I had a younger sibling or, at least, an older sibling.

"That's cool. What are their names?"

"My sister is Jaclyn. But, everyone calls her Jax. Liam's sister in Angela, but everyone calls her Angie. Do you have any siblings?"

I shake my head slowly. "No. It's just me."

Kamryn gives me a face of sorry. "Well you should come hang out with me...and these guys. They're always together. Then again, Liam and I are always together."

I give her a quizzical look.

"No. Not like that. Liam and I have been friends since elementary school. Our dads work together. It spiraled to our family's vacationing together and me introducing him to baseball."

A pang of jealousy hits at the realization that they've been friends for almost a decade. What's it like to have a friend who knows almost everything about you?

"Oh." That makes sense.

The rest of the lunch period is spent with them getting to know me. Asking what I like, and what I don't like, and listening to Liam and James go back and forth with playful jabs. I'm a welcome bystander as I witness the easy-going friendship between the three of them.

Before I know it, lunch is over and we separate for our

final two classes. My excitement is barely contained as I walk into my third class.

Orchestra.

Orchestra is my favorite class. I've been waiting for this class since I stepped foot in the school. It's even more comforting knowing I'm in a group of freshmen so we're not too overwhelmed.

When my parents introduced me to the violin in elementary school, I didn't love it. I assumed it was a way to keep me occupied while they were working obscene hours. But it wasn't until the night we saw *Phantom of the Opera* on Broadway. We were sitting up in the balcony at a show when I was about ten and instead of watching the show, I watched the orchestra in the pit. The strings moved me. From then on I've been entranced.

As a freshman, my classes are relatively easy. I took honors classes in middle school and luckily I was able to continue with them in high school. But music is simple. We spend the majority of the time doing introductions when I'm just itching to unzip my case and play. Unfortunately, we never get to that and the little light I had when I stepped foot in the expansive room dims by the time the bell rings.

I file out of the classroom and walk down the music hall to my final class of the day. My fourth class is one that I'm excited about.

Honors English.

I know that having two lawyer parents would make me more interested in history, or possibly math, but I've loved English and reading and writing since forever.

And as the groans from the other students sound around the room as the teacher mentions reports on our summer reading, I feel joy. Not that the other kids didn't do the readings, okay maybe a little, but because this is the first class where the teacher is actually teaching.

With the hustle and bustle of that, my first day is over. Now I just have to remember my bus number.

~

"How many brothers did you say you had?" I ask him as we wait for the bus.

We've been in school for two days and James and I are slowly making more conversation. I'm still slow to open up and his patience is a godsend. But still, in these two days, he's made me laugh more than anyone has in a while.

"I have an older brother and three younger brothers. Brandon is nineteen and is in his second year of college, Malcolm is nine, Evan is six, and then the baby is Ford who's three."

I look at him like he's sprouted three heads. "There's five of you? I can't imagine—you must strive for quiet."

"I don't mind the noise." James starts as he plucks wild-flowers from the ground and links them together to make a bracelet. "But the quiet finally gives me a chance to think, to breathe. So I don't regret the noise but I appreciate the quiet probably more than I should."

James and I both came to the bus stop early. I think we made an unspoken pact to talk before we went our separate ways at school. I'm learning that we're both introverts but once we get to talking the nerves are soothed away.

"I always wished I had siblings. It would've made for an even more enjoyable childhood. Especially during the summers and even Christmas..." My voice trails off as James grabs my arm and links the daisy chain around my wrist.

The gesture is so tiny, but causes my heart to skip a

beat. I look up at James as he continues to look at my wrist. His cheeks have taken on a rosy hue.

"You remind me of a wildflower. Soft but strong and pretty."

"Thank you," I tell him.

"You're welcome."

Emily

The rest of the week went the same as my first day. Having James to sit with on the bus and his friends at lunch, has made me rethink my choice to stay a loner.

"Are you coming to the football game tonight?" James asks as we're walking down the hallway after the last class of the day.

It's the first JV home game of the year. The energy throughout the school was infectious and made it difficult for anyone to focus.

"Um, I wasn't planning to. Why do you ask?"

It's taken me a bit to warm up to talking with James. He's the first boy I've had as a friend. He's my first friend in general as my shy personality scares people off.

James scratches the back of his neck. It's something that I notice he does when he's nervous to ask a question. We may have only been friends for a few days, but he's one of the best friends I've ever had. "No reason."

Deciding to be brave because I think that's what we both need, I ask him. "Did you want me to come?"

"You don't have to. But if you want you can sit with Kamryn." He rushes out as if he's afraid I'll turn him down. The thought crossed my mind as I'm not used to socializing with kids from school. My school spirit level equates to a trip to the dentist to get my wisdom teeth pulled.

"I'll come to the game."

He releases a huff of air before responding. "Cool. Is it okay if I text Kamryn your number?"

James and I exchanged numbers after the third day of school. He mainly texts me and I text back emoticons. I'm a terrible texter but with James, I think I can get better.

"Sure."

"Okay." Our steps slow down right before we get to the exit doors to the buses. "Well, I'll see you after the game."

"Yep. Good luck James."

"Thanks, Em." He's slow to backup and I lift my hand in a small wave.

Walking to the bus, I mentally run through a list of what I want to do this weekend. But since I'm now going to a football game tonight, I'll have to rearrange some things. Is that a bad thing? I can't figure that out yet.

Unknown number: Hey, it's Kamryn.

Me: Oh, hey.

Kamryn: Did you want to sit with me at the game?

Me: That'd be great.

Kamryn: Awesome! I usually sit with Liam and James' family, so you'll be a nice mix- in.

Me: Thanks? I think.

Kamryn: It's a good thing. Did you want a ride to the game?

Me: If it's out of the way you don't have to.

Kamryn: It's no problem. I get a ride with Liam's parents, so I'll ask them if it's okay.

Me: If you're sure…

Kamryn: 100% sure. You live next door to James, right?

Me: Yeah.

Kamryn: That's perfect. Their families usually hang out at James's family's house anyways.

Me: Okay. Cool.

Kamryn: Pick you up around 530?

Me: Sounds good.

"MOM? DAD? I'M HOME!" I announce when I walk through the front door. They must be in their office or still at work because the house is dead quiet. I stand in the foyer longer than normal, waiting for any acknowledgment, when I realize that they must be at the office. My stomach growls in protest and I decide to feed myself before getting some homework done before the game.

As I walk towards the kitchen the smell of chocolate fills the air. That can only mean one thing. "Hi, Gloria."

She pulls a baking sheet out of the oven and places it on the island behind her. "Hi, sweetheart. How has your first week of school been?"

I set my backpack on a barstool and slide onto an empty one next to it. "It was good. Busy. Exhausting. I don't think I want to go back." I say only half kidding.

School has only been in for a week and I'm loaded down with homework. They're mainly worksheets and reading assignments, so I don't mind that too much.

"Have you made any friends?" Her focus is on removing the chocolate chip cookies from the sheet and onto a cooling rack so she can't see my smile.

"Yeah. A few."

"That's great. I always worry about you."

Our eyes meet and a mutual look of adoration passes between us. "I know you do. Speaking of...where's Mom and Dad?"

Gloria looks down in regret. "They had to fly back to New York for the weekend."

"Oh," I say, unable to hide my disappointment. "Work stuff. I get it."

"Did you want me to make you some dinner?" Gloria asks and puts her hand on top of mine in a comforting gesture. It's a gesture that usually soothes me but instead makes me want to cry.

I blink fast and swallow hard. "Please."

"Of course, sweetheart." Gloria busies herself with some dinner while I unpack my backpack to get some homework done. "Do you have plans tonight?"

"Yeah. I'm going to a football game with a friend."

"A boy?"

She's not completely wrong. "Not exactly."

"Does it have something to do with the boy next door?"

Crap! How does she know everything? Even my own parents haven't pointed that out. But that would also involve them being out of the office or in town when I get home from school. "What? Who? I mean...I don't know who you're talking about."

"Mm-hmm," Gloria says. She turns back to making dinner and I swear I see a smile lift her cheeks.

James

I like her. As a friend. We barely know each other, but at the same time, I feel like I've known her for forever.

It took more effort on my part to break out of my shell just to talk to her. Despite what people may think, I'm a pure introvert. So like I said, it was a lot of work on my part.

But she's coming to the game tonight. I know this because Kamryn texted me. I think she knows I'm crushing on her.

Wait. Do boys even have crushes?

If so, I have one.

A crush, that is.

I walk in the direction of the cafeteria as the school is slowly emptying. This is where we have our pre-game team meeting and our team dinner. The tradition started years ago and has thankfully continued ever since.

"Did Kam text you?" I ask Liam as I slide into a chair next to him.

He fumbles with his phone. "No. Why? Did she text you?"

I can't help the laugh that slips out. "You've got it bad, dude."

"Shut up." The tips of his ears turn red and I decide that's enough indirect teasing for the day.

Liam has had a crush on Kamryn for about a year. We were all at a friend's house for his birthday and someone had the genius idea to play spin the bottle. It was Liam's turn and the way luck was on his side, the bottle landed on Kam. They both brushed it off. At least Kamryn did. But Liam didn't think I knew how that kiss set it off for him until I saw him looking at her with his love eyes. Now it's fun to rile him up where she's concerned.

"Kam said she'll be at the game. And I asked Emily if she would come too. So I think they're gonna ride in with each other."

He turns his stare on me. But I shut him down. Or at least I try to. "Who's got it bad, now?"

"Shut up."

"ALRIGHT BOYS! First game of the season! Let's get out there and do our best!" Coach yells in the locker room. I think it's part of his pep-talk. He's not an overly emotional guy. And for a bunch of young teenagers who also hate emotion, it works for us.

We all hoot and holler and then run out on the field for warm-ups and then the game is starting.

"I see your girlfriend here." Liam teases from next to me.

"Funny. I see yours here too." I tease back.

That shuts him up real fast.

But me, I'm just going to worry about the game.

And not at the fact that a pretty girl is sitting in the stands.

With Kamryn.

And my parents.

Crap. I think I'm too nervous to play.

I think I forgot how to throw a football.

Just my luck, that of all times I get even more nervous than the last.

"Head in the game, James. We'll see them later." Liam says right after we break from the huddle.

He's right. Besides, I don't even know if Emily feels the same way as I do.

When the referees call the captains to the center of the field, Liam and I walk arm-in-arm with two other team-mates. Since we have home-field advantage, we get to call the coin toss.

We win the toss and elect to receive. Hands are shaken and then our receiving team runs out onto the field to begin.

After a ten-yard drive, it's time for offense. The guys and I head out onto the field. We read the sign from our coach and I call out the play, dropping back I scan the field and launch it to where Liam is supposed to be.

He catches it. Because of course, he does.

Two more plays and we score the first touchdown of the game.

I'm not saying this just because I'm on the team. But if junior varsity had the playing field that varsity had, then we'd totally win it all.

Emily

They won the game. And it's not like it was the championship game or anything. But winning the first game of the season is a big deal. So I've been told.

Sitting with my new friend and my new friend's family, I don't feel so alone anymore.

When the game is over, we all wait by the gym for the boys to come out. I'm not nervous or anything. But my body does have a mind of its own.

"Stop fidgeting," Kamryn scolds.

I stop moving altogether and drop my hands. Looking at her from the corner of my eye. "I didn't realize I was."

Kamryn nods her head like she knows. And it's a little unnerving that she can see right through me.

"What?" I ask, feeling incredibly nervous and unsure.

Kamryn looks over at James's parents and then pulls me off to the side. "It's okay, you know?"

"What's okay?"

"If you like James," she tells me as if we're discussing taking over the world.

"I don't—"

"Yes you do," Kamryn cuts me off. "And for what it's worth, I think he likes you too."

I perk up at the confession. "How do you know?"

"I've known James longer than I've known Liam, and I've never seen him act like this around any other girl. Trust me, there have not been a lot. There's actually been nobody he's ever dated. But he's different around you. I know this is only high school, but I have a hunch that this could be something spectacular between the two of you."

Kamryn's words float around in my mind until the boys walk out of the locker room.

My gaze instantly locks in on James. Like it has since the first day of school.

Do I like James? I feel safe around him. I know that when he's around I never want him or I to have to leave. But, like? Is a crush the same thing as like? If so, then I have THE biggest crush on James. But what do I do? I've never even kissed a boy. I mean, it makes sense. I'm only fourteen, well fifteen in February.

But still.

Am I ready to admit that I have a crush on James? I'll wait for him to say it first. Yeah, I like that.

"You came!" James exclaims when he's right in front of me.

We do that awkward one-armed hug thing.

"I did. You did great." I'm assuming that's the correct thing to say. Judging by his smile, it is.

"Thanks. So are you coming over to my house?" He looks so nervous. Is my nervousness projecting onto him? Or is it the other way around?

"Yes. Only if you want me to though." ·

"I do. It'll be fun."

After chatting idly at the school, we all pile into the vehicles. Me, riding with James and his family, and Kamryn riding with Liam's family to James's house.

I'm now officially nervous. I haven't spoken a lot with James's parents. I sat tucked by Kamryn's side for the entirety of the game so the conversation didn't go further than the simple greetings. But now they do their best to include me in the conversation once we're in the car. For the most part, I just observe the easy-going nature between James and his parents. A pang of jealousy rears its head, but I squash it down real quick.

Ten minutes later we're pulling into the driveway at James's place. I look next door, as we're walking inside, at my house noting the dark interior. No life is being lived in the confines of those four walls.

The inside of his parent's house is homier than I could have ever imagined. It's a big house, don't get me wrong. But seeing that it's warm and cozy and not stuffy like I would've expected is comforting. James and Liam get to pouring drinks and getting snacks for us and then the four of us are heading to the movie room.

"So how'd you like the game?" Liam asks once we're all settled in.

"For my first football game ever, you two didn't disappoint. Although I had no idea what was going on."

"You're a football newbie?" Liam asks in wonder.

I shrug my shoulders in a non-committal response. "It was never something that came up in my family."

"What do your parents do?" James asks from next to me.

"They're both high-profile lawyers. They had to fly back to New York to work on a last-minute case."

"I'm sorry," James says sincerely.

I hold his gaze for a few seconds before responding. "It's okay. I'm used to it."

And that's the honest-to-God truth. It hurts that that's the actual truth. But I can't do much about it.

"So what movie are we watching?" Kamryn asks, breaking up the emotion. I send her a grateful smile for putting us back on track.

BY THE TIME the movie ends, Kamryn and Liam are passed out next to one another. I started dozing off too, but I managed to stop myself.

"You wanna watch another movie?" James asks me.

I shake my head. "Dance with me?"

A small smile graces James's face. After putting on some music, he stands up and offers me his hand. Pulling me into him, we start to sway to the music.

It's official. I like James. The crush I didn't think could be a crush? It's real. I like him, like him. And that's crazy. I don't know the first thing about relationships. Do I ride this out and hope this crush will pass or wait for James to make a move? Do we just wait until we're older?

It's decided that I'll wait for James to make a move. But if he takes too long I'm taking this into my own hands.

"Your heart is beating super fast," I say so low that I'm surprised James even heard me.

I hear him swallow it's that loud. But I'm trying to play it as cool as I can.

"I'm nervous," James finally responds.

"Nervous about what?" I ask him and pull back to search his face for something. Anything.

"You. You make me more nervous than I've ever been.

Emily, I know we don't know each other that well, but..."
He's stalling.

"But what?" I ask him. The suspense is killing me.

"I like you."

He said it! And now it's my turn to be speechless.

James ducks down so he can look into my eyes. "Say something."

"I like you too," I can feel my face heating up.

"So where does that leave us?"

And that's the million-dollar question. Most of the time when a guy says that he likes a girl, he does the complete opposite to woo her, and that in turn woos her. Don't ask me why or how that works, it just does.

"I think we take it day by day. And if this turns into something more, then we'll have to go slow because you'd be my first boyfriend. That kind of freaks me out." I blurt completely nervous.

"Why does it freak you out?"

"Because you turn me into a blubbering mess. And I don't want to ruin what we have right now. Somehow, I know that this has the potential to be more. I'm doing it again." I hide my face against his chest.

James's chuckle vibrates through me and his arm on my back pulls me closer to him. "I don't mind."

When the credits end and the screen fades to black, James and I spend the rest of the night dancing in the home theater while Kam and Liam stay passed out in the theater chairs. My heart rate is back to normal speed as my mind processes all that happened.

I'm no longer a loner.

James

If I were a character in *Glee*, I'd probably wake up singing with a smile on my face as I jump and skip around while getting ready. I'm not in *Glee*. But I do wake up with a huge ass smile on my face. And I also don't sing. Which is a good thing because I can't carry a tune to save my life.

I have no words for last night. When school started, I didn't think I'd end up with a sort of girlfriend less than a week into school. My feelings for Emily aren't forced. It's like my being friends with Liam. It's natural. Of course, I don't have any romantic feelings for Liam. Liam is more like my brother and I don't have sibling-like feelings towards Emily.

Okay. Back to my feelings about Emily. She's not like any of the other girls that I grew up with. I know it's a cliche reason, but it's true. Emily is different. She's a good kind of quiet. Almost too quiet.

But in the short amount of time that we've spent around each other, I'm learning that when she opens up she's a rambler, a chatterbox, and a library of never-ending information. I noticed she carries her violin around almost everywhere and always has a book with her. They're kind of like her safety blanket. I've tracked that her knee bounces when she's nervous and excited.

This is what I've observed and what I've come to like about her.

"Hi, honey," my mom greets, breaking me from my Emily internal thoughts. The sound of my mom's coffee cup being placed on the table is a sign she's giving me her full attention.

"Morning, Mom." I reply, kissing her on the top of her head.

Three. Two. One.

"So Emily," she says by way of starting a conversation. "She seems like a sweetheart."

I look over to my dad who hides a smile behind his coffee mug. So much for the bro code.

"Uh yeah. She's pretty cool." What else do I say? That I'm kind of, sort of, possibly obsessed with her? It's gotta be puppy love. It'll fade soon.

I sit down at the table with my breakfast which is way too quiet for a Saturday morning. Both of my parents are looking at each other and then me with little smiles on their faces.

"What?" I ask.

"Are you hanging out with Emily today?"

"Maybe. Why?" They're acting weird. "You know what, I am going to hang out with Emily. You're both creeping me out."

My parents high-five each other from across the table.

"I'm finishing my food in my room. You can plan the wedding when I'm out of earshot." I joke.

But the look on my mom's face confirms that she's not joking.

"Mom!"

"What?! I won't plan anything until you're six months into your relationship. But I will tell you now, James Michael, that I do not want to be a grandmother so soon," she gives me that mother look that makes my brothers and I cower before she softens her gaze. "Although, I'm positive that you and Emily will have beautiful babies."

My face flames and I cover my ears with my hands. "Mom! Dad stop her!"

"You know how your Mom gets James. Best let her get it out of her system," the rustling of the newspaper being reopened is a good sign. "But I was wondering. Do you want a big or small wedding?"

I rush out of the kitchen with flaming cheeks all the while my parents are cackling at the table.

Parents.

My phone buzzes when I walk into my room with a text.

I set my food on my dresser and plop down on my bed, seeing it's from Emily.

E: Good morning.

Me: Morning. How's your morning so far?

E: Considering I just woke up not too long ago, I'd say it's off to a slow start.

Me: What?! Whatever had you sleeping in so late?

E: Some guy.

Me: Tell me his name. And I'll kick his butt.

> E: What if I said you knew him?

She's adorable.

> Me: I'll still do it.

> E: Fine. It's you. You kept me up.

> Me: *pats self on back*

> E: *rolls eyes*

> Me: What are your plans for today?

> E: I'm gonna get some homework done. And then practice for a recital that's coming up.

> Me: Do you want some company?

> E: Sure. Give me an hour?

> Me: Of course. See you in a bit, Em.

> E: XO

To pass the time until I'm with Emily, I scarf down my breakfast, clean up my room, and take my dirty clothes to the laundry room. Fingers crossed my little brother will add his clothes to the pile and start a load. It's what little brothers are for. It's time he learns how to do his—meaning our—laundry.

I finally change the sheets on my bed, but not because my mom has been bugging me to do it. Okay. Yes. I change my sheets because she's been pestering me for weeks.

I put all of the accumulated water bottles from my room in the recycle bin. Rumor has it, we teenagers like to "collect" water bottles in our room. It's a known fact. My older brother had a whole bunch in his room too. This reminds me that I haven't bothered him in a while so I need to call him.

Walking back into my room I check the time on my phone, I see that it's about time to head over to Emily's house. I hop in the shower to clean off the sleep along with the smell of cleaning products. Once I'm dressed and smell presentable, I gather my books and book bag.

"I'm going to Emily's," I tell my parents when I'm back downstairs and head towards the front door.

"Have fun. Be safe!" My mom jokingly yells.

My feet come to a stop and I look at my parents with pleading eyes before I leave the embarrassment behind for a little while. A light and giddy feeling swims through my body and leads me to Emily's house. I bound up the steps with a hop and ring the doorbell.

Emily answers the door after a few seconds. Her hair is thrown in a messy bun and she's wearing a Columbia sweatshirt that swallows her petite frame. The black leggings she wears mold to her legs and the thick white socks she wears has me believing she's preparing for a cold front to blow through.

"Hi." She says with a shy smile.

So. Adorable. "Hi."

"Come in." Emily says as she opens the door wider for me.

It's the first time I've ever seen the inside of her house. Even with the people that lived here before her family, my family never ventured over here. It's grand. But also warm.

The entryway is painted a muted blue with oakwood floors and a mosaic runner leading to what I'm assuming is the living room. A sitting room is right off to the left with stiff-looking furniture, an unused fireplace, and a coffee table that looks like it was freshly waxed.

Emily closes the door behind me. "Do you want something to drink?"

"Sure."

She walks toward the kitchen with me following.

The warmth of the house doesn't hit until we reach the living room that opens to the kitchen. An expensive, but worn, black leather couch takes up the majority of the living room. Seasonal pillows are spaced haphazardly on the seats with throw blankets in baskets and one crumpled on the couch. Pictures decorate the walls. Some of Emily and portrait shots of the city I'm assuming she's from, along with some beach stills.

"Is water okay?"

"Yeah. That's great. Thank you." My attention moves to the spacious kitchen that overlooks the family room. It's quiet. Way too quiet for a Saturday. "Is it always like this here?" My house is the complete opposite if my brothers aren't still asleep.

Emily turns to answer me with a tinge of pink on her cheeks. "No. Not all of the time. My parents are usually home. But like I said last night, they had to fly to New York at the last minute. And our housekeeper only works for a few hours on the weekends."

"So you're home alone a lot?"

Her shoulders lift up in a shrug. "Yeah. But it's really not a big deal."

I can tell by the tightness in her response that it is a big deal, but I choose to let it go. For now. "Well, I am now claiming myself as your weekend buddy."

"A weekend buddy?" Emily asks with a quirk of her eyebrow as she places my water in front of me.

"Yeah. Every weekend we hang out. Do homework, study, practice, read, watch movies, and eat food. A weekend buddy."

"That sounds like a normal relationship." Emily can't hide the smile even if she wanted to.

I fake think about that for a second. "Woah! I like that better."

"You're silly. Come on. Let's get to our homework."

I follow Emily up the stairs to her room. Which is double the size of mine.

"Wow! Your room is huge."

"I guess. When we went back to New York for the summer, my parents had my room remodeled. They wanted me to have a study room/ practice room. So this part of my room is completely soundproof."

"Really? That was thoughtful of them," I tell her.

"Yeah. It was."

Emily rifles through her backpack for her books and sets them on her desk. I'm sure she can feel the hole I'm burning in her face as I wait for her to meet my eye.

"You can set up on the couch and use the coffee table if you want."

Her mood has shifted fast and I wonder if it has to do with her parents. I don't want to pry but I want the playful girl from last night, the one who asked me to dance as the movie credits rolled. I look at the girl before me, burying herself in her work. Is it a mask? Is she hiding her pain? Does she wish her parents were more involved? I want to know her.

"Emily?" I have to tread lightly.

"Yeah?" She responds without looking at me. Her pencil moves as she writes down notes that probably won't make sense.

"Are you okay?"

"I'm fine. I just want to study." She quickly dismisses me.

"Sure. Fine." I'll table it for now. But I keep that part to myself.

I've never had friends whose parents were gone a lot and I'm not sure how to manage. But I think I'll approach her the way I would a skittish animal. And hopefully, she won't be so afraid to open up to me.

Emily

I dismissed James way too easily. I know that. But how do I admit that my parents being away so much affects me? Because the only person who knows how I feel about my parents being gone a lot is Gloria.

This is the part of my life that I was scared of James to see. What does he think of my lackluster homelife? Does he think less of me? Does he worry about me?

I look at the clock by my desk and notice that two hours have flown by. My last meal was hours ago and I'm starving. I know that James is too. He's a football player for crying out loud. And he's super tall. I peek over my shoulder and see he's engrossed with his studying.

When I opened the door and saw him patiently waiting on the front step, my heart about fell to my stomach. I'm new to this dating thing. And being around boys is a completely new territory for me. I may have ruined what little easy-going nature we had when I snapped at him.

So I spent the last half hour re-reading the same two pages of my History textbook until I couldn't take it anymore.

Taking a deep breath I stand up and walk towards where he's sitting. He doesn't notice me until I'm seated next to him. I tuck my leg under my thigh as I pick at my too-long fingernails and wait for my voice to make its way up.

"Hi," I say to him, awkward, even for me.

"Hello."

Rip off the band-aid Emily. "I'm sorry for how I spoke to you earlier. I kind of dismissed you."

"That's okay, Em."

He's too good for me. Too forgiving. And maybe that has to do with how he grew up.

"No. It's not. I just...I get kind of guarded about my parents and how little they're around. That wasn't fair to you for me to dismiss you like that."

"Apology accepted."

"Okay. Cool. Are you hungry?"

"Starving." James quickly answers, followed by the grumbling of his stomach. He throws his pencil in his textbook and closes it, placing it on the small table in front of us.

"I can order a pizza or two," I offer.

"Are you sure?"

"Positive."

I find the number online and order us two large pepperoni pizzas. "Alright. Thank you." I hang up the phone and turn to James. "Fifteen to twenty minutes," I announce to him.

"What do we do until then?" James asks me.

"I want to show you something." I stand up and make my way to the built-in bookcase that was installed. My parents made me promise not to tell anyone. But I feel safe around James and I know I can trust him. I find the book that's hiding the doorknob. Twisting, I push the door open.

"Woah!" James exclaims.

Once the door slides open, I hold my hand out to him. When James takes my hand I lead him up the short flight of stairs.

"My parents had this installed as a sort of safe place for me. I've always loved the night and being surrounded by it." I explain to him as we get comfortable in the small room. It's sort of like an attic but with a huge skylight. I took the liberty of getting a thick mattress pad, blankets, and tons of pillows up here.

"It's like a cloud," James muses as he settles into the space by my side.

"Yeah. It's perfect for me."

"THIS IS REALLY GOOD PIZZA." James praises between bites.

It really is. "It's from this hole-in-the-wall place that my parents found one day. They took me there and I was hooked. Now anytime we get pizza, it's from Frank's."

"I agree. Best pizza I've ever had."

We continue eating in silence until I tap out. "I'm done. I can't eat anymore."

James sends a victorious squirrel-like smile my way. "I was wondering when you were gonna stop."

"Who said this was a competition?" I challenge him.

"I grew up with four brothers. Anything to do with food is a competition."

"I'll keep that in mind."

A comfortable silence washes over us. I take a moment to study James. He's devastatingly, boyishly handsome. He still has some of the baby fat that most fifteen-year-olds have. Have I mentioned how much I love how much taller he is than me?

"Do I have something on my face?" James asks as he wipes at his face with a napkin.

"Oh no. You don't. Sorry. Do you want to watch a movie or something?"

He eyes me warily before getting up and walking to the couch. He plops down and pats the spot next to him, leaving his arm against the back of the couch.

This boy.

I walk over, swipe the remote, and plop down next to him pulling my feet up onto the couch.

"What do you wanna watch?" I ask James and will my racing heart to slow way back down.

"Anything with Paul Walker?"

"You're a fan of the *Fast & Furious* series?" I ask him, hoping that the answer is a resounding yes!

"Who isn't?"

"Exactly! Probably one of the best series ever!"

"A girl after my own heart."

I blush at James's words and press play on *The Fast and the Furious*. Do I lean back on the couch and lean into James? What should I do? James answers that by pulling me into his side.

"That's better," he says.

Calm your freaking racing heart, Emily!!

After mentally telling myself that our feelings for one another are mutual, my heart rate finally slows down. I take in everything. The movie. James sitting next to me.

In a flash, I see the future and he's in it. Scary. We've only been "dating" for like twenty hours. And it's impossible for me to know that James could be the only boy for me. Right?

I mean, my mom and dad met when they were in high school so it's not totally impossible. Although they never talk about their past, they must have such a deep-rooted history that they stand by each other's side through thick and thin.

Emily

The First Date

"So you two are going to get ice cream?" The sound of the turning page of a magazine comes from my bed.

I see Kamryn in the mirror's reflection behind me. She's laying on her stomach with her feet swinging back and forth and came over when I told her James asked me out for an ice cream date. We've been "dating" for about six weeks. When really our dates consist of hanging out between our houses since neither of us can drive.

So when an ice cream shop recently opened within walking distance of our neighborhood and when James wasn't with me he was doing chores around his house, scraping up some extra money to impress me.

His words, not mine.

My outfit is simple. A maxi dress with a thicker skirt and I'll pair it with some Chelsea boots. Since we're still early into winter, I have a thick cardigan that I can wear over top.

Finishing with my hair, I pull it back in a half-up and tie a bow in the back. When I'm done, I plop down on my bed next to Kamryn. "Yep. I shouldn't be nervous. But I am. Totally nervous that is."

My parents are, yet again, absent for the weekend. I've seen them for all of twenty minutes in the last week. They've been so immersed in work that I haven't told them I'm dating anyone. Truthfully, I don't want them to know. I love my parents. I really do. But I want full-time parents more than I want parents in passing.

The bed is jostled as Kam adjusts her position and sits next to me. "Don't be. Nervous, that is. You two are adorable together. Just have fun."

JUST HAVE FUN, has been running through my head since Kamryn left.

Just have fun, runs through my head as James rings the doorbell for our date. I gather my phone and house key before bounding down the stairs.

I blow out a breath and open the door, "Hi."

"Hi," the boyish smile I've come to adore greets me. "These are for you." James tells me as he holds out a bouquet of sunflowers.

"Thank you," I accept the flowers and hold the door open wider. "Come in. Let me find a vase for these and then we can go."

The quiet snick of the door shutting rolls over me as I walk into the kitchen to find a vase. I can't remember the last time we had flowers in the house, so I hope a vase is stashed away under the kitchen sink. With my luck, I find five lined up in the back of the cabinet and snatch out a blue vase with flowers etched into the glass.

Five minutes later, James and I are out of the house, walking hand-in-hand to the ice cream shop. It's a mild early winter day with the sun shining and sixty-degree weather blessing us. If it were any colder, I'm not sure our date would have happened.

"Least favorite ice cream flavor?" James blurts out.

"Pistachio or peanut butter. Yuck. Yours?" I volley back.

Our hands swing between us. "Wait what's wrong with peanut butter?"

"I'm allergic. Like deathly allergic to peanuts."

"It's a good thing I now know this about you. But my least favorite flavor would have to be rainbow swirl."

I laugh through my question. "Why is your least favorite rainbow swirl?"

"Too many flavors. My brain can never figure out what it tastes like. So I don't get it." His face-dropping is too cute for words. "What's your favorite flavor?"

"Are you sure you're ready for the list?" I challenge him.

"Bring it on," he declares, rubbing our hands together.

"I love classic vanilla. But pair it with a warm brownie or chocolate chip cookies and it's pure heaven on your taste buds. Or a pie, but that's more for holidays. Hmmm, I also can't go wrong with butter pecan. And then I do love a good Oreo ice cream."

"So you love ice cream?" James teases me.

"I do. If I could have it for breakfast, lunch, and dinner I would." I proclaim. "What are your favorites?"

"I'm a simple boy, Em," the nickname coming from him makes me blush. "Chocolate, vanilla, and mint chocolate chip will always be my favorite flavors. But you might sway me to try that Oreo ice cream you're so fond of."

Luckily when we walk into the ice cream shop, there are only a few people in line ahead of us. I inhale the welcome scent of sugar and waffle cones being made to order. James and I take our place behind a mom with her two kids.

The choices are endless and luckily they have an Oreo option, so that's what I know I'm going to choose.

I look up at James and see his eyebrows furrowed in concentration. He really is the cutest boy I've ever known. "Do you know what you're going to get?"

"They have so many choices," he whispers to me. I'm not sure why it endears me that he's shy from talking loud, but it makes me like him even more.

"You're cute, you know that?"

His gaze slides down to me and that boyish smile I've come to like so much graces his face. "You're cute too," he tells me right before he boops me on the tip of my nose and slings his arm over my shoulder, tucking me into his side.

Day by day and week by week, James and I have gotten more comfortable around each other. We're still hesitant with our moves. But as time goes on I'm realizing that everything is safe and everything is better when we're touching in some form.

Is it also crazy that he hasn't kissed me? I mean I've never been kissed so I'm not sure how long you're supposed to date someone before you kiss them. But I want to kiss him so bad. He would be my first kiss so I want it to be perfect.

We place our ice cream orders and accept them across the display counter. Once paid we bundle into a small table. I let James try the Oreo flavor and I begrudge him by tasting the mint chocolate chip. I'm not a fan of his, but he was a fan of my ice cream.

We don't linger too long in the shop and start our walk

back to my house. It's still mid-afternoon and no cars are in the driveway.

"You wanna watch a movie?" James proposes as we walk through the front door. Our shoes and jackets line the wall before we head into the living room. I pluck up the remotes and walk over to the couch.

"You pick." I say, holding out the remote for James to take is like handing him control of a ship.

His laugh is contagious as he flips through until he finds a movie we'll both enjoy. I pull the blankets off the back of the couch and unfold them before laying it over us. Laughter escapes me as I see the opening scene of *Miss Congeniality* displayed on the TV.

I turn to look at James. His smile lights up his eyes and I have this intense urge to kiss him. So I do. I gently turn his head and press my lips to his. His moves are delayed until he kisses me back. I'm not sure what to do so I follow his lead. All he does is kiss me back, but I can still sense his nerves as he does so.

James breaks the kiss. His lips are swollen and red. I'm sure my lips look the same.

"Why'd you kiss me?" He asks, but not in an accusatory way.

"Because I wanted to," is the only response I give him.

James

"I love you." I say to the mirror. Shaking my head I try again.

This shouldn't be so difficult to say. I know what I feel for Emily and it's not just like. We've been inseparable for the last year. She shows up to my games and I show up to her recitals and concerts. When she's lonely in that big house of hers, she begs me to stay. Or I invite her over to mine while my parents and brothers treat her as if she's already part of the family. And in most cases she is.

I square up to the mirror again. "I love you."

A pounding on the bathroom door has me jumping out of my skin.

"Open up casanova," my little brother, Malcolm, demands from outside.

Being the second oldest of five, means my younger brothers have gotten to witness every stage of mine and Emily's relationship. After we hit the six-month mark in our relationship, my parents finally stopped teasing me. And up until a few months ago, I didn't think we could have any embarrassing conversations. That is until the birds and the bees talk.

While Emily and I are in no rush to get to that stage in our relationship, my parents made sure to get the talk out of the way. I shudder remembering that conversation.

~

Nine Months Ago

A knock on my door pulled me from my homework.

"Come in," I replied without looking up from my work. Turning around I see both of my parents enter my bedroom. They've given nothing away with the looks on their faces and it kind of freaks me out. "What's up?"

"Honey, it's time we had that talk," my mom stated.

I look at the back of my dad's head as he closes the door and then avoids my line of sight before sitting next to my mom. "Um, what talk?"

My dad looks all around my room until I see my mom nudge him. "The birds and the bees."

"Do we have to?"

"No." My dad.

"Ben!" My mom scolds him. "Yes, James we have to. As embarrassing as this is for you, your Dad and I do not want grandchildren anytime soon."

I held my hands up in surrender. "Woah. We haven't even made it to that point in our relationship. It's a big step for both of us."

"You both are virgins?" My mom coos.

"Yes..."

My dad looks like he'd rather be anywhere but here having this conversation. Well tough luck for him as he'll have this conversation three more times.

She slaps her hand on my dad's thigh with uncontained glee. "Okay, well we're gonna start off with some basics. And then I'll give you some sites to learn from."

I cover my face in pure mortification as my mom goes on about erections and the clitoris.

∽

Whipping the bathroom door open I see Malcolm standing against the wall with his arms crossed over his chest.

"It's about time lover boy," he huffs as he pushes past me into the bathroom.

I roll my eyes before walking back to my bedroom. Plopping down on my bed, I pick up my phone and see a text from Emily.

> Emmy: Gloria is making spaghetti. Dinner and a movie?

> Me: You've got yourself a date.

I decide to tackle some homework before heading to Em's. I'm halfway through my chemistry lesson when my phone rings.

"Hey, big brother," I greet Brandon.

A huff of laughter slips out. "Hey, shrimp. So I heard from someone that you're planning to say three important words tonight."

"Who did–I'm gonna kick Malcolm in the butt."

Brandon barks out a laugh. "I would've done the same thing if I were him."

I sigh into the phone. "You never said those words to a girl?"

"That would require me to have a girlfriend. So no. But I'm happy to take my cues from you."

"I'm honored. When are you coming home next?"

Brandon is on a full-ride scholarship at Bellmore University in Tennessee. He was a walk-on for the golf team so his bread-and-butter lies in his brain.

I hear the flipping of a page on the other end of the phone. "Um, it looks like Thanksgiving in a few weeks. Do you think you can carve out some time for your favorite brother?"

"If I must," I say off-handedly.

Brandon and I talk about small things. While my brother and I aren't close as we're opposites in every way, he's still one of my favorite people to talk to.

It's only when I look outside to see the setting sun that I need to head to Emily's. "Hey, Brandon I'm heading out to dinner. It was good talking with you."

"Oh yeah. Those three little words are threatening to burst free. Good luck, buddy."

I leave him with a teasing quip and throw on a clean pair of sweatpants and a sweatshirt. Padding down the stairs, I let my parents know I'm eating dinner next door as the nerves of those three little words begging to be set free cause me to stumble over my feet.

I give a cursory knock on Emily's front door before letting myself in. Kicking off my shoes, I pad my sock-covered feet into the kitchen and see two of my favorite girls chatting merrily by the stove. Quietly, well as quiet as I can, I take a seat at the island and watch their familial interaction. The relationship between Emily and Gloria is that of a grandmother and a granddaughter. They're both so comfortable in that dynamic that I never want to interrupt these moments between them.

Emily must catch me out of the corner of her eye and an innocent smile with a soft blush covers her face. Coming around to where I'm seated, she wraps her arms around my shoulder and gives me a quick kiss. "Hi."

"Hi, baby," I respond with a quick kiss back to her. "It smells great Gloria."

"Thank you, sweet boy. It's just about done." She announces before giving the food a couple more stirs and then shutting the burner on the stove off.

We each serve ourselves before taking a seat at the kitchen table. Chatter and laughter are ever-present when it's the three of us. Emily's smile never dulls when she realizes her parents are nowhere in this house.

When our bowls are clear, Gloria shoves us out of the kitchen telling us to go put on a movie. With minimal protest and some light towel swatting, we listen.

"What movie tonight, my Emmy?" I ask as we meander down the hallway to the movie room. My arm is slung around her shoulder and her body fits next to mine like a missing puzzle piece.

"*Sweet Home Alabama*," Emily states, shocking the shit out of me.

"Really?"

Our steps are muted when we cross into the carpeted room. "Yeah. I really want to watch one of the best romantic comedy movies to ever exist."

"Is it really the best?" I counter, ready for a debate.

She whips her body around, taking me by surprise, and sternly points her finger at me. "James Michael, don't you dare question this ruling."

"Scouts honor. I would never."

I find the DVD in the genre-specific drawer, because yes Emily is organized like that, and pop it into the DVD opening. Grabbing the multitude of remotes, I walk back to the loveseat that Emily is already curled on. I turn the lights down to set the mood for the movie and curl her body into mine.

Two hours later and I have been schooled. It was a cute movie—one about a second chance between a boy and a girl who were childhood sweethearts. I can see why Emily loves it.

"So what did you think?" Emily asks me as the credits roll.

"I can see why you like it."

"It's the charm of Josh Lucas," she dreamily says.

My eyebrows hit my hairline. "Do you have a crush on him?"

"He is dreamy," she starts. "But my crush is sitting right next to me."

"I love you." I blurt out. "Wow. I did not mean to say it like that."

"I love you too," Emily says with a smile.

One year after asking her to be my girlfriend, the idea of love, which was painted to be this fictionalized ideal that wasn't graspable, no longer terrifies me. Being with Emily has been a whole new experience. Although I feel she's older for her age with how she lives in this house. She also makes me want a sort of domesticity that being in this house temporarily provides.

And if I imagine harder than possible, I can see it all. The house, the kids, the love; all spilled out into a space that we create as our own.

Emily
2009

James: I have a surprise for you.

My phone buzzing breaks me from my violin practice. Even after all this time, I still get butterflies when he texts me.

Me: Is this a fancy surprise or a casual surprise?

James: You'll see when you get home. I'll see you later. I love you.

Me: You know I hate your surprises, right? I love you too.

James: *kiss face emoji*

I still can't believe that it's been over two years since we started dating. And because of it, I love the beginning of the school year. But also bittersweet seeing as James, Kamryn, and Liam graduate this year. They're not my only friends at this school. But they're who I hang out with the most.

Did I know this would happen? Of course. I knew

dating James would come with a solo year of isolation in high school.

But we have time—so much of it.

I get back to practicing as I only have the auditorium for an hour. While my performance isn't until next winter, this is a longer and more complex piece of music. This showcase is where a handful of musicians will perform as an ensemble and then solo for recruiters and professors from some of the top music programs in the country. I still want to go to college and get my teaching degree, but playing the violin professionally would also be a dream come true.

"That's better Emily." My teacher coaches from the chairs in the auditorium.

Amelia has been my private teacher for years. While she's strict, she's also nurturing. My lessons with her are fun, but serious when they need to be. She makes sure my body, mainly my shoulder, can withstand the hour of practice we do a day. Also with this recital, we don't want my body to be overused. So we've dropped down to three days a week and alternating weekends.

"Run through your solo again, and then we'll call it quits for the day."

Since I play in the school orchestra, those pieces have been for fun. They've kept my skills sharp and have helped keep my body loose.

When Amelia and I met to discuss this showcase, we focused on my strengths. And after listening to samples of several solos, we decided on Mozart's Concerto No. 5 in A major. This piece is worlds away from the cute holiday pieces and trendy songs we play at school. It's over thirty minutes and requires my full concentration to remember every single note.

For the showcase, we decided it would be best if I did it

without sheet music. My memory is usually spot-on. But, again, this is a long song. So our hope is that with repetition, that by the time the showcase rolls around, playing will be a breeze. I get my violin into position and flex my fingers with my bow hand. I take a big calming breath and play the first note.

From the first note to the last note, I managed to block out all of the outside noise. It was just me, my violin, and the sheets of music. My body relaxes when the final note echoes out into the auditorium. Only then do I take the bow from my finishing position and my violin off my shoulder.

"Beautiful, Emily." Amelia praises. "I have no notes. For the rest of our lessons, we'll work on you memorizing the music. We'll start line by line before we do that whole sheet and repeat the process so you're not overwhelmed when you do go sheet-less. You're almost there because I noticed you closed your eyes a few times when you were playing. That's a perfect first step."

I preen under her praise and have to manage to hold in a silly dance. "Thank you, Amelia."

The auditorium chair speaks as she gets up, "Now get out of here and go hang out with your cute boyfriend."

Amelia leaves me with a smile and a parting pat on the stage. I tuck my violin under my right arm and gather my sheet music. I'm out of the facility in twenty minutes and on my way home.

Getting my license was a step closer to freedom from a house that isn't a home. While my parents moved us here for me to have a normal upbringing, they've been more absent than ever. I only see them on my birthday and very briefly on holidays. Even then they're barely present as they're constantly on their phones or on their laptops. They don't even take the day off for their respective birthdays. I still love my parents, don't get me wrong, but our relationship is not one like what James has with his family. Or even what Kamryn and Liam have with their parents.

But the feeling of freedom doesn't last when I see my parents' cars in the driveway. Besides them having their names on the deed and paying for the mortgage, I live alone in a house that's empty, cold, and so full of nothing.

> Me: Babe, my parents are here. I'll come over after I see them.

> James: No rush, baby. I'll be here.

Putting my car in park, I take a deep breath before shutting it off and grabbing my violin from the backseat before heading inside. I've always felt comfortable walking into any room my parents were in. But not so much anymore. I feel unwelcomed and forgotten about.

"Emily, can we talk to you?" My mom's voice reaches me from the kitchen.

I dump my bag and set my violin case by the stairs. The realization that I have absentee parents and I'm sick of acting like their workloads don't affect me, starts to sink in. I walk down the hallway to the kitchen which feels more like a death march. When I turn the corner I see my parents sitting at the kitchen table.

"Have a seat, please," my dad instructs.

The early fall afternoon proves to be a different backdrop with them home. Instead of the warmth the afternoon provides, I just feel cold. This house is cold.

"No, 'hi honey' nothing? No asking how I've been or what I've been up to?" I ask in lieu of a greeting.

"Watch your mouth, Emily Marie," my dad scolds me.

I scoff in return. "Wow. Barely been here for the last two years and now you want to discipline me. You said we moved here for me to have a normal upbringing, but we might as well have stayed in New York. Because the only difference between New York and here is that there's grass surrounding the house."

My parents raised me to be respectful. But now they want to talk to me when that's all I've wanted for the past two years. Parents to talk to about my life. Yet in the two years we've lived here, the longest conversation we had was my first day of high school.

"What did you want to talk about?" I'm eager to get this conversation over so I can go see my surprise from James.

My parents glance at each other before my mom takes the lead. "Our workloads are changing."

I scoff at her announcement. "Is that supposed to surprise me?"

It's my parent's turn to look taken aback that I'm talking to them like this. Again, I know they're my parents. I know I shouldn't talk to them like this. I've never raised my voice when they were around. But I'm so tired of feeling like a gnat they can place on some fruit and think she'll be satisfied.

"Do you know I'm preparing for a showcase?" I refuse to wait for them to tell me some lame ass excuse as I see the look of surprise on their faces. I clench my teeth as I slowly nod my head. "That's what I thought. Or that I've been dating someone for two years?" Their brows furrow in confusion. My lips tremble as I fight to hold back my tears.

But my emotions that have reached their peak win out and the tears fall anyway.

"Do you know anything about my life anymore? About what it's like to grow up without parental guidance? To know that your parents would rather be at work than with their daughter. And meeting her boyfriend and getting to know her friends. I don't want some lame-ass excuse of you being able to provide for me. Because I'd rather be poor and spend time together than be privileged and you two be non-existent characters in my life. I want you two in my life as main characters and not some crappy side characters that show up when bad news arrives. I want you two to be introduced to my boyfriend and his family, who have been nothing but welcoming to me in the wake of your absence. I want to tell my friends that my parents want to have a cookout with their families, but I can't do that. Do you know what that's like? To not have any of that because you two choose to not exist in my world?"

Gloria passes me a box of tissues as all of my frustrations at the lack of acknowledgment from my parents come out for the first time. I turn and give her a small smile of thanks. She rubs a soothing hand up and down my back while the emotions continue to run through me.

"So you two love your jobs. That's great. But I want parents who come to my school concerts, are there with me as I cheer my boyfriend on at his games all the while chatting with his parents, and I want to walk into this house to laughter, not the silence that's greeted me for the past two years. You two have no idea what it's been like for me. So no. I won't stand here and listen to whatever bullshit reason about your workload shifting that you decide to grace me with."

The tears come in full force and I can't stay here any longer. My parents muttered protests are ignored as I turn to face Gloria, silently communicating that I'm going over to James's house. Her subtle nod is all I need and without saying goodbye to my parents, as they've spared me the same, I walk back outside and run over to James's house.

James

I've barely finished wrapping up Emily's surprise when I hear footsteps quickly coming up the stairs. I'm walking to my door when it flies open and a tearful Emily bursts through. She's in my arms in an instant.

"Baby, what's wrong?" I cradle her head to my chest and rub soothing circles over her back. Aside from Emily getting her period and crying over the littlest things, I've never seen her cry like this.

She takes deep stuttering breaths. "My parents being home when I got back is what's wrong."

"What? What did they do?" Shock and disbelief coat my words. Em and I have been together for two years. In all that time I still haven't met her parents and I've had dinner with her and Gloria at least once a week since we've been dating. When she mentioned they were home when she got back from rehearsal it took everything in me to not push her to let me come over.

"They wanted to talk. I didn't let them. I berated them for thinking they could just come back here and want to talk when that's all I've wanted for the past two years. I was so mad. And hurt." Her voice is watery and muffled as she speaks into my chest. Hearing the pain in her voice, well I can't imagine how she feels.

"I'm proud of you for standing up to them. I know it wasn't easy. And I know you love your parents. But it was about time they knew how you felt."

Emily has always spoken highly of her parents. Personally, if my parents abandoned me at a crucial time in my life, like high school, I wouldn't be so forgiving. Em's heart is bigger than mine. It's what makes it so easy to love her.

I lift her in my arms and carry her to my bed. Laying her down, I slide onto the bed next to her and tuck her into my side. My shirt soaks instantly with the tears that are still falling.

"Your tears are breaking my heart, baby." I say, kissing the top of her head and tucking her back into me.

"I just want them to be present. I want to laugh with them and do normal family things." Her voice goes quiet as she speaks on the years of hurt her parents unintentionally put her through. "My parents were always good to me. But the further we got from New York, the more they put their work first. I want to matter to them."

It wasn't until last year that I finally got Emily to tell me how she felt about her parents working so much. She said that her parents not coming around became her new normal and she wouldn't know how to act around them.

"Do your parents know where you're at?" I mumble into her hair.

Her head moves on what I assume is her shaking her head, "No, but Gloria does. I don't think she'll tell them where I ran off to."

As much as I hope Gloria doesn't tell Emily's parents where she's at, at the end of the day Gloria works for her parents. But I don't voice it because Emily doesn't need that.

We stay like this on my bed. The surprise I had for her is forgotten as we both drift off to sleep.

What felt like five minutes has somehow turned into an hour when a door closing jolts me awake. I look down and Emily is passed out. With her rehearsal this morning and her parents coming home, I know she's exhausted. Carefully, I extract myself from her hold. Kissing the top of her head, I pull a blanket up over her and head downstairs to see what the noise was.

Turning the corner I halt to a stop when I see my parents and two people I'm assuming are Emily's parents at the kitchen table. My nap is still lingering in my head, so it takes considerable effort to stay put and not cower off back to my room to my girl.

"Honey," my mom's throat clearing brings my attention to her. "These are Emily's parents, Mark and Christie. Come sit."

I eye the vacant chair and wonder how fast I can run back upstairs. But I stay put. Because running away from the people who gave birth to the light that Emily is would be the coward's way out. So with herculean effort, I go and sit in the chair next to my mom.

Surveying the people in front of me, I see a mix of Emily in both of them. She gets her delicate nose from her Mom and eyes from her Dad.

Do I speak first? Or do I have the adults be adults and speak first?

I'm about to open my mouth when I'm beat to the punch.

"For years my daughter struggled to make friends. She's shy and a cautious person. Moving here, I worried about her. And I wish I could say I noticed the change in her. But it makes me a terrible mother to say that while I've been focused on my career I've forgotten about my daughter," her Mom takes a sip of her water before looking me in the eye. "When Emily said she had friends and was dating someone for the past two years, I refused to believe that I–we–could have missed so much of her life." She stops talking as if she's lost for words.

Leaning forward, I place my arms on the table. "It took Emily about a week to warm up to the idea of having me as a friend. I'm also a generally shy person, but something about her made me want to protect and comfort her. The first time we hung out I asked about you two. She shut me down. And told me that she was fine being alone in the expansive house that you two bought to give her a normal life." I look over at my parents and I feel the warmth. "I'm not sure what her version of normal was before moving here. But what I can tell you is that my normal and her normal are nothing alike."

Her Dad leans forward and if I were weak, I would be intimidated by him. But I'm not, so I let him speak. "Young man, I'm not sure who you're talking to. But we love our daughter."

"I have no doubt that you two love your daughter. But is it more out of familial obligation or because you truly love Emily as an extension of you and would move heaven and earth to see her happy?" Her Mom's eyes turn down and her Dad bristles. "Do you know your daughter? Do you know that her favorite ice cream flavor is Oreo and that she loves *The Fast & Furious* movies? Did you know that she started preparing for a winter showcase and will perform it next year? She wants to be a teacher but if she gets the chance to play violin professionally, she would choose to do that." With every word I speak, their faces continue to fall.

"You know all Emily dreams about is normal. She's never outright told me that. But I see her face when my parents mention us doing a family activity together. Having parents who are around for more than ten minutes each week is all she wants. She wants the family dinners during the week and the laughter greeting her when she gets home from school. I want her to blow off our plans because you two decided at the last minute to whisk her off on a family vacation. I truly wish for the day when she blows me off because she's spending time with you two. Every day, whether intentionally or not, you two have taken this beautiful, magnetic, hilarious young lady and made her want the opposite of what you've unknowingly given her."

"James," my dad warns.

But he doesn't need to as I've said more than I needed to. I shake my head and get up, but before I retreat, I leave them with one thing. "I love your daughter," I declare. "I am in love with your daughter. I love seeing the smile that's so wide it takes up the entirety of her face. I love hearing her laugh...her full-on belly laugh, as I think it's my personal cure when I'm having an off day. But what I love most about your daughter is how she dreams and lives her life with no care for how you two may react."

Walking out of the kitchen, I jog up the stairs but stop short when I turn the corner and catch Emily sitting on the top step. Her smile is shaky and her eyes have filled with fresh tears. I walk up the few steps and sit next to her, taking her hand in mine and weaving our fingers together.

"Thank you." Emily tells me before kissing my cheek.

Wrapping my arm around her shoulder, I kiss the top of her head. "For you? Anytime."

We sit at the top of the stairs and listen to the murmuring that comes from the kitchen, followed by the scrapping of chairs. Em and I hold our breath as her parents walk out of the house.

After a breath, Emily turns to me and places her chin on my shoulder. "So you must really love me?"

I hang my head as a huff of laughter comes out. "So much if I haven't said it enough before."

"You have. You've given me a love that I never knew existed. And I thank every cosmic star that you introduced yourself to me at the bus stop. I love you, James Michael Hayes. And I always will."

"Congratulations to the Class of 2010. You did it!" Our principal gives the final remarks for graduation.

It blows my mind that I'm done with high school. Sure college starts in a couple of months, but I'll be living at home and working part-time to save up for an apartment. Hopefully with Emily if all goes according to plan.

I space out thinking about the future when I see caps flying up around me. I take mine off and do a half-toss before I tuck it under my arm and file out with the crowd.

It takes more time than I had hoped to wade through the clusters of graduates to reach the outside where my family and Emily are waiting. I see my younger brothers hitting each other with balloons and my parents laughing with Em. The love I have for her may still be young, but I know she's it for me.

Emily
2010

"Our next performer is Emily Bailey. Performing *Mozart's Concerto No. 5 in A major*."

Smoothing out the invisible wrinkles from my black performance dress, I take another deep breath and flex my fingers before taking the first step back onto the stage. I've already performed in a quartet. But now the spotlight and attention will be solely on me as the final performer of the night. Amelia manages to capture my focus from across the stage and reminds me to remember to breathe.

Turning, I face the crowd and curtsey. Once upright I place my violin between my shoulder and jawline, place my bow in the upward direction, and begin my piece.

The song comes to me like it's my second language. I don't pay any mind to who's in the crowd, who's not in the crowd, or who's paying attention. I let my muscle memory lead me through the thirty-minute piece of music. My fingers float over the strings, my wrist inciting vibrato, and my bow hand keeping up with every stroke along the strings.

My eyes are closed as my body sways to the music this instrument is creating. I sense I've made it to the finale of the song and hold my breath until the very last note fades out into the crowd. Only when I lift my bow off of its resting position does my focus come back to the crowd that's on their feet and cheering.

My face flames with the attention of over a hundred people. I take my curtsey as the pressure from this performance has passed and my smile from finishing this piece cannot be stopped. With a final bow, I make my way off the stage to take the long-awaited cleansing breath that had me locked up from the time I stepped onto the stage to now. And when I'm finally behind the red curtain without a hundred sets of eyes on my every move, does my body relax for the first time all day.

"Emily, that was beautiful," Amelia praises and pulls me into her embrace.

Returning her embrace I tell her, "I couldn't have done it without your coaching and mentoring. Thank you, Amelia."

"It's been an honor to teach you these past couple of years." With a kiss to the top of my head, Amelia breezes out of the backstage.

Packing up in record time, I meet James in the lobby.

My heart kicks up when I see him there with flowers and that boyish smile I love so much. "Baby, you played so incredible. These are from me and Gloria."

"Thank you." Taking the flowers from him, I lean up on my toes to kiss him on the cheek.

I swallow down my disappointment that my parents didn't show up. I thought that after the talk we had, they would be more present. Silly me, huh?

"I wanna take you somewhere," James leads with distraction.

"Okay."

James dropped me off earlier as I needed to do a final run-through of my set. Since we knew we were spending time with each other tonight, him dropping me off was the smart choice.

We stop by the bathroom so I can change out of my performance dress. Taking off the dress, I pull up my maxi skirt that's thicker than the normal skirt and pull the thick dark blue sweater down my body. The thick socks that roll around in my bag slide on my feet along with my flat ankle booties. I pull on my cream cardigan, roll my performance dress into my bag, and exit the bathroom.

James's smile lights up his face when I reach him and then he's slinging my violin case over his shoulder, taking my hand in his. We follow the trickling crowd out to the parking lot into the brisk winter air. "So how do you feel now that your big moment is done?"

I cover his hand with my free hand and lean into his side. "Lighter. I'm not sure if that's the right word. But I worked so hard for this moment only for it to be done in an hour. So I guess I also feel a little empty."

"All your hard work paid off. I'll never get over watching how beautiful you play."

"Thank you, baby," my cheeks hurt from smiling so hard.

"ICE CREAM?" I turn to him with excitement coating my words.

His eyebrows raise with a goofy nod. Slowly leaning

into my space he pecks me on the lips. "I got a craving for some Oreo ice cream."

He leaves me watching after him as he strolls around to my side of his car. "M'lady," he announces as he holds his hand out for me.

"You're such a goofball. And I love you for that."

Shutting the car door we walk into the ice cream shop. James wraps his arms around my upper body and our steps match as we stroll up to the small line which has formed. "It's an honor to be your goofball."

Kissing his forearm, I order our ice cream when it's our turn. After we've paid, we take a seat at our usual table. We people watch as we let the ice cream cool off our already cold bodies and talk about absurd things that will probably never happen.

"You can't say something that insane!" I cough out. The cold from the ice cream makes me sound like I'm sick.

James chuckles. "If it were to happen. Trust me!"

"So you're telling me that if an apocalypse were to occur, the first thing you'd do is rob a grocery store? Of all of the bread? What is wrong with you?" I say and burst out in hysterics.

"When you're starving because everything else got wiped out by the zombies don't come to me for some bread."

"You're so weird. You know that right?"

"I've come to accept that."

I kiss the tip of his nose. "I think I'm accepting it too."

"Where do you see yourself in five years?" James asks.

"With you hopefully. Maybe married or at least engaged." I'm confident enough in us to know that's where our future is heading.

"Pretty presumptuous don't ya think?"

"I don't think anything. I know. I love you. And I know I see our future wrangling our little boys to t-ball practice."

"Boys huh?" His smile is contagious.

My nod is emphatic. "I wouldn't mind having a daughter. But being around you and your brothers has fulfilled me in a way I didn't know I needed."

James leans forward and presses a kiss to my lips. "I like that. Knowing that we've unintentionally given you something precious. And I love you too, sweet girl."

A comfortable silence takes place as we eat our ice cream and people-watch.

James breaks the silence by asking, "Have you talked to Kamryn or Liam lately?"

"Not recently. Why do you ask?" Kamryn texted me a couple of weeks ago and told me about a guy she's been seeing. He's the quarterback at the university she and Liam go to. While I thought them going to college together would spur Liam to confessing how he felt about her, has instead turned the opposite.

James's shrug is a little sad. I know he misses his best friends. But it was his choice to stay close to home for college. "I was just curious. So what have you decided on for college?"

With it being my senior year, I had big options of where to go to school. I could go back to New York, but that place doesn't feel like home anymore. Since my parents are there six and a half out of the seven days a week, I don't want to be anywhere close to them. But I didn't tell James I applied to PhilU. He told me that he could transfer anywhere that I got into.

Is it a mistake to go to college with your boyfriend? Maybe. But is it a mistake if I choose to stay close to the place that makes me feel at home? No.

"I have," I leave him with that and try to hold in my laughter at his wanting more expression.

"Baby, don't leave me hanging." His bottom lip juts out as he silently begs me to tell him where I've decided to go to college.

Finishing off my ice cream, I stack our empty bowls together and scoot closer to James. "How do four years, well three for you, at the same school sound?"

"Really? You got into PhilU?" His excitement is palpable.

"Yeah. Are you happy?" I know the answer but I have to ask him.

"The happiest, baby." He leans forward and our lips collide. We keep it PG for the public. "When did you get your letter?" James asks when he pulls away.

"Yesterday when I got home from school." Gloria was home to congratulate me and make me a celebratory dinner. It was a bittersweet moment that my parents weren't there to congratulate me.

James's face turns morose as he knows the only person I celebrated with was Gloria. He had a big final and I didn't want to disturb him. "I would've come over to help celebrate."

"You had your big test and I don't want you to feel bad. This reaction was what I wanted from you."

He drapes his arm around my shoulder and pulls me closer to him. "So we're both gonna be Grizzlies. These next few years are going to be the best of our lives."

I gaze at him with so much love in my eyes, that I don't think words can adequately express how much I love him. "I love you."

"I love you, too."

I push his hair off his forehead. "Do you promise?"

"I promise I'll love you forever."

I mouth the word, *wow*, "Forever's a long time you know?"

"I'm okay with forever as long as you are."

∼

2011

"Another year has come and gone. Congratulations to the class of 2011." Caps fly up and cheers are contagious.

I beeline my way through my former classmates. Waving back to those who wave at me. Once outside, I find James standing with Gloria. I run into his arms when he sees me coming.

"No more high school," James claims. He sets me on my feet.

The happiness I feel is short-lived as I turn to Gloria and sink into her hug. My body shakes with silent sobs. "I know, sweetie."

∼

January 2011

My parents flew in from New York unexpectedly. They were waiting in the kitchen when I got home from school. It felt like deja vu when I walked in there and saw Gloria was busying herself at the stove. But I knew it was for my benefit, more than for what she was cooking.

"What's going on?" I asked without a proper greeting.

My parents looked at each other before my mom swung her gaze to me. "Your father and I have to go out of town."

"Where?" My question is devoid of emotion.

"Spain." My mother's short response was equal to my short response.

I knew the answer before I even asked the question. But I asked anyway for my piece of mind. "When are you leaving?"

"Tomorrow. For about six months. Maybe more."

I looked up at the ceiling. It wasn't sad tears that burned the back of my eyes. But angry tears that they even had the decency to let me know they were leaving. "So my birthday, graduation, and my first day of college are the events you two want to miss? Any other big events of my life you two want to pencil yourself out of?"

"Sweetheart," my dad started but I shut him down.

"No! My showcase was in December. I played in a packed auditorium. I brought the crowd to their feet. And that little girl who supported her parents with their career was crushed when she finally realized that her dreams meant absolutely nothing to them." The tears fell hot down my face as if this wasn't the tenth time I confronted my parents about their neglect. "But you know, it's good that you two have shown me what it's like to neglect their child. Because I'm making a promise, here and now, that I will never be like you two."

The utensil that Gloria was holding clatters to the floor at the same time my mom's shocked gasp is freed from her mouth.

A bitter smile that didn't quite reach my face and tears that leaked out of the corner of my eyes slid down the sides of my face. "I used to be so proud to tell people what my parents do for a living. How they provided for me in a way they never thought they could. And I confidently said, every time someone asked about you two, that my parents loved me.

Now I feel like such an idiot that they never loved me enough to put me first. So thank you, for letting me know that you two are going out of town. But to be quite frank, I wish you two wouldn't have even bothered. Have a good trip."

I walked out of the kitchen to the front door, slammed it shut, and ran over to James's house. Knocking on the door, James's Mom answered and gave me a sad smile when she saw the tears on my cheeks.

I'd like to say this didn't happen often. But too many times my parents have disappointed me to where I needed to be somewhere that wasn't connected to them. It's sad that my parents are supposed to wipe away my tears when I'm hurt even though they're the ones doing the hurting. I'll never stop wanting my parent's love and attention. But I can't fight for people who won't fight back.

Emily
August 2011

"First day of college. Are you ready?" Kamryn asks from the screen on my computer. She returned to college a week earlier to get back in the swing of things. But I know the true reason is that Mason is down there earlier for football practices before the season starts. So Kam and I have to resort to ooVoo Facetime calls to see each other.

"I'm so ready. But I am surprised you're not sitting on Mason's lap at this moment." I tease my best friend.

"Hardy-har-har," Kam chides. "He's at practice. But we are meeting up later for dinner."

Seeing my best friend in love is all I ever wanted.

"Speaking of boys, hey loser." I turn around to see her addressing James.

James holds up his arms and bangs his fists together. Flipping Kamryn off Ross Geller style.

I can't stop the huff of laughter. "On that note, we're going to head to campus. Kam, I'll talk to you later."

"Okay. Bye, you two!"

Closing out of Facetime, I turn to James with my brow arched. "You two act like siblings most of the time."

"It's so much fun," James claims. "What's on your schedule for the day?"

Pulling out my planner, I turn to August and see my first day lined up. "All intro classes. I have three today, with my last class done at noon. My goodness, I love college."

"And I love you, my little nerd." James says as he frames my face with his hands and leans in to kiss me.

He tries to pry my lips open but I back away because if I don't he'll keep us here all day. "What time are you done?"

"Oh, I only have one class today and that's done at noon, too. I'm going in early to speak with my advisor," he says matter-of-factly.

"If you say so."

"I do. Now get your cute butt in gear and let's get to campus." James pats me on the behind and strolls out of my room to the kitchen to most likely chat with Gloria.

I gather the rest of my things and meet them there.

A breakfast burrito to-go and an iced coffee are waiting for me on the kitchen island. "Thank you, Gloria."

"You're welcome, honey. Now before you go, I put pre-made dinners in the freezer, just follow the directions for how to reheat them. Also, your breakfast burritos are in a freezer bag, you just need to pop them in the toaster oven for about thirty minutes and you're good to go."

Gloria is taking a month-long vacation to visit her grandbabies. I love having her here, but I understand she has her own family to get to.

"Thank you," I tell her again. I mean it. I wouldn't have survived these last few years without her.

"Go, go. You're going to be late."

Kissing her on the cheek, I pick up my food and iced coffee, then I'm out the door with James in tow.

~

> Me: My last class is done early. I'll meet you at the car.

> James: I think my professor is wrapping up. I'll be there shortly.

I FIND a bench and lean back as I reflect on the first day and conclude that it was not what I expected. The professors were chill and interacted with us like peers and not like they were our authority figures. My high school teachers got that fact wrong when they told us our professors weren't casual.

Since I have all intro classes it made for a lighter day, but I know my workload will pile up and according to my advisor, I'm on the right path.

I do love the idea of teaching. But it will be a lot of work.

Am I bummed that I'm not playing violin professionally? A little. But touring with a company would mean traveling. Away from home, James, and Gloria. I'm not quite ready for that.

"Hey, hot stuff." James greets me as he gets closer to where I'm relaxing on the bench.

"Dating a college guy is so hot," I eye him up and down suggestively.

He sits next to me and wraps his arm around me. James leans in and his mouth lands at my ear. "Wanna know what else is hot about dating a college guy?"

"What's that?"

James licks at my ear and a whimper escapes me. "Sleeping with him."

Say less. I snatch my bag and pull James with me to the car.

"Was it something I said?" He teases as he opens my door.

I hop up into his truck and when I'm safely in, James shuts the door and jogs around to his side.

"It's not nice to tease people," I scold him.

A smirk pulls at James's mouth as he starts up. I slide over to sit in the middle of the bench seat and pull the seat belt in place. James tucks his hand between my thighs as he drives us out of campus. It hits me that we have incredible memories in this truck. And the day that he sells it will be a day that I cry.

I rest my hand on his thigh and feel it tense. I hide my smile in his arm as I curve my hand inward.

"Emily," his stern voice sends tingles down my spine.

My pinky brushes over the length of him in his jeans and I see his hands clench around the steering wheel. The familiar street that signifies our neighborhood means we're safe. Well as safe as can be.

"What's wrong baby? I'm merely continuing what you started this morning," I tell him coyly.

James whips into the driveway, throws his truck in park, and fuses his mouth to mine. His tongue seeks entrance right away. I don't care that it's the middle of the day or that we're making out in my driveway. I just care about him.

January 2014

"Happy Birthday, to you!" James croons along with Kamryn and Liam. We're celebrating my twenty-first birthday early before they have to drive back down to school. And I'm lucky they were here to help celebrate.

Since my parents have been as distant as ever, I've made my own family. Gloria woke me up with pancakes in bed and James had flowers delivered every two hours to my house. My room was a variety of colors with sunflowers, roses, orchids, and balloons covering most of the flat surfaces.

I look around at my small but mighty group, my chosen family and then blow out the candles. I don't wish for anything too big as I have all I need.

James places a kiss on my temple and gets up to grab a knife before coming back to the table. I look at Liam and Kamryn whispering secret things to each other. After Mason, I didn't know how Kam would recover. Kam had a rocky comeback but now she and Liam are inseparable.

"Hey, Kam? Do you remember when we first met, and I asked about you two? You said, "Not like that". Well I'd like to say, "I told you so." I pick up my glass of champagne and take a healthy swallow.

Liam and James can't help the laughs that escape as Kam playfully shoots daggers at me. I still remember picking up the phone and Kam announcing they were dating. They were very much in the lovey-dovey phase, and still are if I'm being honest, so I stayed on the phone for the three minutes I needed to without getting nauseous.

We laugh and talk throughout the night before heading to the movie room. It rarely gets used as James and I resort to watching movies in my room. But my parents spared no expense when they first renovated this house all those years ago. The home theater is fitted with oversized loveseats and bucket seats, a deep red color adorning the soundproofed walls, and the TV screen taking up the entire wall. James and I will occasionally have date nights that always end with a movie. Of course, I end up asleep after thirty minutes and wake up to him carrying me to bed. So I can't complain about that possibility happening tonight.

"What's the movie for tonight, birthday girl?" Liam asks when he plops down on the couch. Kamryn grabs a few throw blankets, tossing me one, before unfolding the one she chose and draping it over herself and Liam.

"Iron Man," I declare. James grabs the remotes for the movie, sound system, and lighting.

"Good choice baby."

"Thank you." I accept the praise and unfold my blanket as well. James helps me to spread it over the both of us while the opening sequence plays on the screen. I tuck into James's side and the steady beat of his heart is enough to put me in a catatonic state.

The movie drones on. We laugh when needed and are completely silent during the fight scenes. I feel like I barely breathe during the entire movie. It isn't until the credits start rolling that I take in the proper amount of air.

Kamryn and Liam sit up and turn to face us. "We're gonna head out." She informs me.

As sad as I am at my friend's leaving, I'm more than excited to have alone time with my boyfriend.

"Okay," I tell my friend and hope I did my best to disguise my excitement.

We shut off the movie during the end credits and walk them both to the door.

"Five more months until you're graduating. That's insane!" I tell Kam as we walk out of the theater.

Her arm is looped through mine and our steps fall in sync. "Truth is I'm ready for college to be done. It's been exhausting, as you know. And I'm more than ready to move back up here."

"You and Liam seem to be happy together."

"Is this what it's like to go from friends to more?"

I think of James and me. And how every day with him has gotten better. "The can't stop floating feeling? Yeah."

We all get to the door, hugging and making promises for the summer. James makes sure they get to the car and shuts the door when they do.

"Alone at last!" James exclaims before pouncing on me and tossing me over his shoulder.

He begins the trek upstairs with my body slung over his shoulder like a sack of potatoes. My hands land on his waist to keep myself stable.

"I like this view," my voice is a little nasally as the air is strained.

He brings a hand up and swats me on the butt causing me to yelp. "Don't even think about it."

"Just a little squeeze," I taunt. I won't do it for fear of him dropping me. He never would.

"Emily Marie, don't you dare."

His footsteps are hurried as he gets us to my room and shuts the door closed with his foot. I go flying as he tosses me on the bed. James follows me and crawls up my body.

"What's the matter? Didn't want a little butt squeeze?" I do my best and give him puppy dog eyes.

He wiggles his way into the cradle of my legs. "I'll give you something to squeeze."

My eyes widen, but before I can offer up a retort James

crashes his mouth to mine. His hand slides to cradle my neck as our tongues intertwine. Kissing him is like realizing I'll never need anything else, not even money, to help celebrate the good times.

James is my partner in the good and bad times. He sees me at my best and sees me at my worst. And through it all, our endless trust and love for the other, has made being with each other easier than taking the next breath.

Emily
2015

"I can't see a thing." I note as my hands wave around in front of me as James leads me somewhere.

It's our eight-year anniversary and the year I'm graduating. I managed to take summer classes a couple of times, so it put me ahead by a semester. James has been working at a local news station with the sports department and I've been student teaching. He's practically moved in with me at my parent's house, but it still feels like we're both guests.

"Keep your eyes closed, I have to unlock a door." I feel the immediate loss of his body heat, but hear the telltale sign of a key being inserted into a lock. "Okay, give me your hand." I do as he says all the while keeping my eyes closed. He pulls me inside and the door behind us closes and I wait with bated breath.

"You can open your eyes now."

I do what he instructs and suck in a breath. "Oh my god. James, what is this? Where are we?"

"Well, this is my, hopefully, our, apartment."

My head whips to him. "Are you asking me to move in with you?"

That boyish smile that makes me fall in love with him every day makes its appearance. "Yeah. If you want to. I mean it's been great living at your parent's house and we've both saved a ton of money living there. But I want us to take the next step. Plus Gloria deserves to spend time with her grandbabies."

"Yes." I tell him instantly and jump into his arms, wrapping my legs around his waist. This is the next big step for us. Although living at my parent's place has been convenient, it's also not ours.

"Hold that reaction. I have one more thing to show you." My body slides down his and he waits until my feet are solidly planted, then holds his hand out to me again.

I'm all off balance so the confusion is ever-present. But I lay my hand in his and let him lead me down the short hallway. James pushes open the door to what I'm assuming is the bedroom and I stop short a few feet inside of the room.

Rose petals and flameless candles surround the space. I turn around to ask him what this is, but the gasp that comes out is cut short when I see James on one knee.

James

"Emily Marie Bailey, it's been eight years since you came into my life. You made it better. You made my life more vibrant. I won't do a big speech because it's our actions that do the talking. But I will ask you one big question. Will you marry me and make me the happiest man in the world?"

A watery, "Yes" comes out of her mouth. I barely see

anything, except for the sliding of the ring on her finger. Emily is my first everything. First kiss, first time, and my first and only love.

She leans down to kiss me, and I stand up to my full height, lifting her and wrapping her legs around my waist. Without breaking stride, I walk us over to the only piece of furniture I had the foresight to have in the apartment. I kneel on the bed and gently lay her down in the center.

"Are you about to make love to your fiancé?" Emily's eyes are glassy as she asks me a question that sends goose-bumps over my body.

"I am. Are you okay with that Ms. Bailey soon-to-be Hayes?" Her arms go up with a silent request to take her shirt off, so I do. When it's off, I reach behind her and unclasp her bra, letting her breasts spill free. Rolling a nipple between my thumb and middle finger, Emily's breath hitches.

Her hands tangle in the sheets, too consumed with plea-sure to say anything right away. "I'm more than okay with that my soon-to-be-husband."

Who makes the next move, I don't remember. We love each other until the sun starts to set.

AFTER THE PIZZA I ordered following our love-making, we lay in bed as Emily looks at her ring. Does it make me a caveman if I want to beat on my chest that she's wearing my ring?

"If something ever happens to me, I want you to be happy. I want you to move on with your life."

I'm ruining our celebratory night with sad thoughts. But it needs to be said before I forget about this.

Emily sits up and I hate the cool air that hits me. "Where is this coming from?"

"I don't know," I confess to her. "Actually, that's a lie. I do know. My parents sat me down to talk about their Will if anything were to happen to them. And it got me thinking about us and the future I want us to have."

"But why are you bringing it up tonight of all nights?"

I take her left hand in mine and fiddle with the ring I put there. "Our relationship has been as easy as breathing. And I thank my lucky stars that we work so seamlessly together. But the real world is so unfair to those who've never done anything wrong. When my parents were talking about their Will it got me thinking hard about us. And what would happen if one of us if the other left too soon."

"Nothing is going to happen to you. Or to me." Her voice is tight and I realize it's taking everything in her to not blow up at me.

"Baby, nothing is guaranteed. I need you to promise me that you will live a full life. I need you to promise that you'll love again and laugh as hard as you possibly can. Emily, I need you to promise me that."

She shakes her head and the tears well up as if what I said is blasphemous. And it is. Because I can't think of a time I would want to be apart from her.

"No. I won't promise you anything. Because nothing's going to happen to you."

This is why I love her. Her fierce determination to not let something like a promise keep her down.

"Emily," I turn and face her, boxing her face in my hands. "Baby, I need you to promise me that. I need you to promise that you can make it in this world without me. Please."

I swipe the tears that have started to fall. Her trembling

lips as she struggles to grasp the only wish I've ever made of her.

Emily brings her hands up to my wrists and holds on. As if holding onto me in this moment will keep us in this space for the rest of our lives.

"I promise," she breathes out. "I promise to live a full life. I promise to make it without you."

Hearing those words, as much as I needed to hear them from her, breaks my heart that one day goodbye will come whether we're ready or not.

Emily
2017

"Hey, what's up?" I hear James speak into what I'm guessing is his phone.

I go back to planning out activities for my class. I've been a kindergarten teacher for two years now. It's been exciting, but also exhausting on top of planning our wedding.

We're three months out from the big day. My dress has been chosen, along with the venue, guest list, the DJ, and our honeymoon hotel confirmation email was delivered to us this morning. I think James is just as, if not more, excited for our wedding. He's been intrinsic in the planning and it's a great sign for life as a married couple.

James's voice rises as he tries to calm down whoever is on the other end of the phone. Putting my pen on the table, I get up and walk back to the bedroom to see him getting his shoes out of the closet. He must sense me because he looks up and mouths *Liam*, and it explains everything.

Kamryn and Liam have been on rocky ground for the past year. Whatever happened recently must have shaken him up. I go back to the kitchen table and pick up my phone to text Kamryn.

Me: Hey, is everything okay?

Kam: No. Would you mind coming over?

Me: Not at all. I'll be there soon.

Walking down the hall to the bedroom, I go to the closet and get my shoes right when James hangs up his phone.

"Liam and Kamryn must have broken up," James announces.

My shoulders drop. "Huh. That must explain why Kamryn was so agreeable to me coming over. Are you going to see Liam?"

"Yeah. But first I wanna make out with my fiancée," James claims as he reaches for me.

I gasp faux scandalized. "You're engaged? How could you do this to me? I thought we were getting married?" I wrap my arms around his neck as he maneuvers us back to the bed.

"You're the one I'm marrying, ya goof. And then after we're married we can have all the fun in the world trying to bring little you's into the world."

The butterflies that swarm at his words take flight making me fall deeper in love with him. "Oh, Mr. Hayes, you say the sweetest things to me."

My breath is stolen when his lips meet mine. We breathe into each other for seconds before James's tongue is probing at my lips, begging for entrance. He devours me like a man starved and I meet his intensity as I rise to my tiptoes. His hands slide to the button of my jeans and flicks them open, pulling the zipper down as his hand dives into the front of my panties. His fingers find my clit, circling, before dipping into my entrance.

James's arm is banded around my waist as he continues to kiss me like he'll never get enough. Like he's starved for air and I'm his supply of oxygen. His fingers slide in and out of my pussy as his thumb rubs circles and flicks my clit. The pressure he applies is enough for my orgasm to flow through me.

My body shakes as I pull my lips from his to take a much-needed breath. "I thought you just wanted to kiss me?" I tease him.

"You should know I can never stop at a kiss." He pulls his hand from my pants and sucks his fingers into his mouth. "Delicious. But I want more. Get naked."

I shimmy my pants off as he works his own off his legs. My shirt and bra are next, and his top joins my clothes in a pile on the floor.

"On the bed Emily," James demands.

I sit on the bed and slide back until I'm in the middle. Spreading my legs, I trail my hand down my torso; teasing my nipples until they're hard peaks and down to my pussy, dipping a finger inside until it's covered in my juices, pulling my finger out and swirling my fingers around my clit.

I watch him as he watches me. His hand goes to the base cock and squeezes. The perfect mushroom tip of his slightly curved cock glistens with pre-cum. James pulls and twists, his forearm flexing with the movement, as I circle my clit and build my pleasure back up by shoving two fingers in my pussy. The obscene sound pulls a moan from me as I throw my head back.

"Christ. Stop, baby. Are you trying to make me come

before I'm inside you?" James crawls up the middle of the bed, stopping at the apex of my thighs.

My fingers are still moving in and out until James grabs my wrist and pulls my fingers into his mouth, licking them dry. When he deems them clean, he places my hand on the bed next to me and lays down, sucking my clit into his mouth with an enthusiastic energy that has my hips lifting off the bed. He wraps his arms around my thighs to keep me in place and holds me open with his fingers. Stiff swipes of his tongue against my clit has my hands fisting in his hair. He slides down and his tongue enters me over and over bringing me right to the edge when he pulls away and drives his cock into me.

"Oh god, you feel so good," I moan out. My legs wrap high around his waist and I pull him down to where our lips are millimeters apart. The movement has James sliding deeper and I can't stop from meshing our lips together. Moaning as I taste myself on his tongue, our tongues dance together as he makes frantic love to me.

We stopped using condoms a while ago and now rely heavily on my birth control shot. And nothing compares to feeling James lose himself inside of me. Like we have all the time in the world to stay tangled in these sheets.

James pushes up on his hands which angles his cock right at my g-spot causing me to moan his name. "That's it, baby."

His thrusts are now motivated with the sole need to make me come. He moves and sits back on his heels, grabbing and lifting my hips as he pounds into me. James knows what makes me lose my mind and this is the way.

"Fuck, Emily. Does that feel good? *My* cock claiming this pussy over and over? *My* cock painting your pussy with my cum. Does that feel good?"

My hands and fingers pinch and pull at my nipples as his dirty talk lands on me.

"Does my girl need to come?" *Thrust.* "Does my girl need to scream?" *Thrust.* "Does my girl need my cum sliding down her legs?" *Thrust.* "Does my girl need to feel me long after we're done?" *Thrust.*

Tears leak from the corner of my eyes as I know this orgasm is about to be a powerful one. "James let me come, please."

His thrusts don't slow down, but they don't speed up. "I need you to come too. Play with your clit and nipples, baby. I wanna feel your pussy fluttering around my cock."

I do as he says because I need to come more than anything.

"That's it, Em." His thrusts get harder and sloppier as the sounds of our arousal and skin slapping together fill our bedroom.

"Oh, fuck James! Right there baby," my orgasm hits me at full force and James pulls out. Sliding his finger in my pussy and prolonging my orgasm.

"Can you give me one more?"

My body is bone tired. But his body, his cock, his filthy words spur me on and I nod my head.

"Good girl. Ride me." He demands as he lays on the bed.

Before straddling his body, I can't help but wrap my hand around his cock. Our mixed arousal proves to be enough lubrication for my hand to slide up and down his erection. I bring my mouth to the mushroom tip, I swallow him to the root and slowly tease him with my tongue. Swirling the tip of my tongue over the slit of his cock as garbled curses spill from his lips.

James grabs hold of my hair and gently pulls me off his length. "Your pussy, baby. Let me come inside of you."

I tease him with one last lick before moving up and straddling his hips. Teasing my opening with the head of cock before sliding down. I give myself a few seconds to readjust to him before I begin to move.

"That's it, Emily," James admires as his hands go to my hips and help me move.

My hands fall to the headboard as I bounce up and down on his length. James pulls a nipple into my mouth and my hips stutter their movement before finding it again.

"This view is incredible." I look down and see James's gaze fixated on where we meet.

"I wanna come again." I'm almost desperate. My legs are shaking as I move up and down his length.

He flips us so suddenly I get dizzy. "You're gonna come at least two more times if I have anything to say about it."

My legs fall open as he holds my hips down and pounds into me. The force of his cock driving in has my toes curling as my orgasm pulls me over the deep end.

"Yes, baby. I'm right there with you." His thrusts are more erratic as he chases his high until his body goes taut.

I feel him pulsing inside of me as our release spills out of my pussy. He continues to thrust lazily until our orgasms have faded. My walls are still fluttering with the after-shocks, keeping his cock semi-hard inside of me.

James's hands slide up my torso and he peppers my chest and neck with kisses. Trailing up to my lips. I hold him to me and my hips move involuntarily.

"Baby, I would need at least thirty minutes to recover and our friends need us." With another hard kiss, he pulls his softening cock out of me and looks down seeing our mixed release spill out of me. "Fuck that's hot."

Our eyes meet before a devilish smile takes over as he looks down again. His hand moves and swipes our release up before pushing it back inside of me. I'm still sensitive, bordering on tired and yet my pussy sucks his fingers in as he works my body the only way he knows how.

"I can't come again," I whine.

"Your pussy says that's a lie." James spreads out next to me and tips my face to his. "One more, baby." He coaxes as our lips hover a breath away.

My hands trail up the side of his neck before I weave my fingers through his hair. Pulling his mouth to mine, our tongues tangle as the kiss deepens. His fingers massage my inner walls as he takes it slow. Slowly building me up before all of the attention of his fingers is on my clit.

Squirming, my hips lift off the bed as he pinches and flicks, strumming and rubbing my clit, over and over until I fall over the edge for the third time. My body is loose and I moan into his mouth before James breaks our kiss, looking down at his fingers. I feel a gush of wetness as my orgasm hits me again.

"Jesus Christ, baby. That's hot," James muses before moving and sliding back down my body. I hear him slurping up my release as my orgasm refuses to stop.

My head falls fully into the pillow as my body releases the last drop. With a kiss to my mound, the bed moves as James gets up to the bathroom. I hear the water running and then he's back with a washcloth, cleaning me with care while observing the mess we made up.

"We're gonna have to change the sheets." He claims with his hands on his hips. James realizes the washcloth is no use and I can't stop the laughter that escapes as I decide to rinse off in the shower and get dressed again.

~

THIRTY MINUTES later I pull up to Kamryn's tiny house. It's a cute place for one person. It's where she's made a home that's all for her.

Me: At Kamryn's. I'll see you in a little bit. I love you.

James: At Liam's. He's not doing too well. I'll see you tonight. I love you always.

Turning off my car, I take my keys out of the ignition and walk up the front walkway to Kam's door. Knocking twice, before she pulls open the door. My good mood instantly plummets as I've never seen her look so beaten down.

"Hi, friend." I greet her and open my arms for her to walk into.

We stand embraced on the threshold before I release her, walking over to her couch and I get her to spill. When she tells me everything that's been going on between them, I'm shocked. I never expected them to have these kinds of problems.

"He did not say that!?" My voice is full of surprise.

"He did. I know what I want. He wanted it too, but something changed with him. It's like when his dreams failed mine should too. Am I overreacting? Am I being too hard on him?" It seems she's never voiced these questions out loud until now.

"Kam, you know that boy adores you. I've talked to Liam and it looked like the stars were put in his eyes every time someone mentioned you. You also have a right to feel the way that you do." I tell her as her phone starts ringing.

"It's Liam." His smiling face looks back at us as her phone is lit up.

"Answer it!"

"Hello."

I pull out my phone to text James.

> Me: Everything okay with Liam?

> James: Not even close to okay. He just started rambling. And wanted to go for a drive.

> Me: Try to get him to pull the truck over.

> James: I'll try, baby.

I tune back into Kamryn's phone call. "Liam, what are you doing?! That's not what I want! Liam stop the truck!" Kamryn yells into the phone. Fear takes hold of me as the realization that Liam's erratic driving with James in the truck is a recipe for disaster.

I whip out my phone to text James again. The tears in my eyes make it hard to see.

> Me: Baby.

> Me: Please get him to stop.

> Me: James, I don't have a good feeling about this.

> Me: Please get him to stop the truck!

> Me: You prepared me years ago, but I'm not ready.

> Me: I love you too much to live in this world without you.

"Liam please!" Kamryn pleads with him, *begs* him to stop the truck. "I want you in my life. I need you in my life, just not like this!"

I can't stop the tears that are streaming down my face as I hear the back and forth of a volatile argument that James and I unknowingly got dragged into.

"Liam stop the truck!" I glance at Kamryn's face and see it's gone ghostly white. The phone falls out of her hand. Clattering to the floor.

It's then that I know.

As the shock turns to numbness.

When I'm sure that the string that tethered us together is now severed.

Without anyone telling me.

That the love of my life is no longer a part of my world.

Emily

I sit in the pew between Brandon and my mom. It's been five days since James was taken from this world.

Five days since I've taken a full breath.

Five days since I saw his boyish smirk that I fell in love with at fourteen.

I've been in a state of complete disbelief and denial that I'll never see him again. That the happily ever after that we were so close to having was taken away.

Fading into the nether of the almost.

I hate that word.

Almost.

And as I sit with silent tears trailing down my face, I stare at his closed casket and I think about our 'almost'. Our almost happily ever after.

My mind takes me back to the moment at the hospital. Seeing his handsome face and the jawline that I traced countless times covered in scars. I begged and pleaded for him to wake up. For him to push through the sedation they had him under because of the pain. But the begging and pleading fell into the abyss as his body slowly let go.

When my focus shifts back to the church, I see the priest looking expectantly at me. My heart drops as I walk the few steps up to the podium. I unfold what would have been our vows. I didn't plan to speak. But the Hayes family deserves it.

I deserve it.

"Hi," I weakly start. "I didn't have a big speech planned because I never planned for this to happen. If you don't know, my name is Emily. James and I were set to marry in a few months." I clench my teeth as the tears well up and slide down my face in two fast tracks. "And instead of letting these words that I planned to say to him on our wedding day never see the light of day, I figured it would be best to say them today."

I wipe away the fallen tears and tuck my hair behind my ears. "James, today is the day that I officially become yours. From white clover bracelets to wedding rings, we have been through it all. Thank you, for talking to me on that first day of school. Neither of us knew it but that was the beginning of us. You've made a lot of promises for our life together but now it's my turn. I vow to always stock the freezer with Oreo ice cream. I vow to buy the largest blankets for us to cuddle under for movie nights. I vow to never go to bed angry with you. I vow to grow old with you. I vow to love you until I can't anymore. James Michael Hayes, I vow to be your partner in life, the mother of your children, and the best friend that you will ever have. Today is the day that the rest of our lives begin and I'm so happy it's with you."

My knees almost buckle as I finish reading my vows. Swiftly, I take my paper and walk back down the two steps to the pew. My mom wraps my hand in hers and Brandon slings his arm over my shoulder.

I detach myself from the space that I'm in as the funeral draws to a close. Only family and close friends are allowed at the burial site. As much as I wish I wasn't going, I need it.

Dressed in black we walk like a treacherous wave down the aisle and to the waiting cars. The sniffles from the mourners in the church as this is their final goodbye to the man who lit up a room.

My parents flank me in the hearse as I stare blankly ahead. The world could be on fire and I wouldn't even know. My dad makes sure I get out of the car and holds me tightly to his side as we walk to the site. I blank out as the casket that carries James's physical body inside of it is brought to the center.

His physical body.

Because in my mind he's still here. In my mind, he's preparing for his ten o'clock staff meeting that he has every Thursday. But my mind plays tricks on me.

I fiddle with my engagement ring. The one I haven't taken off since he put it there. The ring I thought I would wear for the rest of my life.

More words are spoken, but I still don't hear any of them. I'm lost in the grief of losing the man who was set to be my husband. I'm lost in the grief of knowing parents just lost their son. I'm lost in the grief of knowing four brothers just lost the glue.

When it comes time, we head up, one by one, and scoop up a handful of dirt as his casket is lowered.

"*I love you*," I say to myself as I cup a handful of the cold, thick dirt from the pile off to the side. "*I love you. I love you. Now I have to make it without you.*"

~

February 2018

"I promise I'll love you forever."
"Forever's a long time you know?"
"I'm okay with forever as long as you are."

I wake up from my dream gasping for breath, drenched in sweat, and wondering why this dream felt so real. It's been a while since I've dreamed about James. Every dream I have of the two of us is more vivid than the last. Like I just experienced it.

It's been six months since he died.

Six long months without the love of my life.

I keep replaying that day over and over in my head. Thinking that if either of us did something different he would still be here. That we would be married. And I wouldn't be in this purgatory-like state wondering when this hell-ish nightmare would be over.

That night as I walked back into our apartment, with fresh sheets on the bed that we had just changed and the old ones waiting to be swapped into the dryer, was it then that my heart disintegrated. The reality of those events caught up to me as I collapsed onto the floor and let the pain of new grief consume me as I cried out with body-shaking sobs and wails as my new reality hit me like a thousand bricks.

How had it been hours ago that I was sitting at the dining table grading papers?

How had it been hours ago that he and I were making love before going off to help our friends?

How had it been hours ago that I kissed my fiancé for the last time and not know it?

The day of his funeral was the second hardest day of my

life without him. It was the day I was officially saying goodbye to the love of my life. To the boy who was my first everything. My first boyfriend, my first kiss, my first time, and my first love.

Not long after James' funeral, I retreated to my parent's house in New York for a while. While our relationship wasn't always on solid footing, they understood my need to retreat to a place he and I had never stepped foot in and were supportive of my need to withdraw from life.

During my stay there, I managed to ask them if they would look for someplace else for me to live. We may not have seen eye-to-eye while I was growing up, but they stepped up for me when I needed it the most. My parents were the parents I so desperately needed in those moments when I could barely string a sentence, let alone a thought together. They hired movers and contacted the leasing office at the old place, explaining my situation. Thankfully the complex was understanding and let the lease break early.

I was told that grieving didn't have a timetable. That you could be on your way to healing when all of a sudden it hits you. The tears you thought were dried are renewed as you think to contact him for the first time in months, those tears fall with no intention of stopping.

I mourned the would-be wedding and honeymoon that quickly arrived on the calendar. I mourned our would-be happily married life. I mourned for a life I could have had.

I left my would-be life in Philadelphia. That's when a new grieving period happened. And now I'm somewhere new. Trying to heal without my other half.

Emily
2019

"Don't forget, that open house is tonight. I'd love to see your faces and meet your parents." I announce it to my kids as a final reminder at the end of the day.

"Bye, Ms. Bailey," they say in unison as they walk out of the door.

My fourth year of teaching has just started and I'm feeling good about it. These kids make my days better. Yes, they can test my patience like no other, but when it comes down to it they're all eager to learn. And I'm eager to teach them.

They may be first graders, but I plan on slipping some real-life information into their brains. And that's what I plan on talking about at the open house. I want the parents to know what I have planned for them. Where I studied, where I come from, and why I got into teaching. I want the parents of my students to know that they can come to me with whatever.

A knock on my door pulls me out of my head. "Hey, are you ready for tonight?" Melissa the teacher across the hall asks me. Since we both started teaching the same year at this school, we've become close.

"Yeah. But I'll probably come back before and finish setting up. Are you up for dinner before then?" I ask while putting some of my things in my tote bag.

"Mm-hmm. Just let me go home and get a shower to change and then we'll meet up."

"Sounds like a plan. See you in a bit." I wave her off before putting my focus back on my things.

Before I walk out of my classroom, I make a physical list of what I need to do before tonight. It's not much, but once I have all of that down, I head out.

I'M so thankful that my apartment isn't too far from the school. It's about fifteen minutes, but with traffic, the drive can take up to thirty minutes. That's living in the city for you.

When I open the door to my apartment my cat, Biscuit, greets me with a meow for food. "Hi, sweet girl."

I pick her up and smother her with some kisses before setting her down to get ready.

I'm still living in the apartment that my parents chose for me when I left Pennsylvania. It's got exposed brick on the walls that line the fully equipped kitchen, an airy living room, a spacious primary bedroom, and a guest room that primarily serves as Biscuit's room. Each floor only has two units which makes living here a peaceful place. I've thought about moving and getting a house, but it's just me and my cat. I have no need for a bigger space when everything fits in my room and the spare room.

Thirty minutes later I'm dressed and ready to meet

Melissa. We meet at a fast food Italian restaurant and then talk about little things. Melissa is from Arizona, but she went to school in Ohio. She never planned to move back home unless she had to, but the stars aligned for her and here she is. She and her boyfriend of four years live together and they have plans to start looking for a house soon.

Do I feel a pang of sadness...even jealousy when I hear this? Of course. Because that should be me and despite the envy, I'm happy for my new friend.

An hour later, we're both back at the school along with some other teachers putting the final touches on our rooms. Music is blasting through the intercom making our tasks that much easier. At fifteen minutes til, the principal comes over the intercom to turn off the music and let us know that it's almost time.

I never remember my open houses to be like this. This nervous energy of meeting the person who's responsible for your child for seven hours. Of course, I can hardly remember that far back...so maybe I'll have to ask my parents if they remember anything.

Whipping out my phone, I quickly send a text to my girls.

Me: Drinks tonight? I have an open house and I'm gonna need something stronger than water.

Jax: I'm in!

Sarah: Me too!

Kam: No question about it

Me: Yay! I'll let you know when I'm done. Usual place? Monty's?

Jax: *thumbs up emoji*

Sarah: Ditto

Kam: *pointing up arrow*

~

"I KNOW it's tough to put this much trust in a fourth-year teacher. It's even difficult because I'm still young. But I promise, I will help your child through everything," I address the room of parents that have raised some concerns.

"What about loss? I know this isn't your area of expertise, but I'm wondering how you'll handle it. My teachers never really understood. So, say an older relative passes and our child is sad about it. You're not a counselor. But are we supposed to think that you're equipped to handle something like this, or have even gone through something like that?" A parent voices.

I take a cleansing breath and walk over to sit on top of my desk while addressing the parents. "My fiancé died in a car accident. I heard every form of condolence and sayings that *you're still here*. As if telling me that I'm still here was going to help. It was tough to go through. I retreated for a while and I'll understand if your kid does too. I'm not saying that my loss is any different from any of your child's potential losses, but I will help them through that. Without knowing it, your kids have helped me immensely.

"When you pull your child out of class, I will understand. I will work with them when they return to catch them up. If your child breaks down in class because they miss them, I understand too. I'm not here to judge your children. I'm here to help them and teach them. Real life experiences are never too soon to begin even with them being so young. And even for them to learn that loss does happen, and that they will get through it."

I get appreciative nods from some of the uneasy parents. And hopefully gain their respect.

Before more questions are asked, the principal comes over the intercom announcing that our two hours are up.

A few of the parents walk up after the open-house has ended to speak personally to me. It touches me to know that their child likes me and the way that I teach. I walk the last parent to the door and look across the hall to see Melissa still talking to some parents.

I go back into my room and gather up my stuff and send a wave to her when she glances my way. Then I send a text to the girls.

Me: I'm out! See you soon!

I WALK into Monty's and search for my girls. It's a Tuesday night so the bar is empty. With a quick scan I come up empty and determine that they're still on the way. So I take a seat at the bar to pass the time.

"What can I getcha?" The bartender asks me and places a small napkin in front of me with a glass of water.

"May I get a Moscow Mule with Stoli, please?" I ask and peel my jacket off before laying it on the back of the barstool and climbing up, keeping my clutch next to me.

"Coming right up."

Expressing to the parents the loss that I've been through was harder than I thought. I hadn't talked about James openly like that in a long time. I also had no plans to. It was both comforting and unsettling.

"Here you go, sweetheart. Start a tab? Or close it out?"

I ponder that for a minute before I slide my card to him. "Thank you. Start a tab, please."

Once he walks away, I continue to wallow in my misery. They say misery loves company. But I have no company. Just my misery.

It's been two years, Em. I tell myself. Yeah but two years of him gone does little to erase the ten years of memories that we have together.

Had together.

~

OCTOBER 2009

"What was the surprise you had for me?" I ask James.

With my crying from my parents, I forgot that's why I was originally supposed to come over here.

He gets up from the top step and holds his hand out for me. "Come on. Let me show you."

Placing my hand in his, he pulls me up and together we walk back towards his bedroom. I shake off my parents being here and James's big declaration and focus on him. We walk back into his bedroom and he closes the door behind him.

"Now that I think about it, it's not a grand surprise. But the idea came to me and I ran with it." James confesses when we're back in his room.

"You know I'll love anything you gift me." I lean up and kiss him on the cheek, then I go and sit back on his bed cross-leg.

"Close your eyes."

"Baby, seriously?" I look at him as if he's serious.

His arms cross over his chest making the sleeves pull taught. As he's gotten older he's continued to fill out. With him choosing to not playing a sport in college he's been hitting the gym to keep in shape. But with our personal extracurriculars, I've told him that should be enough. That earned me three extra orgasms. I didn't complain at all.

I narrow my eyes at him before relenting. My hands go over my eyes too, just to appease him. "Does this work?"

"Yes, smartypants," I hear a rustling and then nothing. "Okay, you can open your eyes now."

He places the box in my held out hands. I give it a little shake just for reassurance.

"Just open it, ya goof."

James sits on the bed next to me and waits with bated breath as I lift the top off the box.

A collage of our time together greets me in a picture frame. Movie ticket stubs, photo booth pictures, a napkin from the ice cream shop, a picture of me practicing, James in his football uniform with me after a game, and so many more mementos of us in the three years we've been together.

"I love it," I tell James with tears in my eyes. "I love you." Leaning forward I place my lips to his but he pulls back.

"I love you too, my Emmy." He announces.

I love it when he calls me that. "What else do you love about me?" I ask as I crawl into his lap and straddle him.

"How strong you are." James declares and then suddenly flips our positions. His body fits in the cradle of my legs perfectly. He places his arms on either side of my head and traces over my face with his gaze. "I wanna spend the rest of my life with you. I want the house, the kids, the movie nights, and ice cream dates. I want to spend the rest of my life with *you, Emily Marie Bailey. I love you more than the words I just said."*

The tears that were once sad from neglect have turned to happiness from the love that James has given me. I nod and smile through the emotions. Pulling him closer to seal our lips together.

Adam

I noticed her the second she walked through the door of my bar. Light brown eyes with long wavy dark brown hair and an olive complexion. She looked like she was seconds away from breaking if something went wrong. So as soon as I set her drink down in front of her, I gave her some space until she looked up in search of someone.

What I didn't expect was her gaze to completely unfocus and tears falling with no intention of stopping. Thankfully it's emptier for a Tuesday, otherwise, I feel she'd be more than mortified if she knew she was crying in front of strangers.

Tossing the dish rag on the counter, I walk out from behind the bar and make my way towards her. She still hasn't noticed my presence and I don't want to frighten her. So I gently place my hand on her shoulder.

"Are you okay?" I say it as softly as possible, even though she still startles at my words.

A soft gasp comes from her as she looks around before settling her tearful gaze on me.

The woman in front of me breaks my heart and I don't even know her. She swiftly wipes under her eyes as if that'll help erase the evidence of pain.

"I'm sorry," she says and it's the last thing I expected her to say. Her phone pings multiple times before she looks at it. And her shoulders fall from her ears as what I'm assuming her reaction is from regret texts.

"Do you want to talk about it?" I ask when a few seconds of stilted silence are all that pass between us.

Her eyes water as she shakes her head. "I don't think you want to hear it."

My bartender comes back into the bar from reconnecting new beer taps. "I've got time. Come with me."

She hesitates before grabbing her things along with her drink. Silently, she follows me out to the dining patio. It's blessedly empty so I'm hoping it gives her a chance to let out what has her so upset.

Her shaky breaths are the only sound between us, so I break it with words.

"What has you here on a Tuesday? Crying in a bar nonetheless?"

A lone tear slips out of her eye and I watch as it forges a path down her cheek. "I slipped back into a memory with my fiancé."

That puts me on edge and I lean forward in my chair. "Did he hurt you?"

"He can't hurt me when he's dead." I watch as her lips tremble while she tries to hold it together. "Although the fact that his death still feels so raw is cause for me to say he did hurt me."

"I'm so sorry," if I could say anything other than that, I would. "Would you mind telling me how he passed? Maybe talking about him and your time together will help."

She looks down at her hands and begins to tell me her story.

"We met when I was fourteen and were together for eleven years. He was the first person to champion for me. He was there when I got into fights with my parents. He cheered me on at my showcases. At eighteen I knew I would marry him."

What's it like to be that sure of who you're meant to be with when you're that young? If I was so sure I wouldn't be divorced.

"Turns out we were on the same page. But he didn't end up proposing to me until I graduated college. That's what I love, or should I say loved, about him. But I guess the universe had a different plan. He was taken from me three months before our wedding."

If I could take her pain, I would. But no matter the words I say or the gestures I make, it can never take her pain away. "I'm so sorry. I wish I had another word to say."

Her smile is lifeless as more tears flow down her face. "For those days after I was in such denial. I kept waiting for him to walk through the door of our apartment, ready to spout off some sports stat that had been rattling around in his brain. But as the days went by and the door never opened, reality sunk in. It's been two years and some days it's hard for me to remember what it's like to breathe. Or how to exist in a world where he's not a part of it. And I know that's selfish, I know I could heal and move on. But he was my other half." She covers her mouth with her hand as a soft sob breaks free.

If there was ever a higher power to ensure that hearts never broke or suffered from loss, then surely us humans would sign up for that.

"My wife left me. Just decided this slower pace of city

life wasn't for her. I know her leaving doesn't compare to your loss. But I do know what it's like to have that emptiness inside of you."

She looks at me through her tears as though she sees me. It's been years since I've had a heart-to-heart with someone that wasn't my son.

"I'm sorry," she tells me.

"I'm sorry, too. I'm Adam." It's silly, but I hold my hand out to her.

Her hand fits in mine, almost like a missing puzzle piece before giving me a small shake. "Emily. I'd say it's nice to meet you, but I didn't really start off with a great first impression."

I pull my hand back and shake off the tingling from her hand fitting with mine. "I won't judge or tell anyone. So what brings you here on a Tuesday?"

"I had an open house. And wanted to get a drink with my girlfriends. But they bailed at the last minute."

Panic ensues as I knew I was forgetting something. I'll just have to see if Dylan has his teacher's email so I can set up a time to meet.

"So you're a teacher?" I lean my forearms on the table in front of me. It's a very slim chance that she's a teacher at Dylan's school. This area has at least twenty schools varying from elementary to high school. So the odds are slim that she's an elementary teacher.

She takes a sip of her drink. "Mm-hmm. It's my fourth year. The first couple of years were a blur. Not because I was still new, but I was planning my wedding and then my personal life went to shit, I didn't think teaching wanted me anymore."

"I really am sorry, Emily."

"Thank you." I watch her throat bobble with a hard swallow. "Shouldn't you get back inside?"

"Yeah. You're right." I push my chair back and get up. "It was good to meet you, Emily. Stay out here for as long as you want to."

She goes to push her chair back as well. "I should get going. It's been a long day."

I walk us both toward the door that leads back inside. Looking around the restaurant, I see no new customers have entered. All signs lead to getting work done and making it home before midnight.

"Can I pay my tab?" Emily asks when we're at the bar.

Shaking my head I tell her. "It's on the house."

"What? I can't let you do that." She goes to take cash out of her wallet.

"Emily," I start and place my hand on her forearm. "I insist. Plus it's my bar so what I say goes."

A rosy hue covers her cheeks and it has me wondering if it was from her drink she was slowly sipping on or the brief physical contact. The rosy hue gives her a look of innocence that sucks me in. She looks too young for me. And I have Dylan to care for. Who even knows if we'll ever cross paths again.

"Well, thank you."

I walk around the bar to the register, cancel her tab and hand her back her credit card.

We both linger at the bar. I'm not sure how to depart after spending the last thirty minutes talking with each other.

"You can feel your grief and your pain, for as long as you need to. There is no set timetable for when you need to move on." The feeling that no one's ever told her that grief doesn't have an expiration date is evident in the tears that manage to pool in her eyes.

Her breath stutters before she looks me in the eye. "Thank you, Adam."

"You're welcome."

With a final breath and a short wave, Emily walks out the door. I didn't know what to expect tonight when she walked through the door, but it wasn't a soul-baring conversation.

Shaking myself out of the ghost of her person, I tell my bartender I'm headed to my office to get caught up on paperwork. I tackle the orders that need to be placed, payroll, tip outs and drops, and finalize the schedule for the next two weeks. By the time I finish all of my work, it's pushing ten. I look at the small TV screens that show the front of the house and notice no one in the restaurant or bar.

Quickly calling up front, I let them know to start closing up early so we can get out of here on time.

> Me: Cleaning up the restaurant. Should be home shortly.

> Jenny: Sounds good. Dylan went to bed about an hour ago.

> Me: Thanks, Jenny.

Dammit. I really thought I'd be out earlier. But time just got away from me. I hope Jenny doesn't have an exam tomorrow or I'll really feel like dirt.

I make a list of what needs to be looked at around the restaurant, post a hiring ad for a host, and work with the chef on the menu for the next coming weeks.

A knock on my office door pulls me from my thoughts,

"Restaurant's all clean boss." My bartender, Matt, holds out his money drops for the night to me.

Looking at the time, I see another hour has flown by. Shit! I place his envelope on my desk and gather my things. I shut my computer down and follow him out of the restaurant to lock up.

"See you tomorrow, boss man." He calls before jogging to his car.

"Later."

Me: Time got away from me. I'll be home shortly.

Jenny: No worries.

With no traffic, I make it home in twenty minutes. I thank Jenny profusely for staying later than intended and watch to make sure she gets to her car to leave. I finish the closing shift of my downstairs before heading upstairs and peaking in at Dylan.

A surge of pride rushes through me that this little boy is healthy and happy. How Chelsea could up and leave not only me, but our son, baffles me. His nightlight gives me enough light to see as I walk into his room as quietly as possible. Pulling his comforter back over his body, I place a light kiss on his cheek and back out of his room as softly as I can.

I pad down to the opposite end of the hallway and into my bedroom. Stripping off my work clothes, I head for the shower. All the while I think about Emily. How she broke in front of a complete stranger.

My mind drifts for the second time tonight as I think about the possibility of us running into each other again.

And then I come to the conclusion that Cincinnati is a big city and the odds of us seeing each other again is slim to none.

Emily

Three Months Later

"Okay, class don't forget to finish the work you didn't get to today along with three things that you're thankful for."

The hurrying and rustling of work being shoved into backpacks at the end of the day is a teacher's personal soundtrack. I stand at the threshold of the door and see them off to the bus loop.

"Ms. Bailey?" A small voice asks from the classroom.

I turn to see Dylan Montgomery sitting at his desk. His feet swing back and forth as he looks at me with eyes the color of moss. "Yes, Dylan?"

"I have to go to the bathroom."

A huff of laughter leaves me. He's my most outspoken student, hence why he's still here.

I check the time on my watch and see we have a little bit of time. "Okay, ya goof. Let's go."

He hops out of his chair and together we walk to the

bathroom. I wait for him outside and when he's done, we walk to the front office to see if I have any messages.

"Hi Patricia, do I have any messages?"

She thumbs through her notes before shaking her head. "Not today, sweetheart. But you do have some mail."

Patricia goes to the mailroom and I glance down at Dylan. He's in his own world watching his shoes tap together like Dorothy from *Wizard of Oz*.

"Here you go, honey." Patricia says and hands me my small stack of mail.

"Thank you. Have a great evening. Come on Dylan, let's see if your Dad is here."

I reached out to Dylan's dad about scheduling a parent-teacher conference. He's the only parent of my students that I have yet to meet. Not only that, but Dylan is having a hard time focusing and I'm wondering if it's something at home that's occupying him. Dylan is still young so it's possible his brain is taking in the environment at a faster pace.

Out in the main hallway, we both look left and right before deciding to wait by the front door. I stand off to the side as Dylan runs his finger through the grooves in the cinder block walls as I thumb through the mail I've gotten.

Junk. Junk. Maybe important. Junk. I decide.

"Ms. Bailey, is this really necessary?" I look down to see Dylan still running his finger in the grooves of the wall.

Tucking my mail under my arm I turn my attention to him. "Do you even know what necessary means?"

His eyebrows scrunch together as he thinks and I have to stop the laugh that wants to be freed. "Um...no. But I heard it from my dad and I really wanted to use it."

At that, I can't stop the small laugh that comes out of

me. "Well, it's the right word, buddy. But maybe you should look it up before you throw it into a conversation."

He shrugs his small shoulders in response.

"Is that my big guy?" A voice sounds from the door.

"Dad!" Dylan shouts.

My eyes follow Dylan as he runs towards…Adam. And I do my best to swallow down my shock when our eyes meet.

It's been three months since I met him and as much as I hate to admit it to myself, I've thought about that night too many times to count.

Now that I'm seeing Dylan in Adam's arms, the resemblance is uncanny. How did I not catch that? How did I not memorize how good-looking Adam is? Eyes as green as the forest, dark brown hair that looks like he's run his fingers through it all day, and colorful tattoos swirling up to his neck and peeking out from the cuff of his flannel. Seeing him in the light of day knocks the metaphorical pants off of me. And the well-kept beard that has me fantasizing about running my fingers through it.

He puts Dylan back on two feet and we stand in the foyer of the school. Adam shoves his hands in the front pockets of his jeans. My arms crossed over the mail in front of my chest.

But we both say nothing. Staring at each other.

Silent.

And a little awkward.

Okay, a lot awkward.

A noise from the front office breaks me out of the haze. "Hey, Dylan, why don't you head back to my classroom and look up the word 'necessary'? I just want to have a quick word with your Dad before we get started."

Dylan starts to run, but I stop him before he can get any

further. Although I know once he turns the corner nothing can stop him.

I drop my arms from their crossed position and hold my mail in front of my body as I slowly turn my attention back to the not-so-stranger. "So you're a dad," I state like him being here isn't obvious.

"It appears that way. And you're my son's teacher. It's a small world."

He holds his hand out to me to lead the way and we slowly make our way to my classroom. I might be crossing so many lines right now, but it's completely innocent. We're just talking.

"Is that why you weren't at the open house that Tuesday?"

He tucks his hands back into his front pockets. "My Assistant General Manager went into early labor. So I'm covering my restaurant without her help for the foreseeable future."

"And you were kind enough to talk to the crying girl at your bar?" I attempt to make a joke. We turn the corner of the empty hallway and only the sound of my chunky heels echo around us.

His hand on my arm halts my steps. "That's not the only reason. I just felt you needed someone to talk to."

"You're right. I did," I get lost in his eyes for a second, before stepping back and reminding myself that he's a parent of one of my students. "Shall we?"

Adam looks as if he's about to say something but closes his mouth and falls back in step with me.

~

"Dylan is incredibly smart, quick on his feet, and helps me out when I get stumped on something. But sometimes it's too much. I have a class full of twenty-five first graders and I need involvement from them just as much from him."

Normally my parent-teacher conferences are for kids that aren't meeting their goals. But in this case, Dylan is overshooting every goal I set and not giving the other kids a chance to engage.

"So the problem is with Dylan over-shadowing the other kids?" Adam looks confused, and rightfully so. Usually, when these meetings happen it's because the student is misbehaving.

"To put it short and sweet, yes. I need my other kids to shine just as much as him. He does tend to act out a little when I attempt to get involvement from the other students. I love that he's so eager to learn, but...give me a week. I think I may be able to create a role for him that'll help shine his quick thinking. Not just for my class, but the whole first-grade class. Is it okay with you if I give that a try? I don't want to do anything without you knowing what I have planned."

Adam glances back at Dylan looking through an encyclopedia with awe. "He has always been like that. I say give it a shot."

"Awesome." The breath I was holding releases quickly.

"Do you think you could email me your plans when you have one set?"

"Of course! Any involvement from my students' parents is highly encouraged."

Adam continues to ask questions about what sort of plan could be involved to help Dylan. And I find myself warming up more and more to him. Helping people and finding solutions is what I'm good at.

"I know things get lost in translation, but is it okay if I leave my cell number? Just in case I'm unable to answer my email in a timely manner."

I see where Dylan gets it. The doe-eyed look that gets me to do anything.

Getting up from the table we're at, I pluck a notebook and pen off my desk. Walking back to him he takes the offered material and writes his number down. He takes a little longer than I thought he would, but he closes the notebook before I have a chance to see what he wrote.

"All done?" I question him even though I know he is.

"Yep." His cheeky grin has my face flaming.

Shaking my head, I step back. "On that note, it was good to see you again, Adam. Dylan, I'll see you tomorrow, buddy."

I watch him put the encyclopedia back before getting his backpack.

"Bye, Ms. Bailey."

"Bye, buddy. Adam."

"Emily," his eyes hold mine until Dylan shouts for him down the hall.

Once he's out of my classroom, I lean against my desk.

Flustered.

A little confused.

And left with so many questions.

I flip open the notebook and see he wrote not only his number but a little note.

IN CASE YOU CHANGE YOUR MIND.

—ADAM

Emily

"Emily, you're allowed to be happy," Sarah announces at dinner.

I looped them in on what happened when they didn't show up to the bar and then the other day with the parent-teacher conference.

Maybe it was for the best that they weren't there. Otherwise, I'd have never released more of the grief that I had been holding on to. And I wouldn't have had the chance to talk with Adam.

"Guys, I can't," I admit defeat.

"Well, why not?" Kamryn asks me.

"For one, he's my student's father. And two, maybe I'm not ready to date anyone."

Sarah places her hand on mine. "Sweetie, no one is saying you have to commit to another man right away. Just have some fun. All you do is work, hang out with us, and spend time with your cat."

"Hey! Leave Biscuit out of this." I defend my cat who can't defend herself. Sarah's eyebrows raise as if saying *See?*

and I know it's a lost cause. "How do I even do this? I haven't had to date-date in a long time."

"What did you and James do?" Jax chimes in.

"We went to ice cream or had movie marathon dates." Those were some of the best dates of my life.

I see them all confused.

"What? We were kids with no licenses. What else were we supposed to do? Being with him was so easy. Being with him was effortless. Nobody put pressure on us to go above and beyond what our relationship was."

I think that's what scares me. James and I *were* effortless. And to start over with someone in my twenties was not something I had envisioned in my life plan.

"James would want you to be happy. You know that, right?" Kamryn tells me as if I don't already know this.

My eyes water at the mention of him wanting me to be happy. To that exact conversation we had after we got engaged.

"What is it, honey?" Sarah asks.

"The night we got engaged, he said that if anything happened to him, he'd want me to be happy. He wanted to prepare me to make it without him if that ever happened. And I was so mad that he brought up something like the after when we were celebrating our present." I feel my lips tremble as I remember that moment so clearly.

Kamryn clasps her hand with mine and waits until I'm facing her. "Maybe James somehow knew that you'd need early reassurance if anything ever happened to him. Em, you are one of the strongest people I know. Yeah, these last few years have been a bitch to get through. But you've done it with the poise and grace I saw in you when you were fourteen. You deserve all the happiness that you can hold onto. And James would want that for you."

LATER THAT NIGHT I'm sitting on my balcony with a glass of wine on the table to my right and citronella candles lit around me. Lana Del Rey on vinyl floats through the open windows as Biscuit is curled in my lap. I've been staring at my unlit phone screen, just waiting for the wine to loosen my brain.

After the parent-teacher conference, I programmed Adam's number into my phone as a precaution. Following dinner, my pro-cons list is battling for victory in my head.

"Just do it, Emily. What's the worst that could happen?" Talking to myself is a terrible sign. But here goes nothing.

> Me: Hey. It's Emily.

> Me: Dylan's teacher.

It's not even hot out here and I'm sweating. How do people do this on the regular? Why hasn't he responded? Is he working? I'm so not cut out for this. I'm about to type out another reply, but my phone lights up with a message from him.

> Adam: Hi, Dylan's teacher.

> Me: Is this a bad time?

> Adam: Not at all. Just making another list for what needs repurchasing.

> Me: What all does that entail?

> Adam: Retail, liquor, seasonal menus... things like that.

Adam: But hearing about my list isn't what you texted me for, is it?

Me: No. It's not.

Adam: I have time.

Me: Do you maybe wanna get coffee one morning?

Goodness, I'm terrible at this.

Adam: I'd like that. I just have to make sure Dylan's sitter is free.

Me: Oh, of course. Well, I'll let you get back to your work.

Adam: You don't have to be shy Emily.

Me: I can't help it. It's who I am.

Adam: Hopefully one day you won't be so shy around me.

How does he say all the right things?

Me: Goodnight, Adam.

Adam: Goodnight, Emily.

"Good morning, class."

"Good morning, Ms. Bailey," they chant back.

I walk around to the front of the classroom. It's the day before Thanksgiving break and the kids are restless. As are us teachers.

"Since today is a short day, let's start off with what we're going to be doing tomorrow. Anyone wanna start?" A show of little arms shoots up and I pick on a student.

Her response is rambled as she tells me all of the food she plans to eat. I nod my head and widen my eyes when appropriate knowing she'll only get a sliver of what she thinks she'll eat. Kids have the wildest imaginations. It's why I love teaching at this grade level.

With it being a half day I only have my kids for a few hours. Why the school district tortures us instead of giving us the day before Thanksgiving off, I'll never understand.

I put on a movie for the rest of the time we're at school. It's an easy way for the kids to be entertained and for me to get a head start on grading.

I've timed it correctly because early dismissal happens a couple of minutes after the movie ends.

"Have a great Thanksgiving break you guys," I declare as I walk to the door and open it. The chatter from the hallway filters in the room. "I'll see you next Monday," I tell my students as they walk out of the classroom.

I get to work on putting my classroom in order, so it's less work I have to do next week. Arranging the desks in a new quad pattern keeps my kids engaged and it's fun for me to see which little personalities mesh or clash.

A knock on my door halts my rearrangement. "Hey, are you headed out soon?"

Turning, I see Melissa with her tote over her shoulder and her purse and water bottle in her opposite hand. Looking at my watch I see an hour has passed me by.

"Yeah. I'm gonna finish up here. Are you staying here for the break?" As I ask her this, I realize I have to decide if I'm gonna stay here with my girls or go home to a not-so-pleasant Thanksgiving with my parents.

Melissa shifts her weight to the other side of her body. "I think so. Jeff and I were talking about heading to Chicago to spend it with his family. But something about not having to beat the holiday traffic sounds more appealing to me. So we'll see. What about you?"

"I'm not sure yet. I try to avoid going home as much as possible." Going home means seeing James' family's house and not seeing him. But it also means I get to be a little closer to him.

"I understand that. Well, have a good break and I'll see you on Monday."

Melissa takes a couple backward steps and I follow her to the threshold of my door. I watch her walk off before I deduce that I've done what I can to prepare for next week. So I pack up my things and make the drive back home.

Adam

"Hey, buddy. How was school?"

With Dylan being out early I had to work my schedule around for him since Jenny is taking her final exam. My assistant general manager informed me she wouldn't be returning following her maternity leave so I got to hiring a new assistant. He started a couple of weeks ago and with the holiday causing a lull, I know he's more than capable of handling the restaurant.

His little legs scramble up to the barstool at our kitchen counter. "It was fun. Ms. Bailey asked us how much food we're gonna eat and then she let us watch a movie."

My heart skips a little at the mention of Emily. Dylan is still too young to understand anything about girls and crushes. At least I hope he is. When his Mom walked out, I did what I could to shield him from the abandonment. Chelsea and I may not have been written in the stars, but I always wanted my son to have his Mom around.

"Oh yeah? Well, what do you say we continue on with a movie marathon?"

"Really?"

Nodding my head to match his enthusiasm. "Mm-hmm. Why don't you go get your comfy clothes on and we'll pick a movie out."

He's gone up to his room before I get the last word out.

Me: I heard you guys watched a movie?

Emily: Pretty sure other parents would call that lazy teaching.

Me: I call it improvising.

Emily: I'll make that my word of the day when the kids come back to school.

Me: So you have some days off?

Emily: You could say that.

Me: What are your plans for those days?

Emily: I'm really not sure yet. I could spend Thanksgiving with my best friend and her boyfriend. Or I could head back to my parent's house. Not sure which seems more appealing.

Me: What's wrong with those choices?

Emily: Kam and Mason are great. But they're still in the honeymoon phase. Going to my parents means facing them alone. And I haven't done that in a while.

Me: Spend it with me and Dylan. My parents are RVing somewhere in Oregon so it's just us.

Shit! Why did I suggest that?

Emily: I can't do that.

> Me: I know. My fingers typed before my brain could catch up.

> Me: What about coffee?

The bubbles appear and disappear multiple times. I think she's going to leave me on read when she responds.

> Emily: You're Dylan's Dad and I'm his teacher. Even texting you like this is grounds for an investigation…or even repercussions.

> Emily: The truth is that you're the first guy I've set eyes on since my fiancé passed and I don't take that lightly.

> Emily: If you were anyone else, I don't think I'd be as cautious.

> Me: If you need a friend, I can be one. But Emily, you won't be Dylan's teacher forever. And I'm not going anywhere.

Dylan running back down the stairs has me putting my phone away. He picks a Transformer movie and has his eyes glued to the screen the entire time. I find myself watching Dyl more than the movie. But that's my right as a parent. I always wonder how this tiny human, that barely reaches my hip, can take up so much space in my heart.

It has me wondering when I can open my heart for someone else. I understand Emily's resistance to crossing that solid parent-teacher line. And I would never jeopardize her career. But something about her has me wanting to know more.

Emily

The plane jostles as it touches down. I made the last-minute decision to head back home to Philly for Thanksgiving. I'm not sure if I'll come to regret this decision.

I only brought a carry-on so I make my way to the car rental line. My decision is rooted in not wanting to rely on my parents, or a car service for getting places. With the rental car keys in hand, I find the coupe in the lot and leave the airport.

I'm not sure if it's an invisible string that's pulling me there, but I find myself at the cemetery. My hands are sweaty and my heart rate increases. It's as if my mind is unconsciously dragging me back to that tearful goodbye. Turning off the car, I take the keys and walk the path to where James is resting.

It's not hard to find his spot. He has fresh flowers and the grass around has been cut recently. The sun is just starting to set, showcasing a beautiful scene in front of a heartbreaking reality.

James Michael Hayes
Loving son, brother, and fiancé
November 9, 1991 - August 28, 2017

"Hi, baby." I speak the two words I haven't said since he passed. It's like the band-aid around my heart is slowly peeling off. Letting the pain of his passing seep out. "I miss you so much. Can you believe we would be married? Two years and it feels like my life has been in a plateau state since you left. Colors are not as vibrant, the seasons are bland...I just—I feel like the joy in the little things left the day you left this world. I remember the day we got engaged. You did your best to prepare me if anything happened to you. And I was so mad at you for preparing me to make it without you."

I sit down cross-legged in front of his headstone and let the tears come. "I moved to Cincinnati. I think I still did it as a way to feel closer to you. Holding on isn't the best way to move forward, but it's hard. I'm scared one day I'm going to forget everything. The sound of your laugh is the one thing I miss the most. Some days I think I can still hear it."

The cool breeze rustles my hair as if it's James telling me that it is okay for me to move on. That if I close my eyes I can hear his voice whenever I want to.

"I think I met someone. But he's the Dad of one of my students. I know, it's crazy. And I would never do anything that would ruin my chances of being a teacher. The girls keep telling me his son won't be my student forever. I'm aware of that. But I'm scared of starting over. You and I experienced everything together. And having to make new experiences with someone else terrifies me. It'd be like erasing you from my past and doing so would make the future we could have had erasable."

That's the real issue. Starting over with someone new *is* terrifying. Having to learn their likes and dislikes, not just in a day-to-day life, but romantically as well. It terrifies me that I won't find someone that I can mesh with seamlessly. "God, being with you was as easy as breathing. You made my heart race and I would still get butterflies when you walked through the door. That was a good thing and I'm realizing it's a rare feeling that most people never get to experience. What if I never have that again?" I know it's silly to base your love off of a feeling. But isn't that love? Feeling something you've never felt?

I look at the time on my watch and realize I've been here for almost an hour. I know I need to go to my parent's house. But knowing James is left behind makes it harder for me to get up. Yet staying will make it harder every time I come to visit with him.

"I wanted to say I love you. And not in the past tense. Because when you left, that love didn't just go away. For so long there were times when I wished time machines existed so we could go back and stay in that little apartment forever. But at the end of the day, if I had to choose a more perfect goodbye for us, it would have been that way. We loved the only way we knew how. I miss you. And I always will. No amount of time can take that away."

Getting up from the ground, I dust the dirt and grass off of my pants. Tears continue their descent down my face as I gaze at his headstone. Knowing his life could have been bigger than what he got.

"I love you. I love you. I love you." The final words come out as a whisper. I kiss the tips of my fingers and place them on the top of his headstone. My fingers fall back to my side and with one last glance at his resting spot, I turn and walk back to the car.

> **Kammy:** How's life back there?

> **Me:** Feels like I'm fourteen again with how quiet this house is.

> **Kammy:** I'm sorry, buddy.

I'M BACK in my old room for a couple of days. Honestly, I should have stayed in Cincinnati for the break. Curiosity is a terrible devil that got the best of me and I chose to come home, hoping that a different scene would greet me.

But my wishful thinking let me down. No food was being prepped, no TV to greet me or laughter from my parents...it's like they chose to ignore this holiday. Hiding in their office to work until they couldn't anymore.

While our relationship is slightly better than it was when I was in high school, it's still not overly familial. We don't randomly text or call to check in. It's like we know we're all related so we do the bare minimum.

So I'm up in the little room I brought James up to the first time we hung out. The room that overlooks the backyard, along with the Hayes's backyard, and the stillness between the two is chilling. It's as if no life has been lived for the past couple of years. It's like this part of life has been frozen.

The ghost of my past life swallows me up. Memories from our time spent up here hit me at full force. Pictures of James and I decorate the wall and any available flat surface: ice cream shop napkins, my violin case collecting dust along the wall, and mementos that remind me of us threaten to suffocate me.

My throat closes up at the realization that coming back here was a mistake.

Running out of my room and away from the memories, I run into my dad in the hallway.

"Woah! Kiddo. Are you okay?" He steadies me with his hands gripping my upper arms to steady me.

I can't speak. All I can do is shake my head as tears cloud my vision. My dad pulls me into his chest as the tears fall. I can't do anything to stop them. The sobs of loss take over my body as the grief proves it never intended to loosen its hold on me. My dad continues to hold me in the upstairs hallway of the house. He's never been an affectionate man but knowing that his daughter hasn't stopped breaking for the last two years, has to break down some of his walls.

"I'll never be able to understand what it's like to lose someone the way you did. And I can't say just move on and you'll be fine."

The tears refuse to stop. "Dad, it hurts. Every day my heart hurts."

The ache that made itself known when James was taken still lets me know it hasn't gone anywhere. Now I understand why some people stay widows. It's hard to imagine your life without the one that made you whole.

"I know, pumpkin. One day, while the pain won't go away, you'll find someone to help carry the weight of it. And when that day comes, you'll look in the mirror and smile when you see how your life turned out. It might not be with the boy you pictured, but it'll be with someone who understands your pain and doesn't make you try to mask it." My dad's voice has lost all of the boom as he comforts me.

I feel a presence at my back until I feel my mom sandwich me between them. These are the parents I wanted when I was a teenager. These are the parents who helped me live when living was the last thing I wanted to do.

We stay like this as a family. My parents holding me together when falling apart seems like the better option. Their words of hope and love, that I can one day heal, renews my love for them.

Emily

It's hours later when I finally work up the courage to go next door. I only know they're home because I was in the living room when I saw Malcolm walk inside. Throwing on my dad's jacket and shoving my feet into some UGGS, I head to the door.

"I'm heading next door." I say to my dad as I pop my head into his office.

His head lifts from a contract he's reviewing. "Do you want me to come with you?"

I shake my head, unable to speak.

"Take your time honey," my dad tells me with the softest eyes I've ever seen him display.

With a final glance at him, I walk outside. I take the long way instead of cutting across the yards. It buys me a little bit of time. I take the familiar steps up the driveway and to the front door. Shaking out my hands I press the doorbell. The familiar chime of the bell sounds through the house. If I thought seeing the Hayes family made me nervous, the wait for them to answer the door drives me to panic.

The sound of the lock on the door flicks, interrupting the quiet street, and I brace myself for who I'm about to face.

"Hi," I say when the door opens, revealing James's Mom.

"Sweetheart." Michelle greets.

She pulls me into the house and her embrace. Her lilac and rose scent takes me back to my childhood. To a time when the future was certain.

Footsteps on the stairs pull us away and we look towards the newcomer. I'm barely prepared to see a new face when a body crashes into me. My arms go around the trim frame as one of the boys tucks his face into my neck.

"Evan, let her breathe," Michelle tells her son.

His hold loosens and I hold in my gasp. He looks just like James at this age. It's scary. I look over at Michelle and the tight smile on her face tells me she knows what I'm thinking.

"You're taller than me." *Really, Emily? Two years you haven't seen this family and that's what you say?*

A blush covers his face and it's so much like James I have to bite down on my teeth to keep from crying. I loved all of James's brothers. But Evan stuck close to me when I was here. I think it was his shy personality he took from James that had him latch onto me.

"I missed you, Eminem."

"I missed you too, Evanescence." I say as I wrap my arm around his neck and follow Michelle into the living room.

The sound of the TV echoes down the hallway and taunting from the other boys greets us. It really is like going back in time. My steps are sure but my heart is racing as I see them for the first time in years.

I observe them as a whole.

A silent observer while they interact with one another. Malcolm does a victory dance while Ford glares at him with invisible daggers shooting out.

"Boys!" Michelle starts. "We have company."

Evan is still under my arm as the attention slides to us. "Woah!"

"Um, hi," I say weakly.

Malcolm is the first to break. He jumps over the couch and pulls me into his arms. His breaths are short and I'm unsure if it's from his dancing or jumping over the couch or he's trying not to cry.

"Hi, buddy."

My greetings go like this with all of the boys. I for sure thought Michelle would slam the door in my face. But I'm welcomed back into their home with open arms.

"So ARE you just home for Thanksgiving?" Michelle asks when we're all on the couch.

"Yeah. It was a sort of last-minute thing to come home. Luckily it was a direct flight so it wasn't too bad."

Brandon hands me a glass of wine and plops down in the corner of the couch.

"I'm sure your parents are glad to have you here," Jeff states and I smile in return. "You're still teaching, right?"

I take a sip of wine for something to do. "I am. And it's good. I like the district I'm teaching in and the school that I'm at. The kids are great. Plus, it's not far from my apartment either."

"Do you go to a lot of football games?" Evan asks.

"Since I live so close to the stadium one would think. But no. I'm still not much of a football fan."

Conversation is awkward. Almost enough for me to want to crawl out of my skin. But not enough to leave this house. This place holds too many good memories to outweigh the tragic moment that bonds us.

It's like I can feel James here. And maybe that's why I feel so comfortable in this house.

Michelle clears her throat and our attention goes to her. "I know it's not my business but I want to know more about your life. Who you're hanging out with. If you're dating."

"Um," I think of how to answer that. "I'm still hanging out with the girls. Not much dating has happened in the last couple of years. But maybe soon? I, uh, actually went to visit James when I got off the plane. I don't know, I think he gave me the sign I was looking for."

"That's good honey. All we want is your happiness and we know that's what he would want."

I look down into my wine glass and smile attempting to hold the tears back. "I'm getting there." Is what I finally tell them. "But enough about me. What's new with all of you?"

"Brandon is dating someone but he won't tell us who." Malcolm pipes up from across the room. I can almost see the laser beams Brandon shoots at Malcom.

"Do I know her?" I probe.

He clears his throat. "Maybe."

We silently war with each other and hopefully, my look conveys that he'll tell me later.

"So what else?' I cheerfully ask.

Conversation finally flows. The boys talk over one another as they tell me everything they've been up to. And I don't miss the smile from Michelle as they interact with me.

When James died, I had no clue how to navigate the *after*. While I've always considered James's family my family, that chance was taken from us to make it official.

Although blood doesn't make someone family, having my name tied to them, would have been the next best thing.

I look at my watch and realize I've been here for longer than planned. When I announce I need to leave, groans of protest sound. It makes me laugh because these are the exact reactions they had when we were younger. Michelle makes the boys and I get together for a group picture. The goodbyes take another thirty minutes before Brandon walks me to the door.

"So...who is she?" I ask in the foyer.

His eyes bug out and he holds his finger to his lips to keep me quiet.

I do a happy dance and silently cheer. "I do know her!"

Brandon ushers me outside and walks me down the driveway.

"Tell me. The anticipation is killing me."

"It's, Angie." Brandon says after looking over his shoulder to ensure we're alone.

I go through the list of people we may mutually know. "Who?"

"Angie. Well, Angela to people that don't know her." He holds my stare and the longer he does it clicks.

"Shut up!" I smack him on the arm. "Liam's sister? Wow. Has your Dad even spoken to Mr. Taylor since the accident?"

Like I'm any better. While I wasn't close to the Taylor's, Liam was still James's best friend. And to have your son taken from you unexpectedly, and in that way, has to put a strain on whatever friendship the parents had.

"I know. It just happened. And no, my dad hasn't talked to Mr. Taylor since the accident."

Something dawns on me. "How old is she? And how long have you two been seeing each other?"

"She's twenty-one. And for about six months."

"Nothing happened before, right?"

He looks at me like I'm insane.

"I'm just checking. Grief does weird things to people."

"That it does," Brandon agrees. "She wants us to tell our parents."

I glance down the darkening neighborhood street as the sounds of cars passing on the road hum in the distance, breaking up the relative silence. "What do you want?"

"Em, I don't even know. On one hand, it would be so easy to move away—start over where no one knows our story. And on the other hand, the weight of keeping this from the people we love is killing me." Brandon paces between our driveways. His hands in his hair and tugging the strands tightly I fear he'll rip them out.

"Do you love her?"

That question stops his pacing. "I shouldn't. Her brother drove his truck into the back of an eighteen-wheeler taking my brother's life with him. I'm nine years older than her. She's still in college. So I shouldn't. And yet, the more time we spent fighting against this attraction, the harder I fell."

"How did you two...you know, come to be this?" I cross my arms and tuck my hands trying to keep them warm.

"I went into a bar for happy hour with some co-workers and she was there."

My eyes widen and Brandon sees.

"What?"

I shake my head as his story and mine have some tiny similarities. "Just thinking—of something."

"Something or someone?"

"This is your story, not mine. Back to it." I scold him.

He snorts but continues. "When we walked in I saw her

and immediately wanted to leave. Because how could I stay in a place, and be served drinks, by the girl whose brother took my brother's life? And I know she had nothing to do with what Liam did. But I couldn't separate the two, you know?"

"It's misplaced anger. Or hatred in your case," I interject.

"Don't I know it. I planned to tell her off. But when she saw me approach her, her face dropped. And as I looked closer, at the girl under the skimpy assigned work outfit and the full face of makeup, I saw a girl who was still coping with the loss of her brother. Of the loss of her only sibling. And what kind of person would that make me if I chastised her for her only brother's actions when I still had some of mine?"

I look at Brandon and see he too is still dealing with the loss of James.

"I went back to the bar a few days later and she was working again. I think she was more shocked I was there again than I was that I returned to her place of work. This went on for about a month until we finally spoke. And it was like the sound of her voice wrapped around my heart, kickstarting it into overdrive. So I stayed until the end of her work shift, followed her out to her car, and kissed her."

I watch him process the past events of how they came to be. It's a classic forbidden romance, and not just because of their age difference.

"I'm still friends with Kamryn." I blurt out and his deer-in-the-headlights gaze locks on me. "I know. It would have been so much easier to cut her off. She was a painful reminder of that day. Because instead of grading papers and spending time with my fiance, we got called to go our separate ways to help them manage the fallout from their failing relationship. I stopped talking to her for a while. I stopped talking to everyone.

"The grief that I was attending his funeral instead of the elation over our wedding switched something in my psyche. So while I don't know what it's like to love someone that should be off-limits, I do know what it's like to feel something for someone when you shouldn't."

We walk up the front walkway and sit on the steps in front of the door.

"You met someone?" Brandon asks.

"Yeah. I think I did."

"Why do you sound so unsure?"

I look out across the lawn as I admit to Brandon what I've been feeling. "I feel like I'm not allowed to move on. Like I'm stuck in this purgatory of emotions and constantly in wait. Waiting for him to just walk through the door of our apartment with some sports stat. I think that's what I miss the most. Him telling me something that had him bursting at the seams." I turn to look at Brandon. "But this new guy, Adam, he's the dad of one of my students. Older than me. I'm not sure how much older. But he's the first guy my heart has jumped to since James and I am terrified."

"Em, you know it's okay to move on?"

I turn my head and look at Brandon. "I know. But saying it and doing it are two different things."

"What a pair we are," Brandon announces and slings his arm over my shoulder. We sit on the front steps watching the last bit of light fade from the sky. And as our breath puffs become visible our goodbye comes around.

"You and Angie should come and visit. I'm not sure how easy it will be to see her. But maybe Kamryn would like to see her."

"Maybe," Brandon muses.

With a kiss on my forehead, Brandon strolls across our yards and back into his house. When I hear the thud of the front door closing, I turn to go inside.

Maybe this trip wasn't so bad. Emotionally I'm exhausted. But mentally I've never felt better.

Adam

"I just want everyone to be prepared for the holiday rush."

I called my staff in for a bi-monthly meeting. We've slacked off on working like a team and with Christmas and New Year's Eve rolling around I need everyone to be prepared. As it's still the off-season, Jeff and I switch off mid-day and night shifts. The night shifts, while I enjoy the hustle and bustle, take me away from Dylan too often.

How I came into owning this restaurant was pure luck. When a distant relative I had never met passed away, confusion hit when I was left with a sizable inheritance. It was enough that I could afford to have built a big enough house for me and Chelsea, and eventually Dylan.

The previous tenant in this space had a dwindling business and I saw the potential when my realtor sent me spaces to look at. My offer was accepted and renovations for this place started soon after. My restaurant is located in the heart of the city. We've hosted baby showers, wedding showers, bachelor and bachelorette parties, birthdays, and other events that are worthy of celebrating. During the summer we convert to more of a bar with live music every Friday and Saturday night.

Jeff clears his throat from next to me. "We have a few dinner reservations throughout the week and lunch parties every Saturday and Sunday. The schedule will reflect who's working with whom."

I stand off to the side as I watch Jeff indicate what's expected of everyone. Glancing around, I see appreciative looks from my staff. Jeff took to his role perfectly and every day I thank whomever that they sent him here.

I feel my phone buzz in my jeans pocket and make no move to look at who's texting me. Tuning back into the now, I see everyone nodding their heads before gathering their belongings.

Shit!

Jeff looks at me with a pointed stare knowing that I zoned out. Him and Tammy, my lead chef, are the last two in the main dining room with me.

"Sorry," I sheepishly tell them.

They glance at one another before Tammy speaks up. "Bossman, are you sure you're okay?"

Tammy has been with me from the start. She's closer to my parent's age, so she's seen every face I have to offer.

"Yeah. Yeah, I promise I'm good. If you two are good for the rest of the day, I'm gonna head out."

I ignore their pointed and concerned stares. Patting my jeans I feel for my keys and pull my phone out when I push open the door to leave.

> Emily: Hey. Any chance you want to get a coffee?

It's been a while since I've seen or heard from her. I

thought she decided to blow me off. I know she's resistant to starting a friendship with her student's Dad, but I meant what I said in that I'm not going anywhere.

> Me: Yeah. I'm just walking out from a meeting. Wanna meet at Millennial Bean?

> Emily: Perfect. I'll see you soon.

> Me: See you soon.

I make the short drive to the coffee shop that's located in the Hill, which houses a handful of restaurants and bars that naturally attract millennials and young college students looking for a place to blow off steam.

I love this area. It's where I always pictured myself raising kids. Dylan loves it here, so I love the feeling that I did something right. Anytime we come here, he always begs to go get ice cream. Can't say I blame him. The Twisted Cow has some of the best ice cream I've ever had.

Parking my truck, I look out at the town square and at the small amount of people walking around. It is mid-December and with the chill from the river swooping in it's not shocking with how sparse the area is.

My mind goes into overdrive as I wonder why today of all days Emily reached out to me. I slide my body out of my truck and walk towards the coffee shop. I tug my beanie over my ears and shove my hands in my jacket pocket to keep from completely freezing as I walk to the entrance.

I'm not sure why my heart is pounding. It's just coffee.

With a woman I can't stop thinking about.

In a twist of perfect timing, Emily and I walk up to the coffee shop at the same time.

The wind whips loose tendrils of hair across her face

and her cheeks take on a rosy hue from the cold. I've now seen her at night at my restaurant, at a parent-teacher conference, and now at the coffee shop. She gets more and more beautiful. I have to drop my gaze down to my feet to gather my thoughts.

"Hi," she begins by way of greeting.

"Hey yourself." I volley back. *Hey yourself?* My fingers curl into my palms until the bite of my nails has me clenching my jaw.

She makes an awkward hand gesture towards the door. "Shall we?"

"Oh, right." I move around her and open the door. She gives me a small smile as she walks across the threshold.

The smell of coffee hits me and soothes my mind. Espresso beans being ground mix with the sounds of a contemporary music soundtrack. Only a few tables are occupied. Since it's winter break, the college students have gone home for the month, leaving the locals to come out of hibernation.

The barista greets us at the counter and I can't help but mentally comment on the customer service. "Are we going to be together or separate?"

It seems we both have brain farts because it takes a moment for our brains to catch up with our mouths.

Emily opens her mouth to respond, but I beat her to it, "Together please."

The barista's friendly smile almost makes me forget about the open-mouthed face Emily is trying to hide. Tack on the red flush covering her face and I know she didn't think about this step either.

I motion for Emily to rattle off her order and then I step up to do the same. Once I pay, we both survey the space for a table. Emily makes the first move and picks one right by the window, overlooking the courtyard with the downtown cityscape in the background.

When we're both settled, I survey her. She looks lighter than the last time I saw her. Her eyes no longer hold deep, aching sadness.

"Why are you staring at me?" Emily questions me.

I try to hold back a smile that wants to take over. "Do you really want to know?"

Her mouth twists before she nods her head in response.

"You look lighter."

"Um…"

Leaning forward, I rest my arms on the table. "I mean lighter in the sense that you don't look so weighed down by life."

She surveys me the same way I did her. I'm assuming she found what she was looking for if it's any indication by the small smile that lifts her cheeks. "I decided at the last minute to go home for Thanksgiving break. It was incredibly messy. But also freeing in a way I didn't expect it to be."

My name being called for our drinks pulls me away from Emily. A mutual smile is held between us before I head up to the counter. I place a five dollar bill in the tip jar before grabbing our drinks and head back to the table.

"Thank you." Emily tells me as she accepts her drink.

"Anytime. So you went home for your break? Why was it messy?"

She blows out a breath and leans back in her chair. "My parents and I have a loving but complicated relationship. It's been like that since high school and hasn't gotten out of the 'it's complicated' phase."

"Why was it complicated?"

"They moved us out of the city when I was going into

high school with the reasoning being for me. They wanted me to have the normal high school experience in a home, but that didn't necessarily include them being there. So I was left to be a teenager in a new school without my parent's home to greet me when I got back from school. They missed a lot. And I don't think they've forgiven themselves enough to move forward."

Her eyes take on a slight sheen as if she's remembering that feeling all over again. "But I think we had a turning point when I went home. At least I hope we did."

I can't imagine what it's like to spend critical moments without your parents around. I'm lucky mine were involved when they needed to be. Of course, I don't voice that. Because even now I know how hypocritical it is to state how having involved parents is.

"That's good, Emily."

She smiles a real smile. And it's breathtaking. A dimple peaks through on her right cheek and her eyes crinkle at the corners. Though her eyes are still tinged with a little bit of sadness, it's still a smile. "Thanks. So how was your Thanksgiving? It's hard to get a flushed-out recap with first graders."

"It was lowkey. My parents are traveling and we don't have extended family in the area, it's just Dyl and I."

"I'm sorry," Emily says with a voice that almost makes me want to wrap her in a hug.

I shake my head to shake it off. "It's alright. We FaceTimed with them and I made a turkey in the deep fryer. So it was a solid Thanksgiving."

She surveys me again and I feel like I'm under a microscope. I won't admit to anyone that not having my parents around can get lonely. Explaining to your six-year-old why your grandparents travel more than they spend time with you is a tough conversation to have. Although explaining why his Mom didn't choose him, I'll never be able to avoid that conversation.

"So what about you?" I jump before she has a chance to ask another question that makes me mournful. "What do you like to do when you're not teaching?"

"Uh oh." Emily adjusts her position and leans back, crossing her legs. "This almost sounds like a date conversation starter. And I don't date my students' parents."

"Six months until you're not his teacher anymore. But who's counting?" I wink and her jaw drops.

She leans up to the table. Our faces are only a foot apart. And this close I can see her eyes so clearly. The golden swirls of her irises mix with the brown. The pulse in her neck thumps steadily at our back and forth.

"Are you always this flirty?" Her question comes out in a breathy whisper.

"Are you always this shy?"

Her left eyebrow quirks up. "As a matter of fact, I am."

That doesn't surprise me. "To answer your question, only when I think it'll lead me somewhere."

Emily snorts and takes a few sips of her drink sitting back in her chair. I drop my stare and focus on my own coffee. The rest of our time at Millennial Bean is spent with surface-level talk. I've never been one to pour my heart out to someone I barely know. And it seems Emily is the same way.

But I take away one thing from this coffee date, and if she denies it's a date, I'll continue to call it that for a laugh. Emily is not like anyone I've ever met. In my job, I've studied thousands of people. Hazard of helping out as a bartender when my guys get swamped. I can tell when they'll pour their life story out for me to react. Or if they'll keep everything bottled until they have another place to vent.

I think Emily has so many layers that it could take months to learn her.

If she feels even the tiniest tingle like I do when I'm around her, then one day she won't be so hard to read.

Emily

February 2020

Adam: Truth or dare?

Me: Truth.

Adam: Have you always wanted to be a teacher?

Me: Yes.

Adam and I have been texting more and more. He does his best to cross the line, but I swiftly push him back. He's persistent. I'll give him that.

But with the new year and me turning a year older, it makes me want to forget the line was ever there to begin with. I've always been one to follow every rule set for me. With violin, school, James, and now teaching; it's made my life simple as the structure keeps my head above water.

Me: Truth or dare?

Adam: Truth.

Me: What are you thinking about?

Adam: You.

He's so sure of what he wants. It's me that's terrified. My girl's words ring in my head anytime he and I are talking. I've never been one for casual. It's just not how I'm built.

My phone rings, pulling me out of my freakout. Adam. I answer it in the middle of the third ring. "Hey."

"I freaked you out, didn't I?"

I look out over the water, mulling over my words. "Maybe. Yeah."

"Question before I get to anything else. Why aren't you teaching today?"

"Oh, I always take the day off for my birthday."

I always felt one's birthday should be a personal holiday. So for as long as I was working, and I had the days, I took the day off. While the past birthdays have been a little bittersweet, they've been a day for me.

"Happy Birthday, Emily," Adam responds softly.

"Thank you."

"So what are your plans for your day?"

I do my best to keep my voice from cracking. "I'm not sure yet. I haven't really loved celebrating my birthday these past couple of years."

"And why is that?" I don't detect any distaste in his question, just genuine curiosity.

"James, he loved birthdays. He would go all out for those he loved. But for me, he went to the moon." I think back to my eighteenth birthday, walking into my room stuffed with balloons and pictures of us. "When he died, I never thought about my birthday until the day came. The first birthday after he passed, I had the day off and spent the whole day crying. I could turn a year older but he was stuck at twenty-six forever."

Time is never your friend when you want it to be. It laughs in your face when you want it to slow down. It laughs in your face when you want it to speed up. Time is your enemy when you expect it to be your friend.

"Do you ever think you'll ever love again?" Adam asks me.

It's not an unfair question. I often wonder if I could love so easily before then what's stopping me from doing so now? And it always comes back to fear.

"I want to," my voice comes out in a whisper when the tears threaten to fall. "But I'm scared I'll never have that again. The knowledge that the person you want wants you back. The knowledge that the love you share is unconditional. I'm scared that I'll never experience the rush that comes with love."

He clears his throat. "I think you'll feel it again."

"I'm scared of feeling it with someone new. And knowing that person is one I can't have takes me right back to the starting line."

Am I talking about James or Adam? At this point, I don't know. Before James died, I never thought I'd have to be without him. Not just in the physical sense but in the emotional sense as well. The days go by and they turn into years. Every moment takes me away from him. From the life we shared. From the life we were creating.

The other side of the phone is quiet and I pull it away from my ear to see we're still connected.

I break the silence, "Did I scare you?"

"No, Emily. You didn't scare me. I want you to be

comfortable sharing the uncomfortable with me. Can I...can I see you today?"

"Adam...I'm still your son's teacher. And as much as I want to explore whatever this could be with you, I have to think about my career. For the first time in my life I have to put myself first."

He's quiet on the other end. I don't want to reject him. It twists something inside of me to do so. He's the first man to make me want more after James.

"Are you this hard on all of your friends?" His question comes out teasing, although I detect a little bit of hurt from my saying no.

I pick at a piece of lint on the blanket that's covering my legs. "You and I both know friendship is the last thing we'd want."

"Well, Ms. Bailey, I guess this leaves us at an impasse."

"I guess it does." I think of what to say that won't leave either of us in limbo. So I try to settle for the next best thing, "Friends?"

"For now. Happy birthday, Emily." Adams tells me.

"Thank you. Goodbye, Adam."

"Bye."

"You said, friends!? Friends!? I thought you wanted to wipe your hand across that line you drew?" Sarah is baffled after I tell them about my and Adam's conversation on my birthday. We're doing a girl's night at Kamryn's house since none of us felt like being around other people. Plus with Mason on a guy's trip, Kamryn begged us to come to her house. Movie number three of our romantic comedy marathon is on in the background. It's provided great sound and sight relief when needed.

It's been a few weeks since then and I can't stop thinking about that day and Adam. We still text daily, but I know he's holding back because I made him.

"I got scared. He was saying all of the right things, but then I got scared."

"Em, and that's normal. What Sarah is trying and failing to say is that you've been on the cusp of wanting more with someone for the first time since James. And while it's normal to be scared, you can't run from something when it's right in front of you." Kam's eyes roam over my face. I think she's looking for something that's not there. It must be the almost-psychologist in her. And when she doesn't find it, she continues. "I know it might seem fast for you, but could you see Adam by your side in the near future?"

"I feel like I'm abandoning James if I say yes." The admission hits harder than I expected it to.

Sarah gets up and sits on the coffee table in front of me, taking my hand in hers. "No one is saying you're abandoning him, little bird. James is always going to be with you. And if Adam is the man that he's presenting to you, then he'll never let you forget him either. You deserve so much more happiness than you're letting yourself have."

Happiness is a feeling I didn't know I could feel. Sure I've felt lighter in the sense that the grief I feel daily isn't so heavy anymore. But happiness? That's a feeling I long thought I could never feel.

I give the girls a grateful smile and they go back to chatting while I pull out my phone to text Adam.

Me: Hey.

Adam: Hey, yourself.

Me: Is this a bad time?

Adam: Not at all. I'm just watching one of the live bands we have tonight.

Adam: How are you?

Me: I'm good. I was doing some thinking.

Adam: Good or bad thinking?

I pull my attention off my phone and see the girls staring at me. My eyebrows raise in a '*Yes?*' before they turn back to their conversation. But not before I see the smirks they throw at each other.

Me: Good thinking. About how lines should be wiped away.

I see the text bubbles pop up and disappear over and over before his response comes through.

Adam: Are you sure?

Me: Positive. But that doesn't mean I'm not scared.

Adam: I promise to chase the doubt away.

His words light me up on the inside because it's what I needed to hear to know that I'm making the right choice.

Me: Do you want some company at work?

Adam: I'll be here until way after midnight.

Me: It's spring break, so I have nothing but time.

Adam: Okay. Well, I'll see you soon then.

Me: See you soon.

I tune back into the conversation and wait for the right time to announce I'm leaving. As excited as I am to see Adam, the nerves are coming in full force. Do I rush out of here? Do I take my time? Do I go home to change? Do I show up in what I'm wearing? Is this what it's like to have a crush as an adult?

It's terrifying.

"Why do you look so scared, Em?" Jax asks.

I feel my face flame with a blush. "I texted Adam and I'm thinking of meeting him at his restaurant."

"What!? And you're still here?" Sarah's blasphemous expression would be comical if she weren't 100% serious. And in the years that I've gotten to know Sarah, she never says things she's unsure of. She hits me with a throw pillow. "Get your cute butt off this couch and go hang out with him."

"I'm with Sarah on this," Kam voices along with Jax.

It takes very little convincing to get me off the couch. And without protest from them, I slide my boots back on and head to my car to leave.

"I need you to tell me it's not a bad idea," I say when the phone connects.

"Hello to you too, Em." Brandon greets.

I let out a huff of frustration. "Brandon, this is serious."

I hear murmuring on the other end and then a door closing. "I take it this is about the new guy?"

"Mm-hmm."

"This is a great idea. And I'm not saying that because I'm a guy. But as James's brother, you deserve happiness again."

The streets give way, signaling I'm closer to Monty's. "Do you think he would approve? James, I mean."

"Well, obviously I haven't met him, but if he's making you question right or wrong then I think James would approve. Who knows? Maybe he even set it up so you two would meet."

I have thought about that. Because what were the odds that he was working the night I showed up? I know he said his assistant went into early labor. But still. This could have James written all over it.

"Yeah, maybe. Did I interrupt something?" I ask because I heard a door close earlier.

He chuckles on the other end. "Now you're concerned about being a cockblocker?"

"Ew. Please don't ever say any word with 'cock' in it. I still consider you my brother." I fight a shudder as I get closer to Monty's.

"I was planning to get it wet tonight..."

"Oh my god! Good night, Brandon."

"Good night, Emily," he sing-songs through his laughter.

Shaking off the end of that conversation, I find a parking spot in the parking garage. I take a deep breath and get out of my car.

Adam

Since Emily texted, I've been obsessively checking the door for her arrival while also still doing my job. I shouldn't be nervous. She's been here before. Knowing her a little better makes this thing between us a little more real. Add in the fact that she's decided to cross the line she drew and my nerves have skyrocketed.

While it is in fact spring break, it's still been slow here. Ohio doesn't tend to bring people out of hibernation until late April, so my restaurant has time to breathe before the seasonal rush begins.

Movement from the corner of my eye brings my attention to the door. And there she is. I had no clue what Emily was up to tonight when she decided to text me. But if it brings her and I one step closer to whatever it is we're aiming for, I won't question it.

Her eyes scan the bar until she finds me at a table off to the side. A small smile graces her face and I get up from where I'm seated to go greet her.

I've now seen her teacher attire and her lounge attire. But this outfit is one I think might be my favorite and what I least expected her to wear. Loose dark wash ripped jeans that look like they're well-loved, an oversized off-the-shoulder maroon sweater, and worn-in moto boots adorn her feet.

Emily's smile gets bigger when I get closer. And I swear she takes my breath away.

Thankfully, the band finishes the first half of their set, so we don't have to shout to greet each other. We stand in front of each other in the low light bar, taking each other in like it's the first time we're seeing each other.

"Hi, beautiful," are the first words out of my mouth.

The blush that covers her cheeks at my greeting has my smile not stopping.

Emily returns my greeting with a simple, "Hi."

"Do you want a drink?"

"Just water. That'd be great."

My hand goes to the small of her back as I lead us to the bar. I get Matt's attention and ask him for two waters with lemon. Emily's body leans into mine and my hand slides further around her waist. My thumb instinctively rubs small circles right above the top of her jeans and I feel, rather than hear, the hitch in her breath.

I lean down to where my mouth is right at her ear and inhale the soft vanilla scent that seems to hit me right where it's intended. "So no more line?"

"None," Emily confirms for me.

Our waters are set down in front of us and I don't miss the look Matt sends me. I've done well in evading every-one's questions regarding my love life. But I know when our next staff meeting happens that will be the topic of choice.

With our waters in hand, I led Emily back to the table I was sitting at when she walked in. It's a circular two-seater meant for intimate conversations. We're close enough but not in each other's lap.

When we're seated, I watch Emily survey the space. And it gives me more time to take her in as well. Her hair falls in loose waves down her back and she doesn't have a stitch of makeup on. If I remember the other times I've seen her she wasn't wearing any makeup then either.

Emily is a natural beauty with her soft features and maybe that's what caught my eye in the first place. But it was when she opened her mouth and spoke. The melodic sound of her voice, falling from her bee-stung lips, washed over me and sent my thoughts to less than innocent.

"You're staring." She notes, having caught me.

My gaze slams up to her eyes to see her still perusing the space, but I see the lift in her cheeks.

"You're the best view in this place," I admit with zero shame.

Her gaze falls to me and I wait for her to break our staredown, but she holds strong.

She leans forward on the table and I match her position leaving very little space between us. "So the line I drew is gone and you up your flirt?"

"I have to make sure you don't regret wiping the line away. I'll also pull out all of my best dad jokes to remind you I'm funny."

A soft snort leaves her. "Good to know the charm will never end."

"Never." I declare.

Her eyes fall to my neck where I'm sure some of my tattoos are peeking out. But I can't help but tease her. "Are you checking me out?"

Emily's eyes slam up to mine. "Your ego is insane. I'm looking at your tattoos."

Bingo. "I can always take my shirt off so you can get a closer look."

"Adam!" She looks around as if anyone else is around us. There isn't. My staff knows not to seat anyone around my table. They know I like the solitude when I'm out on the floor.

"That's a yes to taking my shirt off or a no to taking my shirt off? The choice is up to you." My megawatt smile has Emily's matching mine.

"If I wanted to see a Chippendale show I would've just skipped coming here," Emily says with the straightest face.

I'm momentarily taken aback and speechless that she can dish it back out.

"You should see your face." She says through a small laugh.

The band coming back on the stage for the second half of their set halts my reply. They're a local band that started playing here about a year after I opened. They told me they have no plans of going big and that they just like playing. So I said that they have a spot here anytime they want.

Emily scoots her chair closer to me. I like to think it's so she has a better view of the band. But the other part of me hopes that it's so she can be closer to me.

"What's your favorite tattoo?" She asks when she leans into me. Her voice sends shockwaves through my body.

I have to shake myself out of the not-so-G-rated thoughts and focus on the question she asked me. Holding out my arm, I pull up my shirt sleeve and show her a few dates I had permanently inked on my body.

"These."

Her finger traces the numbers and that small bit of contact has my heart racing for the finish line. "What do the numbers represent?"

"The top one is Dylan's birthday. And the bottom two are the birthdates of my parents."

They're the three most important people in my life. So deciding to ink my skin with numbers, wasn't a tough decision. If I had siblings and Dylan wasn't an only child, my forearm would be a database of my loved ones' numbers.

But with his Mom abandoning him and no siblings, I fear I'm doing exactly that.

"What's that face?" Emily asks, pulling me from the insecure thoughts running through my mind.

"What face?"

"The face you made after telling me about your tattoos? Did I overstep?" Her voice takes on a bit of panic. Panic that is completely not needed.

My hand falls to the back of her chair and I lean in to speak in her ear. My lips brush the shell of her ear and I have to fight the shiver that wracks itself through my body. "No, you didn't Em. I was just wallowing in insecure thoughts that had nothing to do with my tattoos. But please, continue to step on me all you want."

I'm close enough that I can hear her laughter over the band. And I've decided that, along with my son's laughter, it's now my second favorite sound in the world.

We stay close like this. Talking into each other's ears as the band continues to play. We learn each other's favorite colors, phobias, and dislikes. Emily playfully teases me while I continue to make her laugh uncontrollably. After our first tearful greeting, I vow to make her laugh for as long as I can. But all too soon, the night starts to come to an end.

"I should go." Emily mournfully says after looking at her watch for the time.

As much as I don't want her to, I have closing responsibilities to attend to. And I need to check in for the night to make sure Dylan is okay at camp.

Nodding, I get up and hold my hand out for her. "I'll walk you to your car."

I'm grateful for the time Emily and I got to spend together. But it still didn't feel like enough. It's like I've barely scratched the surface with her. But I'll continue to eat up every crumb she gives me.

"You're such a gentleman," Emily teases when we're in the parking garage. She swings our hands back and forth. As serious as she's been, I'm beginning to see that she has a playful side to her. Lights on a small SUV go off and her steps slow down. "This is me."

"I'm glad you came here tonight," I admit. Can she tell I'm nervous? I don't want to push her, but she makes me twitchy.

"Adam?"

"Yeah?" My voice comes out high-pitched. Why does it come out high-pitched?

She moves until the tips of our shoes are touching. "You can kiss me."

"Yeah?" I don't know why that's the only thing I can say.

"I think I broke you."

I tell myself to pull it together and that I'm better than this. "You didn't. Are you sure? Because I think one taste of you will have me hooked."

"Positive." She says as she rises on her toes and presses her lips to mine.

It takes a moment for my brain to catch up. My hand slides up her arm and I feel the shiver work through her body. My other hand slides down her back and lands on her lower back, anchoring her to me.

Once my nerves subside, I take over the kiss and my tongue teases the seam of her lips. When she opens up to me, our tongues dance together and the softest moan escapes her throat. If her laughter is one of my favorite sounds, this moan became a close contender. Her arms fall over my shoulder and her hands tangle in the hair at the nape of my neck. Light pulls of my hair send a jolt straight to my cock and a groan climbs up my throat.

This kiss is months in the making. Gaining Emily's trust and her slowly knocking down her walls was what we needed to move forward.

I peek an eye open and walk us back towards her SUV. Pushing her up against her car and deepening the kiss. The way her body moves as my thigh maneuvers between her legs. The sounds she makes as our tongues tangle is a sound I want on repeat.

Breaking the kiss, I trail my lips down her neck. Sucking on the spot between her neck and shoulder.

"Oh, that feels too good."

My lips move up her neck and I pull her earlobe between my teeth.

"Oh god, Adam."

Her pants and moans drive me forward until she gently pushes me back by my shoulders. I take in her swollen lips and beard rash on her neck. Her chest heaves as she catches her breath. Emily's eyes are wild from our kiss. I want to dive into them and never come out.

"I'm glad your nerves are gone." Emily says while still holding me at a distance by my shoulders.

I can't stop myself from wrapping my hands around her wrists. "Totally gone."

"As much as I want to stay here and make out with you in a parking garage," she looks down at her watch checking the time again. "I really have to get home and you have to close up your restaurant."

Logically I know what she's saying makes sense. But tonight was huge for us.

"I wanna cook you breakfast." I blurt out.

Her eyebrows scrunch up. "What about Dylan?"

I love that she's concerned for him. "He's at a baseball camp for the rest of the week."

The color drains from her face. I'm not sure what I said, but I wanna know. Emily blinks and the look is gone. "Breakfast is good."

"Okay." I draw out the word so as not to push her. Maybe tomorrow I will. "I'll text you in the morning."

She opens the door to her car and gets in. Once it's started, she rolls the window down and leans on the edge. "Thank you for tonight. I had fun."

"Just wait until my world-famous pancakes," I state and lean my arms on the roof of her car.

"What makes them world-famous?"

Leaning down, I press a quick kiss to her lips. Even though everything in me wants to lean in further. "You'll just have to wait until the morning to find out. Get home safe."

I step back from her car and watch as she puts the gear in drive. "Bye, Adam."

"Bye, Emily."

I watch as she drives out of the parking garage and I follow the path back to my restaurant. The band should be wrapping up the last of their set. When I walk back in, Matt is standing behind the bar with his arms crossed.

"What?" I pointedly ask, knowing his answer will be in regards to Emily.

"Don't *what* me. You had a girl here. You never have a girl here."

"What are you, five? And she's not a girl, she's a woman."

He holds his hands up in surrender. "I'm just saying, boss man. I've never seen you like that. It's a good look on you."

Shaking my head, I wave him off and head down to my office. If I want to attempt to get out of here before midnight I need to tackle my latest to-do list.

But as soon as I'm at my desk, my mind flits back to Emily and her reaction to me talking about Dylan and base-ball camp. Against my better judgment, I pull up my internet browser and type her name in.

I don't find anything too alarming from a simple search. Just a few articles on her playing the violin, which surprises me as she's never brought it up. I scroll some more until I see a linked article with the headline 'Fatal Car Crash Claims Two'. And against all common sense, I click on the link.

When the article loads, my heart drops.

I WAKE up the next morning with conflicting feelings. Emily will probably never want to talk to me when she finds out I looked her up. It's just wanting a quicker peak behind the curtain of the woman I'm completely infatuated with, won out over logic and morals.

My phone chimes with a text. Reaching over to my bedside table, I see a text and picture from Sandra, one of the team Moms from Dylan's team.

On days when I feel like I'm lacking as a Dad, it brings me joy when I see my son having fun with his friends. He may not have a sibling but I do what I can to make sure he's fulfilled in that area of his life. Once summer hits, our days will be filled with cookouts, baseball games, and trips to the amusement park. Hopefully, with the addition of Emily, as she'll no longer be my son's teacher.

My thoughts go back to the article I read and back to the first night she came to my bar. It all makes so much sense. However, I can't particularly know what things set her off. It's the knowledge that anything can set her off and send her back in time that terrifies me.

Heaving myself out of bed I head to the bathroom and go about getting ready. Without Dylan here the house is eerily quiet. He's not quite at the age where he's asking for a pet, so I don't have a furry companion to keep me company.

When I'm dressed and feel more human I walk back into my bedroom and pick up my phone to text Emily.

Emily

I've been sitting on my balcony looking at his text for the last five minutes. When I left last night, I couldn't stop feeling like something was wrong. Maybe it was the mention of baseball? I've done my best to avoid any and all mention of the sport since James died.

Can I attach myself, by way of Adam, to a sport James loved so much?

I think the other part I'm so hesitant about is that once I let him into my space, my life, I'll never want him to leave.

I add my address in the next text with Adam responding that he'll be over shortly. Turning back into my apartment I try to look at it from an outsider's view. Walking over to the expansive kitchen, I tuck my phone into the back pocket of my ripped light-wash jeans and pull out my espresso beans to get to work on making an iced latte.

When my parents chose this place, they wanted me to have everything. I think they bought me this place as a way to make up for the abandonment. And while it's not fully solvable, it does help. So I live here mortgage-free. Not because of privilege, but because of my parent's guilt. Which, again, is not solvable but it does ease some financial burden as being a teacher doesn't mean I'm rolling in the cash.

I've just finished pouring the milk when a knock sounds throughout my space.

My heart races knowing that it's Adam on the other side.

I push up the sleeves of my camel-colored sweater and pad my sock-covered feet over to the door, but check the peephole just to be sure it's Adam. Seeing it's him, I take a deep breath and unlock the door, opening it to him.

"Hi," I breathe out.

Opening the door wider, Adam steps through with his reusable bag-laden arms. Shutting the door, I lead him to my kitchen and the whistle he lets out doesn't go unnoticed.

My parents had my apartment completely remodeled. Hardwood floors run throughout the living space, dining area, and kitchen. The kitchen, while not my area of exper-tise, holds a top-of-the-line range with gas burners. The refrigerator is a model down from the ones in restaurants. I have a shallow walk-in pantry where I keep the appliances needed to cook meals should I need them. My espresso machine is the only thing I keep on my counter.

The countertops are white marble with gold flecks that reflect the morning sunlight which pours through the massive floor-to-ceiling windows. The kitchen cabinets are painted a dark navy with gold handles and a soft pink backsplash to add more color to the space. While I'm not a cook, this spot is one of my favorites in the apartment.

When he sets the bags on the counters, he does another survey spin of the space and then puts his gaze on me. "Hi."

Those dang butterflies take flight as the bright morning sun shines through the windows, highlighting the green in his eyes. I swear I get lost in them as I picture myself enjoying a summer picnic with him and Dylan.

Woah! Shaking myself out of the daydream, I step back and avoid Adam's puzzled expression. "Do you want some coffee?" I ask as I pick up my drink and look at everything but him and his handsome face.

"Sure. I'll have what you're having."

Placing my drink back on the counter, I make my way back over the espresso machine. I feel like a terrible host. But after last night and now, I'm still feeling thrown off and don't quite know the best way to get back on track.

My back feels the burn of Adam's stare. The espresso beans grinding becomes more and more interesting than making conversation. I get to work pouring ice in a cup and getting the milk frothed. When I've let the espresso breathe, I pour the espresso shots over the ice, followed by the frothed milk and a straw.

Finally turning around, I hold out the drink to Adam. "All done."

I don't watch him take a sip as I put the milk away and wipe down my machine. Only then do I finally face him.

"Is it good?"

"It's good. Thank you." He looks like he wants to say more but opts not to. "Do you have a griddle or something for the pancakes?"

"Right. Sorry."

I find the flat-top in the panty and gather a mixing bowl, measuring cups, and a whisk.

"Do you need anything else?" I'm not sure what goes into his famous pancakes, but I'm sure I have it. I set the flat-top griddle on the counter and plug it in to warm up. When I can't make myself busy, I sidle up next to Adam with the mixing bowl and measuring cups.

His hands get busy pulling his supplies out of his bag before I feel him pull me into his embrace. "Just you."

My arms wrap around his waist and my body relaxes for the first time since he crossed the threshold into my home. As a matter of fact, my body relaxes for the first time since our kiss last night. His heartbeat thumps steadily in my ear and it's enough to tether me to him. I nuzzle into his chest and inhale the scent that's all Adam, cedarwood and patchouli.

All too soon our embrace ends and Adam pulls away from me. "I want you to sit your cute butt on the counter while I get to work and I wanna know what's with the weirdness, Em."

It's a valid observation on his part. One I've been wondering about myself since last night.

I must be taking too long because Adam hefts me up on the counter like I weigh nothing and hands me my iced latte. "Thank you."

"Mm-hmm. So what's got you putting those bricks up again?"

"Baseball. I don't want to keep bringing James up but he

was such a massive part of my life." I watch as Adam expertly measures out the pancake mix almost in a trance-like state. "When you said Dylan was at baseball camp it was like a bucket of cold water was dumped on me. Since James died I've avoided the sport as a whole."

His hands stop mixing and I trail my eyes up to meet his. "I'm sorry."

"You didn't know," I put my drink off to the side. "Adam, I came to love baseball. And one day I won't corre-late the sport to pain or to him. If this thing between us continues the way we're both predicting then I think Dylan's games would be the perfect re-introduction."

Am I getting ahead of myself? Putting the cart before the horse? Absolutely. But if the fire that burns in Adam's eyes as I include his son is any indication that he feels the same, then I said the right thing.

"If you keep saying things like that then we'll never eat."

"You say that like it's a bad thing." I counter back.

He shakes his head with a smile and gets back to the pancake mix. I watch him work in silence. There is no need for small talk as being in the space with him fills up all of the quiet spaces.

I slide off the counter while Adam scoops out some pancake batter on the heated griddle. I walk over to my record player and flip through my vinyls until I find *The National*. Pulling it out of the case, I put it on the turnstile and turn the volume up until the music floats into the kitchen.

Adam looks so comfortable in my kitchen that it makes me envision Saturday mornings at his house. Hopping back up on the counter I see he's already got a small stack of pancakes with butter smothered on top.

"Are you a fan of *The National?*"

"You kidding? They're one of the first concerts I ever went to."

I cross my legs, holding my drink in my hand, then ask him, "Who are your top five artists or bands if that's what you prefer."

He flips the last of the pancakes onto the plate and then moves my way. "Hmm. *The National,* obviously. *Tim McGraw, The Weeknd, Lana Del Rey,* and *Zedd.* Yours?"

I point to the cabinet to the left of the stove and Adam gets two plates down for us. "*Lana Del Rey* is my top artist. She's who I was listening to the first night I texted you."

"Thank you, *Lana Del Rey.*" Adam holds his hands in prayer pose as he looks up to the ceiling and I can't stop the small laugh that escapes.

"You're such a goof. Then it would be *Kendrick Lamar, Hozier, Miley Cyrus,* and *Florence & the Machine.* But I'm not too picky. As long as a song hooks me I'll obsess over it for weeks until a new song comes along. And repeat the obsessive process all over again."

"Solid choices, Ms. Bailey. Breakfast is done. Where should we sit?"

I have a couple of options: the balcony that has a small table or my dining table that can easily seat six.

"Let's do the dining table."

Adam makes his way to the table as I reach into my refrigerator to pull out the bottle of syrup and some napkins.

I join him at the table and sit caddy-corner to him for maximum closeness without sitting on top of him. Although I'm sure he wouldn't mind.

Taking a bite of my pancakes, I let out a moan that

should only be heard in the bedroom. "Holy shit these are good." I see Adam shift in his seat and I hide a smirk that my moan affected him. "Are you okay?"

He clears his throat. "Mm-hmm. So I see you like them?" Adams asks as he shovels food into his mouth.

"Mm-hmm," I respond in the same way and shovel more pancakes into my mouth.

We eat in comfortable silence with only the sound of our forks on our plates and The National crooning in the background. When my plate is clear, I push it to the middle of the table and sit back on my chair. Adam mirrors my position.

"That was good. Thank you."

"You're welcome. So you mentioned your birthday a while back. How old did you turn? If you don't mind my asking."

"I turned twenty-seven," I state proudly.

Adam lets out a whistle of surprise.

"What?" I ask with a small laugh.

"I knew you were young. But I didn't think you were that young."

"And you're so old and wise?" I joke as I get up to take our plates to the sink. Turning the faucet on, I rinse off the sticky residue of syrup and pop the plates in the dishwasher. Adam joins me in the kitchen and places the syrup back in the fridge.

Wiping my hands off on a dish towel, I turn and mirror his stance.

"As a matter of fact, I am old and wise." He stalks closer to me, causing my heart rate to amp up.

I steady my breath. "Just how old are you?"

"Thirty-eight."

Our sock-covered toes are inches from touching as

Adam stops in front of me. My chest heaves like I ran a marathon as he cages me in. His scent, mixing with the syrup from breakfast, is a heady sensation. His warmth cocoons me as I rest my hands on the waist of his jeans.

"You can let me know how forty is."

Adam

I barely let the final word pass through her lips before mine descended on hers and I'm swallowing her gasp. I've been wanting to kiss her again since I walked through the door. But I needed to play it cool and tread carefully. Emily is like a skittish cat that warms up to you until a loud noise causes her to retreat.

The pressure of her hands on my waist gets more noticeable as she pulls my body into hers. My hand snakes up and tangles in her hair, angling her head as I deepen the kiss.

Her tongue teases the seam of my lips, surprising me and I let her in. The moment our tongues touch it's like a fire has licked up the back of my neck. She rises to the tips of her toes and wraps her arms around my neck, fusing our bodies together.

I roam my hands down her body and pick her up by her toned thighs.

"Couch," Emily pants out before diving in for another kiss.

Blindly, I make my way to the couch without tripping

over something. Not trusting myself, I peek an eye open just as Emily trails her lips down my neck.

"Shit, Em. You can't do that while I'm walking."

I hasten my last couple of steps and sit on her couch. It seems that spurred Emily on. Her lips come back to mine and slides her body closer to mine. My arms wrap around her waist and I'm sure she can feel my erection bumping up against her legging-covered core. She sits up and moves closer, putting her pussy over my cock.

I rip my mouth from hers and pull back. "I'm trying to be good and take it slow. But damn you're not making it easy for me." I emphasize *easy* by rutting up into her.

"Okay, okay. I'll stop." She claims but latches her mouth onto my neck.

My eyes roll to the back of my head as her mouth suctions harder on my neck. Quickly maneuvering to where I'm on top of her, I place her arms above her head and hold them there. "Unless you want my mouth on your pussy, I need you to stop. I can only hold out for so long," I say and don't even recognize my voice. "And once I have a taste of you, you're mine."

Her chest is still heaving and her lips are red and puffy from the assault of our lips mashing together.

"Okay, we'll wait."

I hide my disappointment behind a smirk. "Three months. Once you're no longer Dylan's teacher, nothing is stopping me from claiming you in front of everyone."

Her smile is rather bashful for someone that was writhing over my cock. "Okay."

Kissing her one last time I pull myself off of her and relax on her couch.

"I need to tell you something." I hadn't meant to bring

up my little research project last night right now. But if I don't tell her now I never will.

Emily sits up but rests her feet in my lap. It makes me want to beat on my chest that she's already comfortable like this around me.

"What is it?" Her eyebrows pinch in concern.

"Last night when you left, I was morbidly curious about you." I feel her body tense and I place my hand around her ankle to hold her to me. "I looked you up and I saw the article on your fiance. It explained why you tensed up when I told you about Dylan being at baseball camp."

"You could have asked me."

I tilt my head and observe her. "Could I have?

She chews on her bottom lip as she mulls it over.

"I like you a lot, Emily. But you're skittish around me. And maybe that's who you are, but selfishly I don't want that. I know you've had a traumatic past. I just want you to let me in more than what you're giving."

"I like you a lot too. Just so you know." She says and takes my hand, holding it in hers. "I deal with parent abandonment if you haven't picked up on that. Neglect if that's the term you want to use. But my parents weren't abusive. My high school and college years were spent with my housekeeper, Gloria, and James. Anytime my parents would come home it was to tell me they were working more or heading out of the country for a special case."

Emily looks towards her record player but I stay looking at her. "I had many arguments with my parents when I was younger that resulted in me running to James's house and seeking the comfort that he and his family brought me. As I got older, I no longer cared about what lives my parents were living when they weren't around me. I guess that sped mine and James's relationship up."

A child fending for herself and living as an adult.

"We got engaged right after I graduated college. My parents weren't there to celebrate with us, but his family was."

"You don't have to tell me anything else."

She shakes her head. "I wanna tell you it all. The last day we were together, I was grading papers and he got a phone call from our friend Liam. Him and Kamryn, my best friend, had broken up for what seemed like the hundredth time. We spent a little time together and then went to help our friends."

I tamp down the jealousy when she tells me how they spent their last day.

"I got to her house and she was a mess. That's when she got a frantic phone call from Liam. I had this terrible feeling in the pit of my stomach. I was frantically texting James and telling him to get Liam to stop his truck. Their yelling got louder and those last handful of texts I sent went unanswered. My last text to him was telling him I loved him. And when Kamryn stopped yelling into the phone, that's when I knew that the truck stopped."

She doesn't continue. She doesn't have to. The article had pictures of the truck her fiance was in, smashed into the back of an eighteen-wheeler. How she's managing to find happiness again is inspiring.

"I also saw an article about your violin playing."

She doesn't look me in the eye. Instead, she flips my hand and traces the lines on my palm. "I haven't played since I graduated high school. I spent years loving an instrument that walking away from it wasn't as hard as I thought it would be. My parents may have introduced me to it, but I chose to keep pursuing it." Emily looks up at me and her eyes are brighter. "Wow, that was deep."

A puff of air comes out of my nose with a small laugh. "Are you still friends with his family?"

"Remember how I said my Thanksgiving was draining?" I nod my head and she continues. "I finally went to go see them. As hard as it was, seeing them was also like someone took the elephant off my chest and I could breathe for the first time in years. They want my happiness just as much as I want it."

So I also have them to thank for pushing her along. I lean forward and place a kiss on her lips. It's meant to be a short kiss until Emily places her hand on the side of my neck. The smile I try my hardest to hold sneaks out.

"You're trouble." I speak as our lips brush against one another.

She slides closer, almost sitting in my lap. "I like kissing you."

Emily drives her point home by pulling my bottom lip between her teeth. With a groan, I haul her back into my lap and worship her mouth. I drive my tongue between her lips and hold her hips still though I feel them tense as she tries to gain friction.

Em rips her mouth from mine. "I don't know if I can wait three months."

"Fuck. Ms. Bailey, are you suggesting we sneak around?"

"Who said parent-teacher conferences had to happen at school." She barters all the while teasing my hair at the nape of my neck.

I look up to the ceiling and pray to whoever is listening that I behave accordingly.

"What are you doing?" Emily asks and gently pulls my face down by my chin so we're at eye level.

"Hoping my karma is good."

She places her lips to mine one last time and crawls off.

"Where are you going?" I reach out for her but come up with air.

Emily grabs a throw blanket off the back of her couch and lays in across her lap. "Helping you keep your karma good." She says so matter-of-factly.

If I thought Emily was a shy mouse, she has severely proved me wrong. Until she's no longer Dylan's teacher we'll be playing a game of cat and mouse.

Who will be the first break?

Adam

I walk into my restaurant on a warm April morning. Dylan has a month and a half left in school and that leaves me with a month and a half to hire more people. Namely, another assistant manager. So I have a few interviews lined up today with several more throughout the week.

We used to only open for nights during the week in the off-season. But with more offices requesting working lunches and retirement parties, my employees decided that being open more won't hurt because they are the ones who work harder than me.

When I settle into my desk chair, I send out a few emails to the applicants wanting to schedule interviews. Hopefully, I get responses in a timely manner.

With Jeff and I splitting the night shifts during the week, I have free nights for the first time ever.

> Me: Hey, you.

It's the middle of the school day so I don't expect a

response from Emily for a while. I tackle more items off of my to-do list before creating another one. The staff that is in for the day shift and I eat lunch together. It's a way I've managed to keep the closeness up with my employees.

Jeff comes in half an hour earlier to relieve me. I let him in on what's on the schedule for tonight. It's a Wednesday, so it shouldn't be too busy.

I'm walking out to my truck when my dings.

> Emily: Hey, yourself.

> Me: I have a question for you.

> Emily: I may have an answer...

> Me: Would you like to go on a date with me?

> Emily: You mean making out in my apartment isn't your idea of a date? I'm shocked.

> Me: Smartypants.

> Emily: Can't help it. But to answer your question, I would love to go on a date with you.

> Me: How does 7 o'clock sound?

> Emily: Perfect.

> Me: I'll pick you up.

I drive on clouds all the way home. Dylan should be getting home as well, so I get to spend some time with him before I need to get ready.

"Dylan?" I call out when I'm inside the house. Jenny is

at the kitchen table doing homework and I wave to her when she looks up.

"He just went upstairs." She tells me and sets her pen down.

I look to the stairs and then back at Jenny.

"What?"

"I have a huge favor to ask you."

Jenny leans back in the chair and crosses her arms, quirking her brow as she asks, "What's in it for me?"

"Free food and a night with the best kid ever?" I phrase it for her and hopefully, it sells.

"Night, huh? And where are you going?"

I purse my lips and take my hat off my head to ruffle my hair. "I have a date."

Jenny's legs get tangled around the chair as she rushes to me. I hold her shoulders steady and she waves them off.

"You should have led with that!"

It's my turn to cross my arms over my chest. "I'm supposed to consult with my twenty-year-old babysitter that I have a date?"

"Considering it was the Ice Age the last time you dated, yes."

"Watch it." I say and flick her on the nose.

What started as Jenny being Dylan's babysitter, has turned her into the little sister that I never had.

"Ouch," she says and rubs her nose. "But, Adam, this is huge. Oh my god, my group chat is going to freak out." She murmurs the last part as if I'm not supposed to hear her.

"You've been talking about me to your friends?"

"You've been the topic of many conversations for the last two years."

"Is it too late to fire you?" I ask jokingly.

She laughs as if I said the sky was green. "Like you could find a babysitter that Dylan adores more."

Jenny isn't wrong about that. But I'll never inflate her ego more than what it's already at. Heavy footsteps barreling down the stairs has me turning right in time to catch Dylan.

"Hey, buddy."

"Hi, Daddy. What's for dinner?"

"Is that all I'm good for? Cooking you dinner?" I tickle his neck before his squirming gets to be too much and I have to set him down.

He runs to the living room and turns the TV on. I look at him and shake my head. Jenny snorts before getting back to her homework.

I riffle through the fridge for anything that's defrosted. When I come up blank, I pull out a bag of chicken nuggets from the freezer and go about getting them cooked. While Jenny and Dylan are eating, I rush up to my room to get ready for my date.

At fifteen after, I head downstairs to say bye to Dylan. I give Jenny a knowing look when she does a weird dance in the kitchen. That generation is one I'll never understand. I make sure I have enough blankets in the backseat and that the mattress pad isn't too flat. When I'm satisfied, I peel out of my driveway and make the drive to Emily's.

Emily

Iscrutinize my basic ripped jeans and black three-quarter long-sleeve shirt. Adam told me to dress casually, only I have no clue what that means. I'm either in work clothes, sweatpants, or workout clothes; there is no in-between for me. My hair falls in loose waves down my back and my makeup is light. I spritz some perfume on my pulse points and look over myself in the mirror again.

"You look hot, Emily." Sarah says from her spot at my vanity.

With Kamryn whisked out of the country by Mason, I had no one to help me figure out what to wear. In one of our talks when she started college, Kam mentioned her roommate, Sarah, would help her figure out what to wear. So she's my trusted stylist for the night.

"Are you sure?" I've never been so unsure of my choices.

"You're a nervous little bird, Em. And it's understandable. But I promise, whatever you wear is not going to deter him."

My phone chimes with a text.

Adam: Headed your way. I'll be there in ten minutes.

Me: Do I need a sweater?

Adam: Bring one just in case.

"He said to bring a sweater," I muse as I head to my walk-in closet.

"Who needs a sweater in April?" Sarah's question is muffled while I'm deep in my closet.

I find a thick cream cardigan that'll pair well with my dark-wash jeans and black shirt. "Are heels too much?" I call out as I look through my shoe rack.

"Do you know who you're asking?" Sarah quips back with a laugh.

"Silly me," I call out as I grasp a broken-in pair of Christian Loubitans.

Walking out of my closet I toss my cardigan on the bed and slip my heels on. I take another look at myself in the mirror. My face has a new glow to it that can only be described as joy. And I can't stop the smile that appears.

"Hot and happy," Sarah muses as she watches me through the mirror.

My eyes meet hers in the reflection. "Thank you."

"Em, you don't need to thank me," she says and peels herself off of the chair with a groan. "I'm gonna head out. My phone has been buzzing more than my vibrator and I need to take care of it."

"The phone or your vibrator?" I ask when I turn around.

"Both, you silly girl."

We walk to the door and she kisses me on the cheek

before floating down the stairs. No sooner have I closed the door does my phone chime.

Adam: Out front.

Me: Be down in a minute.

I feed Biscuit her dinner, then slide my purse over my shoulder and fold my sweater over my arm. Locking up the door I head down to my first date in years. My heart matches the beat of my footsteps as I get closer to Adam and his truck. He's waiting at the passenger door and the moment he hears my heels click on the pavement, his gaze travels up my body, warming me from the inside out as I see his eyes heat with pure lust.

"God, you're ethereal," he says when I'm a foot away from him.

"Hi, yourself." I tell him and walk into his arms.

Adam's cedarwood and patchouli scent surrounds me as my head fits under his chin, even with my heels on. His body is solid under my touch as I wrap my arms around his waist.

He pulls back. "Are you ready?"

"Yes," I tell him and he sneaks a quick kiss before opening the door for me.

The scent of food invades my senses as I watch Adam round the truck and hop in. I look in the backseat to see blankets and pillows piled high. My gaze swings to him.

"It's not what you think," he states quickly and pulls out of my neighborhood.

"Are you a mind reader?"

"No," he starts and signals to the left, taking us in the direction of the highway. "But I know what it looks like now. When I put everything back there I didn't even think about how it would look."

My chin is propped on my fist that's resting on the center console and I see the furrow in his brow. He turns to look at me and I see the nervousness in his orbs. "I trust you didn't know."

"Are you sure?" He looks at me and then back at the road as he switches lanes.

I reach over and pick up the hand that's resting on his thigh and weave our fingers together. "I'm sure."

Adam picks up our linked hands and presses a kiss to mine.

The rest of the drive to our destination is silent, save for the music. We turn off the highway to a dirt road I'm not familiar with and it's out of the city, so my interest is piqued.

"Are the blankets to wrap my body in when you need to dispose of me?"

Adam snorts. "How many unsolved mysteries do you watch?"

"It's the podcasts that should worry you." I tell him as I give his hand a squeeze.

He barks out a laugh and turns down another dirt road as signs for a Drive-In Movie Theater create a path.

"Get out!"

"Em, I can't. I'm driving," he responds with a lame dad response.

My laugh is silent as I watch the trees open up. A huge screen playing short cartoons greets us. We get to the ticket booth and Adam lets go of my hand to pay for a ticket before he's driving up to find a spot. He does that hot guy thing by putting his hand on the back of my seat as he reverses into a parking spot and my heart rate triples from that small movement.

"Ready?" He asks when we're stopped.

"I'm so ready," I can barely contain my excitement.

We get out and Adam opens the backdoor. I do the same and grab the blankets without him asking.

He drops the lift on the tailgate and places the basket on the door. Adam climbs up and takes the blankets from me.

"Will you get the mattress pad from the backseat as well?"

"Sure." I say and walk back around.

Handing it to him when I walk back around, I watch as he gets to work on making us a comfortable palette.

When Adam is satisfied with his work, he places our food to the side and jumps down. He closes the bed of the truck and turns to stand behind me. "Your turn," he says.

"You're not going to cop a feel when you help me up?" I ask him with a teasing lilt in my voice.

"Oh, I most definitely am."

I smile at him over my shoulder and scoot to the back corner of his truck. Adam's hands engulf my waist as I pop a foot on the corner and pull myself up. His hands trail down the length of my legs and my body goes light for a moment until I'm safely in the bed of his truck. Adam joins me a minute later and props his leg out before pulling our food out.

My gaze fixates on him. And I wonder how, in a time when I needed healing, did this man pick me. His hair is pulled back in a bun and the beard on his face is well-kept. There's something about Adam that makes me want to cuddle into him and never let go.

We eat in comfort as the sun goes down and the movie starts on the big screen. When we've polished off our food,

Adam leans back on the pillows he has set up and gestures to me toward him. I take my heels off and slide over to him. I fit into his side like a lock sliding into place.

This comfort I experience with him is quick. Like what I feel for him I should be me taking it slow. But in this phase of my life, I'm in a 'why go slow?' phase.

Adam turns the volume down on the box that's on the side of the truck. "Tell me something."

"What do you wanna know?"

"Anything." He volleys back.

"I love squirrels and geese," I admit.

His body shakes with a laugh.

"What is so funny about my love for innocent animals?"

He sits up and rests his back against the truck. "It's just random. And not an animal I expected you to like."

"Fine. Expect the unexpected with me, Mr. Montgomery. What's your favorite candy?"

"Twix. I have some stashed at home and work."

"And you manage to keep them away from Dylan?" I ask.

"I like that you're not afraid to ask about him."

I sit up and move next to him. "He's a part of you. And don't tell him I told you, but he's my favorite student this year."

"Did having a strikingly handsome father play a role in that?"

"You are—"

His arm slides around my waist and holds me tighter to him. "Dashing. One of a kind. Exquisite..."

"I'm now going to go with full of himself. And there's no mistaking that Dylan is your son."

"My work here is done." Adam says with a show of crossing his arms and putting them behind his head.

We talk in between the movie finishing. Adam tells jokes that have me burying my face in the blankets so I don't disturb the other watchers. I try and fail to scold him for his spicy jokes. When the movie credits roll, I realize I don't want this date to end.

"This is one of the best dates I've been on." I tell Adam as we fold the blankets.

He hops down from the truck and holds his hands out to me. "Have you been on a lot of first dates?"

"Now that you ask that, no. I've only been on one other first date and I was fourteen." I tell him as I gather some blankets in my arms and move around to the backdoor.

We finish putting the rest of the things in the truck and then Adam helps me into the passenger seat. I watch him walk around to the driver's side and then we're off.

"What was your first date like?" He asks when we pull out onto the main road.

I smile remembering how nervous we were. "It was terrifying. We went to an ice cream shop that was down the street from our neighborhood."

"Classic first date material. I'm impressed."

"I was too. What was your first date?" I ask and turn to face him as best as I can with the seatbelt restraining me. The glow from the dash lights up his face and the green in his eyes is more slime green than forest green.

"It was a bonfire after a football game."

"Did you do a group date?" I ask baffled.

Adam's laugh comes from deep in his chest. "She was not happy. Safe to say I didn't get a second date."

"I can't imagine why," I say dryly.

I see the smile lift his cheeks. The drive to my apartment is quiet. As the scene outside of the truck turns from trees to city, I still can't help but wish that this date never ends.

Adam pulls up to the curb and looks over at me once we're in 'park'. "Do I get a second date with you?"

"It won't be a bonfire with a group of people will it?" I ask him as I unclick my seatbelt and lean onto the center console.

He mimics my position by leaning on the center console, leaving a few inches between us. "Please. Like I'd share you with anyone else."

"Then, yes. You get a second date with me."

Adam's face moves closer by millimeters. My eyes move over his face, but my gaze focuses on his lips more than they probably should. His hand tangles in my hair and ghosts his lips over mine.

"You are so beautiful it takes my breath away," he says before pressing his lips to mine.

What starts soft and sweet amps up to hot. His tongue traces the seam of my lips before I open and our tongues tangle. The moan I let out spurs him on and the whimper I let out when he bites on my bottom lip makes me regret taking us slow. My hand slides up to his hair and I pull the tie out, freeing the strands, and fisting his hair in my hand.

Our tongues dance as I try to get closer to him. I'm halfway across the center console when Adam slows down the kiss.

"Slow, Emily." He tells me as he peppers kisses up and down my neck. My breath hitches and my eyes roll as Adam latches onto the spot between my neck and shoulder.

"I don't want *slow* when you do that." How I manage to string a short sentence together is beyond me. My nipples are so hard they could cut glass and my underwear is completely ruined.

I feel his smile against my skin and then he lets up. Adam trails soft kisses up my neck before he kisses me again. Long and slow until I'm completely breathless.

"It's only fair I tease you the way you tease me," Adam shoots out before he's out of the truck and rounds to the passenger side.

The time he's out of the truck barely gives me enough time to get my bearings. When the door opens, Adam holds his hand out. I grab my purse and place my hand in his.

"Thank you for a fun date," I tell him when I'm on solid ground. I like that I can still look up at him with heels on.

"Thank you for wearing those shoes," he groans out and backs me into the side of his truck. I feel his hard cock through his jeans and I want nothing more than to feel him pounding in me. "You are trouble." Adam kisses me one more time and then directs me to the stairs. "Goodnight, Emily," he says with a swat on my butt.

"Goodnight, Adam."

I hear his exhale as I walk away. When I turn to the stairs, Adam is still standing by his truck, and as I ascend the stairs his truck starting up breaks through the sound of my breathing and the click of my heels.

When I'm in my apartment, I fall on my bed and look at the ceiling. The smile I try so desperately to wipe off my face no matter how hard I try, never leaves. And I have to thank Adam for returning the happiness I never thought I'd see again to me.

Adam

"Hey, Tammy, did you get the menu finalized?" I ask when I come up from my office.

Once a month we hold a speed-dating event for the singles and newly singles in the city. Everyone is also carefully vetted before a formal email is sent out to willing participants. Dating in the city is hard, so if my restaurant can be the catalyst for a relationship starting, then I'm not one to turn people away.

I may be a little clouded with hearts in my eyes because this is where Emily and I met. Love can make people do the craziest things.

My steps stop. Nope! Can't be love. We haven't even had our second date yet.

But she's also all I think about.

It's been tricky with her teaching and being Dylan's teacher. I won't come between her job. I just have to wait a few more weeks.

But, love? No. It can't be.

"You look like you've seen a ghost," Tammy observes from the prep station.

I shake my head out of the thoughts they turned to. "It's nothing."

She regards me carefully. "If you say so. The menu is finalized. We're going to keep it simple but also sensual."

For the next hour, we go over the menu. We make small tweaks and decide which wine and bourbon to pair the meals. By the time we're finished, it's closer to four. When I check my phone, I see a text from Jenny.

Jenny: Class got out early so I picked up Dylan.

Jenny: Feel free to not rush home.

Me: Are you telling me not to come to my house?

Jenny: I'm telling you to hang out with someone else.

Me: Stop talking about me in your group chat.

Jenny: Can't help it. See you later!

Not wanting to head back down to my office, I walk to the bar and take a seat. Jenny is giving me the push I need to see Emily. But do I rush her?

Me: Hey, baby.

Emily: Hi, handsome.

Me: *puffs out chest* What are you up to?

Emily: *takes needle to deflate chest*
Walking to my car.

> Me: How would you feel about dinner cooked by me?

> Emily: I would love that. When are you coming over?

> Me: I'll be there in an hour.

> Emily: See you soon *kiss face*

THE SMELL of garlic permeates the air as *Hozier's* voice floats through Emily's expansive apartment while she enjoys a glass of wine on her balcony.

When I got here she offered to help, but I quickly shut that down. I like cooking for her, and I noticed when I cooked her breakfast, she liked watching me. But tonight I want her to relax. The end of the school year is tough on teachers. So the more weight I can take off her shoulders, the better.

I serve up our food and place everything on the table. Emily must be engrossed in her book because she hasn't looked up once.

Making my way to her balcony, she doesn't even flinch when I squat down next to her. "Hey, baby. Dinner's done." She looks at me with flushed cheeks and blown pupils. "What are you reading?"

"Nothing," she says and tries to lock her Kindle but I swipe it from her.

I ignore her weak protests and read a little of the page she was on. And what I see is explicit. And hot as hell. "What is this book about?"

"A book about a gymnast and her coach." Emily says and takes a sip of wine.

"That's legal?"

"It's fiction, baby," Emily says if I don't already know.

I hand her Kindle back to her. "I would hope so. Let's go, my little reader. And you can tell me all about the books you read."

She tosses her blanket to the side and takes my offered hand. Emily opted not to change out of the dress she wore to teach in and it makes me glad that she's comfortable in her teacher clothes. The dress hits right under her knees and I saw the shoes she wore with them and it gave me the ultimate Ms. Honey vibes.

"It smells so good in here."

I kiss the side of her head and move to pull out her chair. "I'm glad you think so."

"Thank you."

"So tell me more about this book you're reading," I continue and don't miss the eye roll she throws at me.

But Emily tells me about the book she's reading. It's a five-book series following one couple. In this, the gymnast's goal is to reach the Olympics, and she falls for her coach, among other setbacks that Emily has said broke her heart.

"Are you a big reader?"

I take a sip of wine to wash down the rest of my food. "Unless invoices and Dylan's bedtime stories count."

"I can't say that they do."

"Tell you what. You find a book we can read together."

Her jaw drops. "Seriously?"

"Mm-hmm. So make it a good one," I say with a wink.

If our reading together puts a smile on her face, then I'll read with her for the rest of time. Emily peppers me with questions about growing up here and if I ever felt the need to move away. Now that I think about it, moving away from the place I grew up never occurred to me. And I'm glad I didn't move as I get to raise my son here.

When one of my favorite *Hozier* songs cues up, I stand up and hold my hand out to Emily. "Dance with me?"

The smile she gives me as she places her hand in mine warms me to my core. And as we sway to the music, her body melting into mine, and mine curving around hers, I realize that this is peak happiness.

After seven months of knowing her, I feel like she's been in my life forever. While we're still taking it slow, she makes me wanna hit the gas full throttle. The revelation I had earlier today threatens to expose me. But I choke it down and focus on the right now.

Emily

Last week of school. The kids have been feeling it and so have us teachers. It's hard to concentrate on teaching when the taste of summer is at our fingertips. We work hard nine months out of the year for a full three months of relaxation.

It is the end goal when becoming a teacher.

Of course, that's the last goal when our main one is making sure our kids don't fall behind. It will be sad when I say goodbye to this group. And when they move up to the next grade, all I can hope for is that I prepared and taught them enough.

Adam: T-minus 2 days until you're free to be mine.

Me: Stop distracting me.

Things with Adam have been great. However, I'm nervous and excited for our relationship to proceed further than it is.

He keeps me laughing. He lets me feel my feelings

when I need to. He doesn't belittle me or tell me to stop feeling my grief when the wave hits me.

On weekends when his restaurant has live bands, I keep him company. I've yet to introduce him to my friends as I want us in the next phase of *us* before we venture into the outside world.

But my taking it slow and adhering to his good karma has not been easy. Oh, no. Adam makes sure that the nights we do see each other are worth remembering. He kisses me breathless and leaves me with a serious case of lady blue balls. I've never gotten so much use out of my vibrator than the nights he leaves my apartment. And I'm sure it hasn't been easy on him if what I've felt through his jeans is any indication.

When the bell rings for the end of the day, my little ones pack up their things and head to the bus.

"Bye, everyone. See you tomorrow." I stand at the door and watch their eager faces as they leave my classroom and head to the bus one last time.

I smile as the exuberant chatter greets my ears as other students pass me by. When the last of the group is out the door, I look across to Melissa and breathe out a sigh of relief.

"One more day," she announces rather loudly that it incites a round of cheers from the other teachers that have classrooms nearby.

While my kids were doing their color worksheets, I was catching up on end-of-the-year paperwork and report cards. I laugh as I see what they colored and how they colored them. Laughing as I clean up the mess they left behind, I pack up my things and head to the front office to pick up any mail before leaving for the day.

On the way home, I blast *My Dear Melancholy*, by *The Weeknd*, an album that Adam is obsessed with. I'm not usually an R&B fan, but this album is sensual. Maybe that's why Adam is a fan. I get home as the last song is ending and get my things out of the backseat. Walking up the stairs to my apartment, a vase with orchids is waiting for me on my welcome mat.

I unlock the door to my place and pick up the vase right as I open the door. Bringing it to my kitchen counter, I pluck the card off of its holder.

TO MAKE YOU SMILE.
YOURS, ADAM

Taking a picture I send it to Adam.

Me: Mission accomplished.

Adam: I'm glad you like them.

Me: They're one of my favorites.

Adam: What are your other favorites?

Me: Sunflowers and roses.

Adam: Does it make me cheesy if I say that you're the sunflower in my life?

Me: Not at all.

Heading to my bedroom, I pull some shorts out of my dresser and a tank top. Once changed I walk to the other end of my apartment and check in on Biscuit. Although it's veering towards the middle of May, I open my patio door and am lucky when a breeze comes off the water.

It's moments like this, when my life is at a plateau, that I miss the chaos. The silence causes me to slip into the darkness. So I find an upbeat record that never fails to boost my mood. Pouring a glass of Rose, I pick up my Kindle and head to my patio as I let the rest of my day pass by.

~

"Five, four, three, two, one! Summer!"

Cheers are heard throughout the school as summer is officially here. School is done until August and my kids could not be happier.

I'm happy too. But for an entirely different reason.

My kids smother me with hugs on their way out of my classroom. I had a blast teaching them and it makes me a little sad that I won't see them again. When the final kid is out the door I let out a long-awaited breath.

I straighten up desks and push the chairs in. Throwing away worksheets that were left behind. I have three months of freedom.

"Bye, Melissa. Girls night soon!" I say as I pop my head into her classroom.

"You got it, girlfriend."

With a wave, I walk down the deserted hallway and push my way out to the parking lot. I see a lone figure standing by my car. I'm a good distance away so I can't quite make who it is. But when I'm closer my heart rate picks up and I can't stop the smile from spreading across my face.

"What are you doing here?" I ask Adam with a laugh.

He meets me halfway. "I told you I didn't want to wait."

And then his mouth is on mine. Claiming me for the world to see. My bags drop to the ground and my hands fist the bottom of his shirt. This kiss is freeing. Our tongues tangle and send shockwaves down to my toes. I rise to my tiptoes wanting to get closer to Adam.

Wrapping my arms around his neck and weaving my hand through his hair. His hands slide down my body landing on my lower back, pulling me into his groin.

I rip my mouth from him and take in a much-needed breath. "Hi."

My greeting comes out breathy as I search his eyes. They're greener in this light but all I see is my reflection shining back at me.

He leans in for one more kiss. "Hi, beautiful."

"How are you here? Where's Dylan?"

Adam bends down to pick my fallen bags up off the ground and slings them over his shoulder. "I was waiting for him at home. But he promptly informed me that he'll be at Sandra's pool, one of the baseball team moms, with the rest of the team and they're having a sleepover. I was told their pool is better than ours. I even took today off for his last day. But now that he's occupied I have a free night."

We get to my car and I fish my keys out of my bag Adam is holding. "Are you saying what I think you're saying, Mr. Montgomery?"

He crowds me against my car. "What is it you think I'm saying?"

"That you have a free house and an empty pool just waiting to be used."

"That's exactly what I'm saying. Will you join me for an at-home date?"

I feel my smile spread across my face so I turn my head and kiss his forearm. "Yes, I would love to. Let me go home to change and get some clothes."

"Deal," he leans forward and kisses my forehead, then pulls out his phone and I hear mine chirp a few seconds later. "I just texted you my address."

Leaning up to kiss him, I unlock my car and get in.

Sending him a finger wave I drive off. The good thing about the last day of school is that it was a half day. This means we teachers get more than a few hours of sunlight to enjoy the start of our break. And it's a rare weather pattern where it's already sweltering in the early summer.

Adam wasn't joking when he said the last day of school I was his. And if the joy I feel from one slightly public moment at my school's parking lot is any indication of what being his feels like, then I'm in for the ride of my life.

Adam

Once I see Emily turn out of the parking lot, I hurry back to my truck and head to the store. Although I had planned for her to come over, I didn't expect it to be so soon. But I'm not one to complain.

Pulling into the Whole Foods parking lot, I grab a small cart and head to the butcher section. Picking out two slabs of steak that will cook perfectly on the grill, I make my way around the store to pick up more necessities: wine, vegetables, bread, and another bouquet of her favorite flowers.

When everything is paid for, I hightail it home. Placing the wine bottle in the fridge I get to marinating the steak with a dry rub, then pop them in the fridge.

Emily: Headed to you.

Me: See you soon.

I blow out a breath and wipe off my hands. I should not be nervous. I've had my tongue down her throat for crying out loud. But this is the first woman I'm having in my home. And that means something to me.

To take my mind off of my nerves, I head outside and sweep off the patio. Walking into the shed, I pull out the leaf blower and do an air-sweep of the cushions on the cabanas. When all of the fallen leaves, grass, and bugs are gone, I turn the pool lights and hit the switch for the waterfall that's off to the side of the pool. Heading back inside, I jog upstairs to my bedroom and change into my swim trunks, making sure to put some sunscreen on.

My phone lights up from the security camera at the end of my driveway signaling a car. Checking the app, I see it's Emily and grab the towels from the hall closet before heading to the door to meet her.

I hold in a laugh as her mouth hangs open at seeing my tattoos and piercings for the first time. I also have to take deep breaths to keep from sprouting a boner. She's not in anything too revealing, but her legs are bare and it's the first time I'm seeing her not fully clothed.

As she's walking up the front steps, I survey her closer. The scent of sunscreen wafts towards me as a gust of wind ruffles her hair around her face.

"I like seeing your car in my driveway," I speak out loud. If I didn't care to save face I would puff my chest out.

"Funny. I like seeing you without a shirt," she quips back.

I step aside to let her in my house. When I close the door it becomes even more real that she's here.

I lead her towards the heart of the house, the kitchen that opens into the living room, and take her bag off of her shoulder.

"Adam, your home is beautiful," Emily states as she continues to roam her eyes around the space.

I do my best to see my home through her eyes. My biggest goal was to make this home as inviting as possible with color splashed on the wall in the form of accent walls and art mixed with photos of Dylan and me decorating the space. It's a place where I could raise my son as normal as possible and where he would want for nothing.

The living room is fitted with an oversized sectional, that's seen better days. A coffee table that houses this morning's coffee and some of Dylan's action-hero toys. It's home.

"Thank you. Pool?"

Her eyes meet mine and I swear, it's like I've never been with anyone that takes my breath away from a simple look. But she does.

"Yeah. Let's go."

"Don't you need to change?" I ask, unsure if she's wearing her suit under her clothes.

Emily pops a hand on her hip. "What if I told you I swim nude?"

I blow out a breath and run my hand through my hair. She flusters me and I refuse to let her know that. Although I doubt I'm fooling her. "Then I'll be glad I don't have neighbors so close to me."

She shakes her head with a smile and turns towards the open door, crossing the threshold to my outdoor oasis. Shaking myself out of the trance she put me in, I gather our towels and follow after her. I drop our towels on a chaise lounge and turn on the radio. When I turn around, my mouth hangs open at the sight of Emily's dress pooling around her feet.

Her bathing suit leaves little to the imagination. The dark blue of her suit is a strapless top and her bottoms showcase the very asset that's taunted me from the beginning with the color of the suit bringing out the warm undertones of her skin, despite the colder months that plagued us.

"Do you trust that top of yours?" It's a valid question.

"Do you trust those bottoms of yours?" Her gaze goes to my very defined crotch. And I love that we can volley like this.

"Not in the slightest," I tell her.

Emily walks backward to the pool with a smirk on her face. "Well Mr. Montgomery, I for one think I need to cool off."

She executes a perfect dive into the deep end of the pool. When she surfaces, she pushes her hair off of her face and searches for me before finding me still on land.

"Adam, get in the pool," Emily demands.

Kicking my flip-flops to the side, I cannonball into the pool and the sound of her laughter hits me right as I go under. Opening my eyes under the surface, I swim to where she's treading water.

My hands trail up her legs before I resurface to take in a much-needed breath. As I'm breaking the surface, she swiftly swims away from me. Indulging the playful side of her, I chase her until she slows down. Sinking under the water I snatch her leg and pull her back to me.

When we both come up for air, I greet and wrap my arms around her waist. "Hi."

Her arms go around my shoulder and her legs go around my waist in return. "Hi. Anyone ever tell you how hot you are?"

"Sure," I start and she narrows her eyes at me. "The line cooks tell me all the time."

She tugs on my hair which in turn sends a jolt of awareness right to my cock. "You're such a jokester."

Lifting up on my torso she lays her body backward gracing me with a spectacular view. I let her enjoy the water of my pool and the weightless feeling that comes with submerging yourself.

"How were your summers as a kid spent?" Anything I can get to know from her, I'll take it.

Her abs flex under the bright sunshine as she returns to an upright position. Her legs slide back down my torso and I swallow a groan when she lays her arms over my shoulders again.

"Honestly? My summers were spent either cooped up in our New York brownstone or I was left alone on some island while my parents worked in the office. It wasn't until high school when I was making a life for myself that I told them to stop the pity invites. I was sixteen when I enjoyed my first true summer break."

I twirl us around in the water and lower us further into the water to soothe the burn from the sun. And my heart hurts for the woman who never enjoyed the true freedom of summers. "Consider this me making it my goal to give you the best summer ever."

"What all does that entail?" She questions.

I feel water falling down my back as Emily pours water on my drying hair. "The zoo is a top one."

"Oh, of course. What else?"

"Carnivals."

Her hand runs through my hair and I revel in the feel. "I have always wanted to ride on a Ferris Wheel."

"Consider it done. Then we have amusement parks and water parks. Although the water park may be more Dylan's speed."

Her forehead scrunches. "How do we tell him?"

"Hold on," I don't answer her confused expression as I swim us over to the shallow end of the pool and walk us to a cabana.

I set her on the cushion next to me and pull a leg across my lap.

"I haven't dated anyone since my divorce," I confess.

She rears her head back. "No one? So you've been…"

"I didn't say that," I try and fail to hide my smile but it still manages to slip out. "But it's been about two years since the last."

"What a pair we are." Emily muses.

I lift an eyebrow and she nods at my silent question.

"As for how we tell Dylan, maybe I should do it first? I don't know any other way to do it."

When I started dating I never thought it would be with his former teacher. So trying to explain to a six-year-old that I'm dating his teacher is a conversation I'm not exactly looking forward to.

"Hey," she moves closer and slides her hand into my hair. I wait a breath and look over at her. "We don't have to decide right away. But if I do remember, you said once I was done with school everyone would know I'm yours. So maybe we just play it by ear before flaunting all over the city."

Nodding my head absentmindedly I focus on her calling us a 'we' and decide that Emily is right. I need to ease Dylan into my dating again. He barely knows his Mom, and I'm wary that any woman I bring around he'll get overly attached to her.

"Deal. And where does this put us?"

Emily gets up and straddles my lap. "Well, first we get to know each other a lot better. You know? See if we're absolutely compatible." She tugs on my hair, pulling my head back to expose my neck.

My hands slide up her toned thighs and roughly grip her waist, "What else?" My voice comes out like I swallowed a bag of sand and my heart thuds so hard in my chest I fear she can feel the effect she has on me.

Her tongue trails a path from the hollow of my neck, ending her ascent by dipping her tongue in my ear and I can't stop the shivers that roll through my body. "We both end our dry spell over and over."

I move before I can overthink, I flip our positions and lay her on the chaise lounge. Fusing my mouth to hers, her legs wrap around my waist and I grab one, pulling it higher around my waist and grinding my cock into her heat. The moan she lets out is music to my ears. My tongue traces the seam of her lips begging for entrance. She opens easily and yep, the moan that comes from her when our tongues tangle is a sound I want to hear on repeat forever.

My hips push into her center and she breaks the kiss to let in a ragged breath. I take advantage of trailing my lips down her body and press open-mouth kisses to her clavicle and the tops of her breasts. Her hands weave through my hair as I worship her body with my mouth.

I trail my hands down her body, feeling the goosebumps pebble her skin. My hands stop at the waistband of her bottoms and I wait for her permission.

"Yes." She breathes out.

Leaning on one arm, I pull her bottoms down and off her body leaving her exposed in the afternoon light. I trace the divots of her stomach with my fingertips and create an invisible path to where she's bare for me. Our mouths connect again right as her legs fall open and her chest heaves as I trace everywhere but the spot she wants me at most.

She rips her mouth from mine to protest but is cut off when I circle her clit with my finger and dip into her opening. My tongue enters her mouth at the same speed as my finger pushes in slowly to her channel. I swallow down her moans as I collect her juices on my finger and pull out to play with her clit.

Her hand slides up to tangle in my hair. Pulling on the strands when I find that spot that makes her moan. The sound of her moan has me grinding on her leg to alleviate the pressure.

Adding a second finger, the whimper she makes almost has me coming on the spot. I groan into her mouth and our tongues slide together in a sensual dance that makes me lose my mind. Her hips lift to meet my fingers and I feel her walls tightening, a sign that she's getting closer.

"I feel your pussy clenching around my fingers," I pant heavily against her lips. "Sucking them in. Not letting me move. Does my girl need to come?"

Emily's whine travels up her throat. "Yes. God yes."

"Fingers or tongue?"

"Both. Tongue." She makes a point to push me off and down her body.

I throw her legs over my shoulders, making it a point to wrap my arms around her thighs and open her up to me. Her pussy is glistening with her arousal and her scent is enough to drive me to insanity.

Taking a swipe through her opening has me swearing as I taste her for the first time. The quiver and moan that Emily releases is my go-ahead sign. My tongue plunges into her opening, drinking up her essence as the sound of her pants and moans only grow louder. I rub her clit with my thumb and she pushes her pussy into my face, as if I need more convincing to eat her like a man starved.

"Adam, more," she pleads as she squirms under the assault of my tongue and fingers.

I suck her clit into my mouth and push two fingers inside her channel. Curling as I pump them in and out.

Adding a third until she's deliciously full of me. I flutter my tongue against her clit and alternate with stiff swipes. My fingers curl and rub against her g spot. Her body stiffens and I look up to see her jaw slack with a silent scream.

Her inner walls spasm as she floods my hand with her release. I lap up every drop of her cum and work her through until she's completely spent.

Pulling my fingers out of her I suck them into my mouth to clean them off. I crawl up her body, placing open mouth kisses on her chest and neck. Before pushing the hair off of her face and falling to the side of her body. I could look at her content gaze all day long if it meant the outside world didn't exist.

"You're good," Emily says when she finally comes to.

"You taste pretty good too," I tell her even though it's far from what she was getting at.

I reach down and pull her bottoms back up her body. She looks at me like she sees more than a summer with me. Like what we've been doing the past few months has the possibility to be a permanent thing between us. And as I unflinchingly gaze back at her I realize the permanence doesn't terrify me.

She's the first to make my heart stutter when she enters a room. As long as it's taken us to get to this place, I realize I never want to leave it.

Emily

"Some days I miss playing the violin," I tell him.

My head is resting in Adam's lap and I feel so content and relaxed around him that it sort of terrifies me. That orgasm loosened something in my brain and has me wanting to tell Adam everything.

He links our hands together and studies my fingers and nails as if it'll clue him into teenage me. "Why did you stop?"

"Because I didn't reach a goal I had set for myself."

My need for perfection had to have stemmed from the lack of attention from my parents. I'd have to ask Kamryn about that, but along the way with me playing, I fell in love with the instrument. But when the emails and calls never rolled in after that final showcase I knew I needed to let that dream go. Maybe it was a way of letting that part of my parents go as well. As sad as I was to not become employed playing professionally, I love that my job now allows me to shape young minds in an influential and direct way.

"And what goal was that?"

I hold his hand, palm side up, and trace the lines in an

effort to gather my thoughts. "I wanted to play in the Phil-adelphia Orchestra. I had this big recital my senior year of high school. Professors from different colleges were invited along with conductors from the Big Five."

"What's the Big Five?"

"Have you heard of the New York Philharmonic?"

Adam nods his head. "Of course I have."

"They're one of the five. Along with Boston, Chicago, Cleveland, and Philadelphia."

"Sounds like a gang."

Laughing at the observation, because I had that thought more than once. "It does. But the term isn't used as much anymore. Anyway, I wanted Philadelphia because it was close to home."

I realize now I was living in a world that was created by a child. I was living in a world where I thought if I could just shine brighter, my parents would notice. That world was created from pure innocence. No pain had reached her or affected the trajectory of her life. She lived in a fairytale. I lived in a fairytale.

"And you haven't played since?"

I shake my head as best as I can while still lying in his lap. "No. I want to though. It was a big part of my life. It taught me discipline and poise. Patience was also a big learning lesson. Rhythm and keeping the beat for a song is also something that'll never leave me."

"Would you ever play again?"

I look up into Adam's eyes and don't detect a lick of judgment, just curiosity. "Is it strange if I say I'm scared? Because I spent years loving something only for me to be fine without it."

The first time I picked up the violin, this nervous-antici-pation feeling flowed through my body at an electric speed.

It was a new experience. And as I got older that nervous-anticipation feeling morphed into breathing. I could place my violin in the playing position and my breath would follow the beat of playing. When I closed my violin case for the final time, I had no idea that the spring concert at school would *be* my final time.

A warm breeze ruffles my hair around my face and Adam tames it as best as he can. "I think it's normal to be scared."

"Yeah," I muse thoughtfully. "I'm wondering if our pasts will always be this thing that's in our relationship with us."

"So we're in a relationship?" Adam asks with a barely contained smile.

Sitting up, I push him back to where he's lying down. I crawl over his body and straddle his lap, running my hands over his torso, tracing his tattoos and flipping the hoop of his nipple ring, feeling his cock jump under me, I state, "Well I'm not dating anyone. I assume you and Dylan will be enough for me to handle. And if I recall, again, you said once the school year ended that you were making me yours. Do I need to keep reminding your old man brain?"

"That I did," Adam agrees. He's about to continue speaking when my stomach grumbles loud enough to be heard over the music. I fall into the crook of his neck, laughing because what a time for an interlude.

"Okay," he says through laughter. "Food first and then I make you mine."

"Deal," I agree against his lips and hold on as he makes to get off the cabana. Holding on tighter as Adam gets up and walks us into the pool, our lips still loving together with the cool pool water a welcome salve to my hot skin.

My legs wrap tighter around his waist as we sink deeper into the pool.

"I thought you were hungry?" Adam asks. The sun has brought out the freckles over the bridge of his nose and cheeks and I mentally trace over each one.

"I am. But I wanna kiss you a little more."

His eyebrows raise and the smirk that took my breath away the first time appears. "You do, do you?"

"Mm-hmm. Is that okay with you?"

"Yeah, baby. That's okay with me."

His smile and half-mast eyelids disappear when our lips mesh together. Our hands roam as the summer sun shines down on us, heating our barely-cooled skin.

THE SMELL of steak cooking on the grill rouses me from sleep. After Adam kissed me silly, he swiftly retreated from the pool and I pulled my body onto a pool hammock to let the summer sun warm my body. Looking around, I spot him on the deck with a look of concentration on his face and a beer grasped in his hand.

I never pictured myself dating a single dad. Let alone a man with tattoos and whose nipples are pierced. But I'm finding that all three of those things make Adam, Adam. And I like those things about him. Doesn't hurt that he likes me the way I am. Trauma and all. He listens to me, talks with me and not to me, and he was especially respectful of the boundaries I had in place.

Sliding off the pool hammock, I swim my way to the pool steps. Climbing out of the pool, the food completely abandoned on the grill as Adam looks on when I walk up the pool steps.

"You are every wet dream come to life." He tells me.

I snag a towel from the patio chair behind him and wrap it around my body. "Have a lot of wet dreams, do you?"

He takes a healthy sip of his beer. "Not at all."

"Okay, macho man." Dropping my towel, I pull on a white coverup dress.

It's just around three in the afternoon and the summer sun has yet to let up on the shine or the heat. I apply a light layer of aloe vera lotion to help soothe my reddened skin and the relief is instant.

Walking up next to Adam, I loop my arm around his waist and peer over his shoulder.

"Steaks are almost done," he announces. "The corn on the cob and potatoes are done."

"It smells really good." I praise.

"Thanks, baby. I have a few wine choices, but I think a red will pair best with the steak."

"I'll get it," I announce and place a kiss on his shoulder. "Where is it?" I ask as I walk backward to the patio door.

"In the wine fridge on the far wall. And the wine glasses are in the cupboard right above."

With a nod and a wink, I make quick work of getting the wine and glasses. I make another quick perusal of the space and realize this isn't just a house where he raises Dylan. It's a home where he and Dylan grow.

I walk with a spring in my step back out to the patio, placing the wine and glasses on the patio table. The wine opener sitting on the table beckons me to uncork the bottle. Adam places our food on the table as I fill my glass with a hefty pour of the rich red wine. His body heat encompasses me as I fill his glass up too and place the bottle on the table.

"Cheers," Adam claims as he holds up his glass. "To new beginnings."

I pick up my glass and clink it to his. "Cheers."

We hold eye contact as we each take a sip of our wine.

"So you got your first tattoo at eighteen?"

Our empty plates sit abandoned at the end of the patio table. Conversation was at a minimum as we ate our food in comfortable silence. I decided that if Adam wanted to cook for me for the rest of his life, I'd happily sit with a glass of wine and watch.

"Yes and if Dylan gets one the way I did, I'm grounding him. I won't care that he's technically an adult."

His dad-side coming out makes me laugh. "How did you get your first tattoo?"

"At a house party when I was eighteen," he says with a grimace on his face.

"Oh, Adam. If I was your mother I surely would have grounded you."

"You would have?" He leans into the table to ask.

"Mm-hmm. And then again once I found you got your nipples pierced. Although they are the hottest thing I've seen and not at all what I expected from you."

Adam pushes back from the table and grabs our plates. "What did you expect?"

"The tattoos were unexpected but they're growing on me." I voice as I gather up our polished-off wine bottle and empty wine glasses, trailing behind Adam into the kitchen.

"Duly noted," he tells me as he turns the water for the kitchen sink on.

We work as a team with rinsing our dishes and loading them into the dishwasher. I wash off the tongs and wipe down the counters while Adam scrubs down the grill.

"More pool?" Adams questions when he's joined me back in the kitchen.

Glancing outside I shake my head. "How about a movie?" I meet Adam's eyes as he nods his head. "Any chance I can shower?"

"Is that an invitation?" He queries as he crowds my space.

My hands land on his chest in an attempt to hold him back. "No."

"Okay," he agrees with a kiss on my forehead. "You can shower in my bathroom."

I pin him with a stare that usually has my students shaking.

"Just to shower, Ms. Bailey. I promise."

"Lead the way, then," I say with a flourish of my hand.

He grabs my bag from the kitchen island and I follow him like a needy cat. My eyes travel over the pictures lining the wall as we head up the stairs. Dylan in all stages of life, candids of them both, and some landscape shots. It's another tiny peek into their life as a family of two.

At the top of the stairs, Adam turns right and heads to the only door at the end of the long hallway. He leads the way into a spacious primary bedroom with a sitting area off to the side that catches the setting sun. His room is swathed in shades of blue and warm wooden touches. A fluffy cream rug adds texture and warmth to the wooden floor that I'm sure gets cold in the winter. The bed is a huge dark oak four-poster king-size bed with a cream-colored linen duvet and an even amount of pillows that I could sink into.

"It's just your room on this end, huh?"

The thump of my bag being set on his dresser pulls my focus to him. "Yeah. After we lived in our last apartment I realized that Dylan and I needed rooms that weren't next to each other. Having a 6 AM wake-up call after working the closing shift for work proved me to be insufferable."

"I'll bet. Well, everything I've seen of your house is beautiful. You should be proud, Adam."

"Thank you." He accepts the praise and crosses his arms over his chest. "Bathroom is through here and there are towels in the small linen closet."

Adam steps aside to allow me entrance to his spacious primary bathroom. It's safe to say he loves color.

White hexagon tiles give the floor a clean feel that's not overly sterile. A thin rug runner sits in front of the double oak wood vanity that contrasts beautifully with the dark navy blue backsplash that runs from the vanity to the standup shower. A massive soak-in tub sits in front of the bay windows providing an uninterrupted view of the dense forest lining Adam's backyard. The gold handles and knobs compliment the wood tones of the bathroom vanity and the white countertops complete the room.

"Is it your goal to get me to not want to leave?" I ask him as I run my hands over the gold faucet of one of the sinks.

"If I say yes, will you stay?"

I meet his gaze in the reflection of the bathroom mirror. "We'll start with sleepovers."

"I can work with that. Well, I'll let you shower and then we can pick out a movie."

"Okay." I watch him push off the doorframe and leave his bedroom, closing the door with a soft click.

Adam overwhelms me in the best possible way. And as I turn on the waterfall shower I realize that jumping into something with him could either end in love or disaster.

Adam

It took herculean effort to leave my bedroom while Emily showered. Just picturing her naked body with bubbles running down her petite frame made me want to propose marriage. So I walked down the hall to Dylan's bedroom to tidy it up to keep my mind off of Emily in my shower and my hands busy with something that doesn't involve her body.

My dad-hearing was up to par when I heard her pad downstairs, as casually as I could, I walked back to my bathroom to shower. With my towel wrapped around my waist, I walk into my closet and pause when I see her bag on my closet floor. Seeing her bag occupying space in my closet gives me hope that one day more than just her bag will be taking up space in my closet.

Pulling on sweatpants and a t-shirt, I toss my discarded towel into the hamper and head downstairs.

My steps falter as I descend the last couple of steps when I find her curled on the couch looking completely at home in my home. Her damp hair leaves water on the hoodie she must've stolen from my closet. Seeing as it dwarfs her petite frame causes me to wonder if she's wearing anything underneath. And when I walk towards her, the scent of my soap and shampoo requires me to adapt my breathing exercises I hadn't used in years. Emily in my hoodie and smelling like me is taking every bit of willpower in me not to maul her.

Heading over to the bay windows, I pull the curtains closed to set the movie mood. Walking to the couch, I swipe the remote off the coffee table and take my place by Emily. She's got a blanket settled over her lap and her phone in her hands.

"Who are you texting?"

"My best friends. They're curious about you." She tells me and throws her phone to the other end of the couch when she deems herself done with their conversation.

I sit back on the couch and prop my feet up on the coffee table. "What have you told them? And what do you want to watch? I have no clue what your movie interests are."

"That does seem like something we should have covered. But I'm good with anything. Except for slasher films and war documentaries."

"Okay. Gonna nix those from the list," I joke.

Emily lightly shoves me. "But as for my friends. I've told them next to nothing."

Nodding my head slowly to hide the disappointment.

"Honey," she gently tilts my chin to her. "It's not that I'm ashamed of you. I am so far from ashamed of you that it's not even funny. Like I'm kind of obsessed with being around and with you. But I didn't want to say anything to them until I knew for sure that this thing between us was worth pursuing."

I grab her hand and kiss her palm. "I wanna meet them."

"I know. I want that too."

Satisfied with her response, I put on *Transformers* and settle in. Emily spreads the blanket over my lap and wraps herself around my arm. Leaning down I kiss her forehead and watch as the opening sequence fills the screen.

Emily watches the movie as if she's never seen it. And she would have fooled me had she not quoted the movie line-for-line.

"Want some ice cream?" I ask Em when the first movie ends.

"Yes, please." She stretches and mewls like a kitten.

"Is vanilla okay with you?"

She nods her head and pulls back the blanket to allow me the freedom to get up. I head to the freezer and pick out the almost empty carton of vanilla ice cream. Deciding against a bowl, I instead snag a spoon and warm up the ice cream as best as I can in my hand as I make my way back to the couch.

"You're being a rebel," Emily announces and lays the blanket back over my lap when I sit back down. She grabs the remote and presses play on the next movie.

"Hey. I didn't want to use unnecessary dishes. And it's almost empty so we can finish this off as the movie plays."

"I guess I'll allow it." She vows and turns sideways, tucking a foot between my legs and eyeing the ice cream carton like it's a winning prize.

"Should I be worried about you and ice cream?" I eye her suspiciously as I pop the lid off and place it on the coffee table.

"Absolutely not."

"You didn't even look at me when you said that."

Her eyes fly up to mine. "Sorry. I just really like ice cream."

I scoop some out on a spoon and hold it out for her. "In that case, you get the first spoonful."

"And they say chivalry is dead." She muses.

I feed her a scoop and then me. Going back and forth until a single serving is left. We eye each other like we'll fight for it. I scoop the last of the ice cream on the spoon and hold it out to Emily. She eyes me warily. But this, feeding her ice cream, has been a delicious game of foreplay. Her mouth wraps around the spoon and when she releases it, I place the empty carton and spoon on the table. Grabbing the back of her head, our lips meet with my tongue seeking entrance.

Emily matches my energy and pushes me back, moving until she's straddling my lap. The movie is long forgotten as the cool from her tongue gives way the longer we kiss. Since I surprised her on her last day of school, we've been playing a game of cat and mouse. Wondering who will be the first to break.

It was me.

I was the first to break.

My hand slides up her back and tangles in her hair. Holding her to me as we breathe each other in. Her hands slide down my torso and land at the hem of my shirt, pulling it up and off, tossing it over her shoulder. She kisses me again before moving to my neck. Moving her body away from me as she slides down, paying attention to my nipples. Her tongue flicks the ring and my cock twitches against my thigh.

Her hand squeezes and rubs my cock through my sweatpants. I stop her before she gets any ideas.

"Baby. If my cock gets anywhere near your mouth I won't recover." I let her know as I pull her back up on the couch with me and kiss the frown on her forehead.

"You tell a girl you'll claim her and then, nada." Her breathing has deepened and her sole focus is on my mouth.

I quickly flip our positions. Laying her on the couch and settling between her thighs. My cock rubs her pussy through the barely there shorts I see she has on.

"God, that feels good." Emily pants out as I rock into her core.

Her hands slide up my arms and wrap around my neck, pulling me down until our lips are a millimeter away. I wrap one of her legs higher up on my hip as my thrusts continue a steady rhythm. Erasing that millimeter of space I press my lips to hers. Our mutual groans of satisfaction when our tongues meet again is nothing short of spectacular.

My lips leave hers, trailing down her jaw to her neck. I run my hand down her torso and under my hoodie. Her stomach tenses as I run my hand up and grab a handful of her breast. Emily weaves her fingers through my hair as I trace a nipple.

Loving the sounds she makes as I roll her nipple between my thumb and middle finger.

Loving the look of pure ecstasy on her face as I keep up with my thrusts and the ministration of her nipple.

"Adam," Emily whines out my name.

"Emily," I taunt. I'm ready to burst, but I want to take this at her speed. Which at this point is nonexistent.

She pushes me back and whips the hoodie off her body. Emily doesn't give me time to gawk before she pushes my shorts down my hips as far as my knees and the couch will allow.

I halt her progress and grab her hands in mine, putting them above her head. "Tell me what you want Emily."

"I want you." She states as she tries to break free from my hold.

Smirking, I flex my fingers around her wrist. "You have me. What else?"

"I want your cock."

"It's yours, baby."

I lean down and press my lips to hers. Letting go of her hands, I pull her barely-there shorts down her legs and drop them on the floor. The smell of her arousal is a mind trip. She helps me pull my shorts off the rest of the way and then we're both bare.

"Condom?" I remember to ask as the blood whooshes to my other head.

She shakes her head and my furrowed expression gives way to my confusion. "I have an IUD and I was tested at my last checkup."

My brain short circuits at the realization that means. "Baby, are you sure?"

"More than sure. I don't want anything between us." Her hands frame my face when she says this. And I see nothing but complete and pure adoration in her expression.

"I'm clean too," I tell her before I get lost in her.

My fingers go to her clit, teasing until she almost breaks the skin on her bottom lip before going down to her pussy to make sure she's ready. And when I slide my fingers between her heat, I can't help the groan that sounds as I bring her closer to the edge. I rub my fingers, which are coated in her juices over my cock and rub it through her wetness. Tapping the head of my cock to her clit before lining up to her entrance and sliding in halfway. I pull out, bringing us both to the edge over and over as her pussy tries to hold me in and then slide my cock inside of her.

"Adam," she says on a gasp as I settle inside of her. I give her a few seconds to adjust to my size and the intrusion before she's tapping on my waist. "Move."

"Give me a second," I groan into her neck. Reciting the roster for the Bengals calms me down enough to flex my hips into her tight heat. "Em, you feel too good."

"Make me feel good. Make me yours." She vocalizes in my ear and turns me to goo when she sucks my earlobe between her teeth.

Rising up on my forearms, I take her mouth in a bruising kiss and start a lazy thrust of my hips. Her hands roam over my back and nails dig into my shoulder blades. The pain mixes with the pleasure coursing through my body. My thrusts get more wild as the heels of her feet ground into my ass, spurring me on.

Hooking her knees around my arms drives me deeper into her body. Emily's eyes are closed in euphoria, her chest and neck a shade of red.

"Look at me," I demand.

Emily slowly opens her eyes, her gaze landing on me. This moment with her, the start of us, no more secrets and hiding or pretending like what this is between us isn't real. Our eyes hold and convey so many words as I continue to thrust inside of her. The glazed look swimming in her eyes is one of pure lust.

I let a leg go and lean back down to kiss her. The movement has me sliding deeper and Emily moaning into my mouth as our tongues meet in a dance that we've somehow perfected. Her hands weave through my hair. Pulling the strands as I feel her inner walls start to quiver.

"Do you need to come, baby?" I ask against her lips.

Her pupils have blown wide as she whispers, "Yes."

I rotate my hips on shallow thrusts, causing her breath to hitch. "Then beg for it. Beg to come on my cock like I know you want to."

"Adam," my name is a whine off her lips like the sweetest melody of a song unwritten. It's almost enough to make me give in. To give us both what we want. "Let me come. I need to come."

I lower my face until our lips brush over each other as my thrusts get longer and slower. "Rub your clit for me, baby. Come for me and take me with you."

Her fingers move to her clit and brush the base of my cock as I continue to move in and out of her. With the swipe of her fingers against her clit, Emily's moans of my name get louder until I feel her body seize up and then let go. The strength of her orgasm pulling mine out. Rising up, I hold her hips, thrusting erratically as I chase my own release and come on a roar.

I collapse on top of Emily, making sure not to crush her. Her walls are still fluttering around my cock keeping it semi-hard. I'm too spent to move and my body has relaxed as Em lightly runs her nails up and down my back.

Kissing her neck, I peel my body off of hers.

The forgotten movie playing in the background brings reality back into our bubble. I look over to Emily and see her still lying down. Eyes on the ceiling.

"Did I fuck you into unconsciousness?"

I see a slight movement of her eyes as she looks in my general direction. "Considering it's been a while, maybe."

"I'd say I'm sorry. But I'm really not." Grabbing the remote for the TV, I turn it off and pull my shorts back up my legs. "Let's head upstairs. I saw you eyeing my tub when we went up there."

The smile she gives me is shy as if I wasn't inside of her five minutes ago. I pick up her shorts and toss them to her, but she forgoes them and pulls on my hoodie instead. Pointing to my back, she reads my sign and crawls over, wrapping her arms around my shoulders and legs around my waist. Standing up from the couch, I walk us both upstairs where I don't plan to let her out of my sight.

Emily

The steam from the bath along with the scent of essential oils mixed with the mountain of bubbles on the surface of the water, relaxes me into euphoria. Adam brought up our phones and the second bottle of wine while the water filled the tub.

I feared there would be awkwardness after what we did on the couch. But after those moments with him, where it was us and nothing more between us, I want more. More secret moments that no one else is privy to.

Adam runs his fingers up and down my arms. The action brings goosebumps to my arms despite the heat from the water.

"What are you thinking?" He asks, breaking the silence.

I turn my face into his neck. Ghosting a kiss at his pulse point and inhaling the scent that's all Adam mixed with eucalyptus from the oils. "How I like these moments between us."

"Me too, baby." Adam places a kiss on my forehead. "Tell me about your friends."

I lean my head back on his shoulder and dive into my

world. "I've known Kamryn since I was fourteen. I actually met her through James. She's a fashion designer. Scratch that, she's an extremely successful fashion designer. And she just got back together with her ex, Mason Brooks."

"Woah. She's dating the Bengals new quarterback?"

"Mm-hmm. I take it you're a football fan too?"

Adam links our fingers together and I feel the excitement coursing through him. "The NFL package comes in handy at the restaurant. Man, Dylan will freak when he finds out."

"Hey, I didn't tell you to show off."

"I know." His arms wrap around my middle, pulling me closer to him. "What about your other friends?"

"Sarah was roommates with Kamryn at CSU. She's become someone very important to me in the time we've become friends. Sarah is feisty and blunt, but she's also sensitive. She works in PR and always complains about the athletes who get themselves in hot water. And Jax is Kamryn's younger sister. She runs a YouTube channel that does extremely well and helps Kam on the marketing side of her brand."

I felt a hum low in his throat. "You've surrounded yourself with driven women."

"Not only that but they've seen me at my lowest. When I couldn't get out of bed they were there to get some food in my system."

"I'm glad you have them."

"Me too." I kiss the top of his hand and relax into his body. The afternoon sun slowly fades beyond the tree line of the dense forest giving way to, what's looking to be, a clear night. Adam was right when I eyed this tub like it was candy. It's a great place to relax and decompress.

Movement rouses me from my ultra-relaxed state.

"We need to get out of the tub before we turn into raisins."

"Okay," I relent and scoot forward so Adam can get out of the tub first.

I watch him dry off his body of art before he turns and holds out a towel for me. Our teasing smirks are that of playfulness and mischief. When I'm standing, with water sliding down my body like a waterfall, I hold my arms out to the side and wait for the towel to envelope me. I don't miss the heated glare as Adam dries off my body. It gives me a thrill that we're equally affected by our baring it all to the other.

"So Dylan's Mom hasn't tried to reach out?"

We're lying in his bed with the TV on at a low volume. After we both dried off from the bath and got dressed, hunger struck so Adam whipped up a grilled cheese for us to share. Conversation has steadily flowed. But neither of us has felt the need to disrupt the silence when it hits.

He shakes his head. "I wish more than anything she wanted a relationship with him. Me, I could deal with her leaving. But Dylan? He's just a kid that needs his Mom."

"Moms are important." I never had the classic mother-daughter bond that Kamryn and her Mom had. It's one thing I was jealous of her for having.

"This is not me telling or even asking you to fill that role."

"I know," I reassure him that I never fathomed that thought to cross my mind. With as confident as we both are with our relationship progressing, that line will eventually be erased and allow me to cross over to it. "No chance she would ever pop in? Is it ever something you worried about?"

"Every day for the last six years. But I've given up hope that she'll ever come back for Dylan."

Leaning back into the mountain of pillows, I survey his face. The light from the TV dances across his features. "What happens if she does?"

It's not that I'm even considering the option of running. I have no idea of the way they left things. Does she still love Adam? Does Adam, deep down, still love her? Has she changed her mind about having kids? Where would that leave me if the answer to all were a yes?

Adam looks over at me and adjusts himself to where his head is in my lap and his arms are wrapped around my waist. My hands automatically go to his hair. The brown strands soft to the touch as I run my fingers through his hair. His body deflating at the touch gives me an ego boost I didn't know I needed.

"I haven't given much thought to what would happen if she came back. She signed over her rights when she served me with divorce papers. And that was that."

"Selfishly I'm now glad that she did. Because then we wouldn't have met." I murmur so low I don't think he heard me.

"Silver linings, baby." His response doesn't need a retort from me.

We stay twined in bed, letting mindless TV prove to be an excellent backdrop. When Adam's breathing gets deeper, signaling to me that he's fallen asleep, I let my mind wander to five years in the future. To the day we can walk down the street, hand-in-hand, and not have the whispers of me being his son's teacher. I imagine the future until sleep takes me too.

~

"Yes, Adam," I moan out.

This is the hottest dream I'll probably ever have. His tongue spears my pussy. Eating like I'm the only thing around to satiate his burning hunger.

"Does that feel good baby? My tongue in your cunt?" His husky voice asks.

I flinch, waking myself out of a dream that's not a dream. Adam is buried beneath the covers fucking my pussy with his tongue. "Fuck, Adam."

"Do you want me to stop?" Is what he asks as the heat from his breath hits my clit.

"Don't you dare."

"That's my girl."

Adam dives back in. His mouth suctions to my opening as his hands travel up under the sweatshirt I'm still wearing. His thumbs circle over my nipples with the lightest of pressure as his tongue dips into my entrance. My hands grip his hair, holding his mouth to me as I chase my release.

"Adam," I breathe out.

"Come for me, baby." He demands.

Proving I'm weak to his demand as my orgasm hits me like a freight train. Adam works me through my high as if he's done it a thousand times. When the last of my orgasm has faded, Adam shimmies up the bed. My legs cradle him as his lips meet mine in a searing kiss.

The taste of me lingers on his tongue and all it does is turn me on. My legs wrap around his waist. Holding him to me.

I take control of the kiss and flip our positions. Adam grinds his boxer-covered erection into my pussy.

"Ride me," Adam says between kisses.

Breaking the kiss, I trail my lips down his body. Dipping my tongue into the hollow of his neck as my hands roam over his torso. Paying attention to the hitch in his breath when I swipe my thumbs over his nipples the same way he did me.

His hands go under my arms and pull me back up so we're at eye level. "Don't tease me, Em." His tongue licks at my bottom lip as we're both panting. The smell of sex is the only scent in the room. "I want my cock buried so deep in you. I want your cunt to squeeze my dick so hard I lose consciousness. I want my cum leaking out of you. Ride me. And don't stop until you're screaming my name."

If it's possible to orgasm with just words, Adam mastered it.

My lips fall to his. His mouth opens and our tongues meet and dance as I pull his boxers down. My body shifts forward, our kiss never breaking, as Adam takes his boxers off the rest of the way.

Lifting up, I circle my hand around his length, his breath hissing out in the process. I tease my entrance with the head of his cock. My insides tense at the almost intrusion.

"Put it in, baby. Put my cock inside of you," Adam says through clenched teeth.

With another swipe of the head through my arousal, I line him up at my entrance and slowly lower. Inch by agonizing inch as his cock stretches me. Gaining entrance to my body is his sole focus. His hands wrap around my waist, holding me steady as I slowly sink down on him, letting me set the pace as my body adjusts to the angle and intrusion.

Adam's hands grip my waist so hard I know I'll have bruises.

Placing my hands on the headboard, I lift my hips and watch as his cock is exposed before slamming back down.

"Ride me, Em."

My hips move with their own rhythm. Lifting and swiveling, chasing my own high. Taking my own pleasure.

"Just like that, baby." Adam praises.

It's like the praise went right to my clit. "You feel so good."

I place my hands right next to his head and drop my lips to his. Our tongues tangle as my hips move on top of his length. Adam takes hold of my hips, keeping them steady, as he pounds up into me. Gripping his hair and moaning into his mouth as my orgasm rolls into me. My toes curl as I fall off the orgasmic cliff. Adam pounds into me three more times until I feel the warmth of his release. My hips move slowly as I work us both down.

Our lips never break as we reach the peak.

Adam flips our position and I wrap a leg around his waist as he moves his semi-hard cock inside of me.

This.

Us taking it slow.

How we started is a metaphor to how we end the night.

Adam

The sizzling of the bacon overtakes the beating of my heart. School has been out for about a month and in that time, Emily and I have snuck in more time together. But sneaking around and making excuses to run out of the house have become exhausting.

"Baby, I'm tired." Emily tells me as we watch the sunset.

I know she's not metaphorically tired, so this must be about how our relationship has been closed door.

"I know," I start and wrap my arm around her, pulling her closer. "I think I'm gonna tell him tomorrow morning."

Her hand weaves through mine. "I don't want to rush you if you're not ready."

"I'm ready. I want my two favorite people in one spot."

"I want that, too."

I flip the bacon and get started on the pancakes. Am I trying to butter Dylan up with his favorite breakfast foods? Does that make me a bad parent or a smart parent? I'm thinking through the best way to tell Dylan I'm dating his teacher when he barrels down the stairs.

"Hey, buddy."

"Hi, Daddy."

Taking the bacon off the stove, I place it on the island and face my son.

"So I wanted to talk to you about something," I start and turn back around to flip the pancakes.

Dylan's munching on the crispy bacon drowns out my ragged exhale.

When I turn back around his eyes are solely on the bacon and if I don't take the plate away, he'll eat it all. I do just that and his eyes finally meet mine.

"I'm dating someone."

His little forehead scrunches as he tries to figure out what that means. "Like boyfriend and girlfriend?"

"Yeah. Like that."

"Is she pretty?"

His question brings a smile to my face. "Yeah, buddy. I think she's very pretty."

I plate the pancakes and eggs on the island. Dylan loves strawberry jelly and butter on his pancakes so I get that out for him along with the syrup for me. He slathers on the strawberry and I look on in mock horror. I'll never know where he picked that taste up.

"When do I get to meet her?"

Oh, right. We were talking about my dating. "I was thinking at your game on Saturday?"

Dylan shovels a piece of pancake in his mouth and chews, then tries to talk with his mouth full but it comes out garbled.

"Chew your food first, kiddo."

I chew my food as Dylan chews as fast as he can. I

watch with amusement as I see his little jaws work overtime.

"Who is she? Does she like baseball?"

That's a tough question to answer. Dylan is too young to understand permanent loss. So I can't say that she used to until she lost someone close to her.

"You know, I don't know if she does. Do you think you could teach her how to like baseball?"

His eyes light up. "Yeah, I can do it, Dad."

"I don't doubt that for a second, buddy. But do you remember your teacher? Ms. Bailey?"

"Yeah," he responds.

Just do it, Adam. "She's my girlfriend."

"Do I have to call her, Ms. Bailey?"

I ruffle his hair and huff out a laugh. "No, buddy. Maybe call her Ms. Emily or Emily. You'll have to ask her."

"Okay," Dylan responds. And that's that.

We finish eating and then Dylan is off to the living room with the sound of Transformers interrupting the quiet of the house. I clean up from breakfast and then head out to the backyard. I keep the doors open and pull up Emily's number.

"Hi, baby," she answers on the second ring.

"Hi, sunshine. I told him," I come right out and say it.

I hear her suck in a breath. "How did he take it?"

"Pretty good. But I think he's still too young to know what me dating someone is supposed to mean."

"That's understandable," she agrees with me. "So what next?"

I sit on the chaise lounge she and I shared one of our first moments on. "Well, he has a game on Saturday and I told him you'd most likely be there."

"Baby steps. This is good."

"You're nervous, aren't you?"

Em blows out a breath. "A little. Not because of Dylan—"

"But, baseball," I finish her sentence.

"Yeah."

I didn't forget about Em's need to go slow when it came to baseball. And while I'll never understand the need to ease myself back into something, I'll also never rush her.

"What are your plans for tonight?" I change the subject to something lighter.

I hear a clink of glasses through the phone and it's almost as if I'm in her kitchen with her.

"The girls and I are doing a girl's night," Emily tells me with glee.

"And what goes on at these girls' nights?"

"You know, the usual. Talks about boys and how much we don't really need them. Gorging ourselves on greasy food and drinking wine."

"Huh," I start. "So women don't need men to satisfy your needs?"

Her laugh is audible and I fear I missed out on the joke. "You naive man. That's what vibrators are for."

I damn near choke on my tongue. "Is that so?"

"You're picturing it, aren't you?" She asks teasingly. "Me using my vibrator on myself after one of our many makeout sessions before we crossed the line. My body climbing higher and higher to release until I remember the way you teased me and I fall over the edge." Her voice has taken on a huskier tone and it makes me want to climb through the phone and use that bloody device on her.

My silence over my loss of words must be entertaining. But it's only because the blood has rushed to my cock.

"God, I love breaking you," Emily taunts over the phone with a laugh.

Dylan rushing outside is like a bucket of cold water on my body. It's a welcome reprieve but this phone call was getting somewhere good.

"Hey, Dad?"

I hear Emily's laugh as I pull the phone away from my ear, "Yeah, buddy?"

"Can I sleep over at Jackson's house tonight?"

My son is a mastermind. "Let me call Sandra and make sure it's alright with her."

"Okay," and then he's off back inside the house as fast as he came outside.

"You heard all of that, didn't you?"

"I have no idea what you're talking about. Goodbye, Adam," Emily sing-songs before hanging up the phone.

WITH THE HELP of the younger employees, they convinced me that 'theme nights' would draw in a crowd during the weeknight. I was skeptical at first. But these 'theme nights' have been running smoothly for the last few weeks.

As it's a Wednesday, it's Wine Down Wednesday with the women drinking at a discount. We have the menu catered to complement the wines on our menu so nothing goes to waste.

Jenny: Dylan sprinted out of my car when I pulled up to Sandra's house.

Me: Of course, he did. Thank you, Jenny.

Jenny: Anytime. See you later.

The night goes by with groups of women just getting off work, a 21st birthday party, and a last minute bachelorette party. I help Matt out behind the bar when he needs it and converse with a few men who braved the theme night. Or dare I say strategic on their part?

When the night slows down I retreat down to my office to check my email and see what slots need to be filled in terms of entertainment, food, booze, and apparel. I see an email from the head of the city in regards to a block party during the Fourth of July weekend. It looks as if all of the restaurants on the street, along with vendors, will be in attendance. Half of the proceeds made from the weekend will be donated to shelters in the area, with food deliveries for the rest of the year.

My office phone rings and the time shows that an hour has passed. I let them know to clean up and that I'll be up in a bit to lock up.

> Me: Sober up, sunshine.

> Emily: I don't know what you're talking about.

> Me: So if I were to drive over to your place you'd be sober enough?

> Emily: As a skunk.

> Me: Drink some water.

I shut down the computer and head up the narrow staircase. The kitchen is cleaned up from the day and I wander out of the closed kitchen and to the bar. I hear keys jingling to my left and see everyone waiting for me.

"It's about time old man," Matt whines.

"Watch it."

Together we leave and I lock up and we make sure the girls get in their cars before we're both heading opposite ways. I peel out of the parking lot and head to Emily's. I'm never one for speeding. But when I get a chance, I'll break all the rules for her.

I pull into a parking spot right next to her little SUV. Taking my keys, I jog up the single flight of stairs and knock on her door. It opens five seconds later and I bulldoze my way inside. Taking her face between my hands, our lips crash in synchronous harmony. The door closes behind me and I push her up against the wall.

Emily wraps a leg around my waist and I take her other leg, hoisting her up against the wall. My cock is painfully hard against the zipper of my jeans. But the warmth of Emily's pussy is like coming home.

"Bedroom," Emily says against my lips. Her legs tighten around my waist and I turn, walking us to her bedroom.

I close the door to her room when I cross over the threshold and kneel onto the bed. Not breaking the kiss as I'm finally breathing better after weeks of chaste kisses. Between work at the restaurant and baseball with Dylan, all we've gotten were small moments when Emily would drop by my work.

This past month we've been together has only made my craving for her unstoppable.

I break the kiss and trail my lips down her neck. Her heavy breaths and mixed moans are enough to make me lose my mind. When I get to the waistband of her leggings I stop.

"Adam?"

I place a kiss on her lower stomach. "Do you wanna play a game?"

A smile spreads across her face as she nods her head quickly against the pillows.

"Good girl," I praise and crawl off the bed. I move over to her nightstand that houses her toy collection. Emily's eyes grow wide when she sees where I'm moving towards and I'm guessing in her wine-induced haze that our conversation from this morning slipped her mind.

I take my time perusing through the drawer and hold in my retort to her collection. I have an idea of what I want to use on her and when I land on a little device that's meant for clitoral pleasure, I know what to do.

Looking over at her. Her chest heaving and lips puffy from my kiss. Something animalistic runs through my body.

"Clothes. Off." I demand.

Emily hesitates for a breath before she slides off the bed and strips. She holds my stare as each item of clothing comes off. This is what I love about her.

Woah.

Love?

The feeling of love that slammed into me a while ago comes back at full-speed.

When Emily is bare before me, I step into her space and slide my hands through her hair. Tipping her head back and gazing into those beautiful eyes of hers.

"I love you."

Her eyes well with tears as the hands resting on my waist and her bottom lip trembles. "You do?"

"Yeah, baby. I do," I wipe away a stray tear. "I think I fell that night when you came to my restaurant and wiped that godforsaken line away. It was made clearer to me the next morning. I love you, Emily Marie Bailey."

"I love you, too. I love you for showing me that I can

love again. And that I get to love *you* means more than I could ever have imagined."

Our lips are a breath apart. I inhale what she exhales. I soak in what she pours out.

Ghosting my lips over hers I say, "On the bed, baby."

She sneaks a chaste kiss as she brushes past me. I pull my shirt off and toss it to the floor. When Emily is settled back on the bed I strip down to just my boxer briefs. I hold up the toy that I grabbed from her nightstand drawer and hold in the laugh as her eyes widen.

"You said you wanted to play, so we're gonna play," I announce as I crawl back up the bed and lay out beside her.

The toy I was holding sits between us as I trail my fingers up and down her body with featherlight touches. She holds her breath as she anticipates my next move. I drop my lips to her collarbone. Licking and sucking at her skin. Emily turns her head to meet my lips and I take the toy, trailing it down to her pussy. I can smell her arousal and it's enough to make me want to say *to hell with the game* and make her come with my cock buried inside of her.

Breaking the kiss, I look down at where her legs are spread and place the toy over her clit. With my thumb over the silicone button, I turn my attention back to Emily and watch as a red flush instantly runs up and down her neck and chest.

Her hands fist in the sheets as I keep suction on her clit. Her teeth bite down so hard on her bottom lip that I fear she'll break the skin.

My name is moaned from her mouth.

My cock is as hard as stone.

Her breath comes in pants as she gets closer to release.

I pull the toy off of her clit and give her a moment to

breathe. When her chest is no longer heaving for breath, I place the toy back on her clit.

Emily's hand slides up her torso and grabs a handful of her breast. Pinching her nipple as the pleasure gets to be too much.

I pull the toy off her clit again and the breath of relief from her is bone tired.

"One more baby. You're doing so good," I whisper in her ear. Praising her for playing along as I push and pull her from the edge.

"Adam," she weakly says my name.

"One more. And then I promise to bury my cock so deep inside this pussy."

I place the toy back on her clit and turn it on. Emily whimpers as I press the device closer.

"Oh, fuck." She exclaims when I bump the speed up to the next setting. Her hips move as if she's looking for more friction.

I bump the speed to the third, and highest setting, and watch as magic happens.

"Adam!" Emily yells as she comes.

I look down, seeing her feet curled into the sheets as her release squirts out of her. This is the hottest thing I've seen and I maneuver myself between her legs and continue to lap up her arousal. Her hands fly to my head as she keeps coming. My name a cry on her lips as I still haven't removed the toy.

I let myself have a few more seconds to her soaked entrance. Then I'm turning off the little device, sliding up her body, and slide right into her tight heat.

"Baby," *thrust*, "you did," *thrust*, "so good."

I pull a boneless leg up around my waist as I slow my pace and make love to her.

Emily

Nervous? Me? Not at all. I'm lying to myself. I'm totally nervous. I've been thumbing through my closet trying to find something to wear to Dylan's game tomorrow.

Walking back into my room, I pick up my phone and call Sarah. Hopefully, she's not still working.

"Hi, little bird," she greets.

"What do you wear to a little kid's baseball game?"

Sarah laughs into the receiver. "Isn't this something you ask Kamryn help for?"

"Yes," I confess. "But you're the one at all the games for your clients."

Sarah manages some of the biggest names in sports in the Cincinnati area. She managed to take on Mason as a client right before his injury forced him to retire. With Mason on her roster, she now has basketball, hockey, baseball, and another football player she manages. How she does it I'll never know.

"Hmm, well since you'll be outside roasting away, you

can't go wrong with a sundress or shorts and a tank. I take it things are going well with Adam?"

I walk back into my closet and pick out a muted sage green dress, that thankfully has a built-in bra, with a form-fitting bodice and adjustable spaghetti straps. "Things are going really well. I'm almost scared to say it out loud or even introduce you all to him." I find some sandals in my collection and lay out my outfit on my vanity chair. "He told me he loved me the other night."

"What?" Sarah's shock matches mine.

"I know," I agree.

"And do you? Love him, that is?"

"I do."

Sarah squeals, a very un-Sarah-like thing to do. "I'm so happy for you."

"You're the first to know."

"What? You haven't told Kamryn?"

I sit down on my bed and pet Biscuit. "No. Kam would want me to be all open-hearted with her. And even with James, I was never like that. Do you think she'll be mad at me?"

"I think she'll be hurt more than mad."

"Love after loss," I snort. "I don't recommend it."

Sarah snorts into the phone. "Noted. So when are you going to tell her?"

"Soon." I declare.

When I get off the phone with Sarah, I pick up my phone again multiple times to text Kamryn. I went out with the group back in April and back then, nothing between Adam and I was as deep as it is now. But I know when I do see Kamryn I'll have to confess everything.

~

I woke up extra early for someone who doesn't have a child playing a sport. Why these games start at the asscrack of dawn I'll never know. I made sure to slather on sunscreen as I wasn't sure of the shade coverage. I'm a huge fan of summer, but a sunburn is where I draw the line. I nixed the idea of wearing a dress and went with shorts and a tank top that I paired with slip-on tennis shoes. I pulled my hair up in a ponytail and threw a Phillies hat on top.

> Me: Pulling into the complex now.

> Adam: We're parked on the far left side of the lot.

I slow roll through the parking lot until I get to where Adam said he's parked. I find his truck easily and find a spot close by.

> Me: I'm nervous. Now what?

> Adam: Now we meet at the entrance and I'll kiss your nerves away.

Blowing out a breath, I take my keys out of the ignition and snag my phone. My car lock beeping twice does little to calm my nerves.

I follow a small crowd of parents and little baseball players up to the entrance. And when I see Adam there in his own baseball hat he causes my heart to stutter. I could blame the sun for my skin feeling on fire as his gaze trails over my body. He's seen me in far less and never fails to make it feel like the first time.

"Hi, sunshine," he greets me when I'm close.

"Hi, handsome," I greet back. "Seeing you in dad mode

really is such a turn-on." I'm wary of tiny ears so I keep what I tell him PG.

"I'm always in dad mode," he tells me as he reaches out for my hand.

His hand is my lifeline where I feel like a fish out of water. My steps are light as I follow him to a field that's just about ready to play.

"I like you being in dad mode," I confess when we get to a set of bleachers. Thankfully it has some shade over it so we won't bake like cookies.

Adam leads the way up the bleachers and settles us in a row in the middle. I look around and see other parents sitting in lawn chairs with some not-so-subtly glancing our way.

"Still nervous?"

My knee bouncing up and down, a nervous habit since childhood, does little to disguise my nerves. "That obvious?"

His hand rests on my knee and rubs soothing circles. "Soon enough the game will start and their attention will be off of you. I promise." He emphasizes and presses a kiss to my cheek.

My nerves soon subside as the game starts. Not much of a game considering how young the boys are. There is a tee by home plate that is used when the little ones can't hit the ball that's tossed to them. I sense Adam tense when Dylan steps up to the plate. His helmet bobbles as his little legs carry him there.

"Eye on the ball, buddy!" Adam yells from our spot on the bleachers.

Yeah. Totally hot.

I sit quietly as the coach pitches the ball to Dylan. He swings and misses on the first pitch.

"It's okay Dyl. Get it next time," Adam coaches from here.

Dylan's head moves in what I'm assuming is a nod. The coach holds the ball up so Dylan can see and then it's tossed towards home plate. Dylan swings and the bat connects with the ball.

"Go, Dylan! Run, buddy!" Adam chants as I cheer next to him.

He runs as fast as he can to first base, pumping his arms and legs as fast as he can to get there before the ball does.

Seeing Dylan's smile and Adam's enthusiasm for this game erases any of the hesitation I had about this sport. Yes, it's tee ball. But it's still baseball-adjacent. I watch as Adam high-fives some of the parents sitting around us.

"EMILY, this is Sandra. One of the team moms. She's whose house Dylan runs off to any chance he gets." Adam introduces us when the game ends. The boys are sitting in the outfield as the coach gives them a speech. They won the game but it wasn't about who won or lost. As long as the boys had that was all that mattered.

"It's so nice to meet you," I tell her and hold my hand out.

She swats my hand away and pulls me into a hug. "None of that. It's so nice to meet you, sweetheart."

I return her hug, albeit a little shocked by her outright affection. Mommy issues. It happens. "You, too."

"So how did you two meet?" Sandra asks us.

"Parent-teacher conference," Adam says and slings his arm over my shoulder, pulling me into his side.

I squeeze his side. "He's lying. I came into his bar on the night of the parent-teacher night at school."

Sandra looks between us with love only a mother can give. "Well, you two are a beautiful couple."

The compliment makes me feel things, more than the love I have for Adam at knowing that this, meeting his and Dylan's other world is off to a great start.

"Hey, boys," Sandra says as she looks behind us.

My body tenses and Adam notices. "You're fine, baby," he tells me before letting me go and turning around. "Hey, buddy. Great game."

I turn around and see Dylan looking at his Dad with a smile and then he turns his eyes on me. "Hey, Dylan. Long time to see." When I get nervous, I spout things like that.

"Hi, Ms. Emily."

Phew. That's easy.

Adam takes his bat bag from him and slides it over his shoulder. "Wanna go get some ice cream? It's hot out."

"Yeah," Dylan responds and then looks at me. "Are you coming?"

I look at Adam and he nods his head. "Sure. I love ice cream."

And so we walk to our cars like an almost family. Me with my former student and his Dad whom I very much love.

I've never been shy with Dylan. But that line was firm with a student-teacher relationship. Now I have to muddle through the girlfriend and boyfriend's son relationship.

"We usually go to the *Twisted Cow*," Adam offers when we get to my car.

"I do too. I'll meet you two there."

Adam leans forward and kisses me on the cheek. "Breathe, baby. He won't bite," he whispers in my ear.

Nodding my head, I give them a small and awkward wave before hopping into my car and starting it up to cool down.

"When did you start playing?" I ask Dylan.

Now that we're all seated and I have something to do with my hands, I'm not as nervous. Plus the *Twisted Cow* has Oreo ice cream and it calms me.

"Daddy, put me in it last year," he tells me. His face is covered in chocolate ice cream. Adam lets him keep with the mess because cleaning up little boys is futile. "Do you like baseball?"

"I do," it comes out more like a question. "I haven't watched a lot of baseball in a while."

"Why not?"

I scoop some ice cream into my mouth before answering. "Someone very close to me was a big fan of baseball. And it felt wrong to watch it without him."

Dylan looks at me like that's crazy. At this age, I still don't think kids understand loss. Sometimes I still don't understand it. Losing someone. It's like saying they're lost in the store or at an amusement park.

"Does he still watch?"

"I'm sure he still does," I confirm with a small smile.

Adam frees a knowing smile that soothes my nerves. Not just being with him and Dylan in a casual environment but talking about James.

I pepper Dylan with questions until his eyes begin to droop. Adam and I stand from the table, he picks Dylan and I gather our trash to toss.

Walking to our cars, I stand to the side as he tucks

Dylan into his seat. Adam buckles him in and starts up his truck to cool the inside down.

"That wasn't so bad," Adam tells me.

"For you," I confess.

He pulls me into his embrace and my arms wrap around his waist. "We'll give it time. We still have your summer bucket list to complete."

"That's right. Now that Dylan knows, we just have to set some time aside." I tilt my head up and rest my chin on his chest.

Adam pecks my lips with his, once, twice until he sinks into a kiss. My lips part and our tongues meet as they dance and tangle. My body moves closer to his. He pulls on my ponytail causing a moan to slip free. That's when I know we need to stop our kiss.

I pull away, breathless and flushed. But not from the summer sun. "Go take him home. I'll see you later."

"Spend the night," Adam blurts out.

"I would love to. But we just told him. How would that look if I was just there?"

"It would look like a relationship." Adam deadpans.

"Okay, smartass," I pinch his side again. "In a few days."

"Deal. I love you."

The smile that hits my face is uncontrollable. "I love you, too."

Adam watches as I get in my car. I wave as I drive by and head home light. So light it's as if I'm floating and nothing can bring me down.

But what I've come to learn is that when life is going too good, the other shoe is bound to drop.

Emily

Two Weeks Later

"Hi Mom," I say into my phone.

The other end is silent until she speaks up.

"Honey, it's Gloria. She's in the hospital."

Tears instantly flood my eyes. For so long I thought that after James the people in my life were invincible.

"Is she okay?"

"No. Honey she didn't want me to tell you, but she has cancer and it's terminal. She doesn't have long."

I hold my hand over my mouth as I try to hold back a sob. It doesn't work. I'm going to lose the final piece of my childhood.

"Where are you at?" I ask, breathing through the emotions.

"In New York. At Rutherford Hospital."

Sitting on my couch I feel numb. Like I'm so numb to losing people but it still hurts.

I run my hand through my hair, stopping when I

remember it's in a braid. "Okay, I can try to be there tonight. I just need to pack and book a flight."

"I can do that. You pack and I'll send you your flight information."

I blow out a relieved breath. "Thanks, Mom."

"You're welcome, honey. I'll see you soon."

I stare at nothing on my wall as I come to terms with another loss. Picking up my phone I find Jax's number and send her a text. Jax and I live in the same apartment complex but at different ends.

Me: Hey can I ask for a favor?

Jax: Sure, what's up?

Me: I have to go to New York. I'm not sure for how long. Will you watch Biscuit for me? She just needs food twice a day and clean water.

Jax: Of course. I'll head over now to get your key.

Me: Thank you.

I get moving and pack my suitcases. I'm not sure how long I'll be there, so I pack for two weeks just to be careful. I'm putting my toiletries in my suitcase when I hear a knock on my door.

Checking the peephole I see it's Jax and let her in.

"Is everything okay?" She asks when I close the door.

Shaking my head, I walk towards the bowl with my keys and fish out my spare apartment key. "No. Gloria is sick. She's been sick. And she hid it from me."

The anger I feel at being the last to know pours out as the tears fall down my face. Jax rushes towards me and holds me as I break down. It's selfish to be angry over someone not telling you they were dying.

"Please don't tell Kamryn," I say through my tears.

Jax's hands stop moving on my back and she pulls away. "I won't lie to my sister if she asks if I've seen you."

I nod my head because that's fair.

Jax leaves and shortly after my phone dings with a message from my mom with my ticket confirmation and a notice that a car is here to pick me up.

I heft my suitcases downstairs and then I'm off to the airport with no idea what's to greet me when I arrive.

THE FLIGHT into New York was uneventful. But I was antsy the entire time. I have no clue what to expect. And the hurt and anger over losing another person I love, I can't mask that.

When we deboard the plane, I follow the line right to the luggage carousel. While waiting I turn my phone back on and a message from Adam is waiting.

> Adam: Hi sunshine.

> Adam: Any plans this weekend?

> Me: Hi baby.

> Me: I can't this weekend. I'm in New York.

My phone buzzes with an incoming call from Adam.

"Hi," I answer.

"What's wrong?" I hear the concern in his voice.

I step away from the crowd but still keep an eye on the luggage carousel. "It's Gloria. My mom told me she has cancer and it's terminal. She's in the hospital. And I," my voice squeaks out. "And I don't know how to say goodbye to my childhood. To the last person who saw me when all I wanted was to be seen."

The truth is she's my last honest connection to James. She was there as we grew up and fell in love. Gloria was there for every milestone and she was equally devastated when he passed away. He was another grandchild to her and I could never try to understand the beautiful bond they had.

"Do you want me to fly out there?" Adam asks. And it's sweet of him to ask.

"No, baby. You don't have to. Being back here is hard enough for me. Plus I don't want this to be the first time you're meeting my family."

"Okay. Well, I can be on a flight whenever you need me."

"Thank you, baby." The signal for the luggage dropping sounds. "I have to get my luggage, but I'll talk to you later. I love you, Adam."

"I love you too, sunshine."

I hang up and collect my bags. My mom must have had a car called for me here because there was one waiting for me at the curb.

"Thank you."

WALKING through the hospital's sliding glass doors, I head for the reception desk to get Gloria's room number, when my name is called out. Turning to the side, I see my dad by the elevator bay.

I rush over to him and fall into his embrace. Tears

prickle the back of my throat, making it hard for me to swallow.

"Hi, pumpkin."

"Hi, Daddy."

He pulls back and presses the button to take us up on the elevator. My dad holds onto me as we enter the open car.

I have no clue what to expect. Gloria has been my grandmother in all the ways that counted since I was a kid. The bond we have. The love she so freely gave me.

When we get up to the sixth floor and turn to the left, I see my mom pacing in the hallway. My hands start sweating because I've never seen my mom act this way.

"Emily," my mom greets me with a hug.

"Hi, Mom."

"She's in there."

I look at the door nervously. But my mom wraps her arms around my shoulders. Resting her chin on top of my head.

"It's okay to be scared, honey. It's okay to be sad and angry."

With a deep breath, I pull myself from my mom's embrace and push through the door. And what I see breaks me down.

Gloria is lying in a hospital bed that's three times too big. Her body frail and pale as she stares out the window. When the door shuts, her attention shifts to me.

"Come here, my sweet girl."

I go to her instantly and climb onto the bed next to her. Settling into the bed, I wrap my arms around her waist and she runs her hands down my hair.

"Don't cry."

"You can't leave me. I'm not ready to say goodbye to you." I cry out.

"One of my greatest blessings in life was helping to raise you. I got to watch you grow up into a beautiful majestic bird. I got to watch you perform your heart out to a packed auditorium. I got to watch you fall in love."

My childhood plays behind my tear-filled eyes. Every big moment, Gloria was there. When she goes, the best parts of that time in my life will only be alive because of me.

"Tell me about your life in Cincinnati."

"I started dating someone," I tell her.

"What's he like?"

"Kind. Patient. He has a little boy who's going into the second grade. He loves me."

"What's not to love about you?" She pokes as she continues to run her hands through my hair. "What's his name? The both of them."

"His name is Adam. And he's thirty-eight. His son's name is Dylan and he's...they're both amazing."

I talk with her about how we met and how he never gave up on me when I was determined to keep him as a friend. I talk to her about how hard it was to love again but that Adam made it incredibly easy.

"Emily," her breathing has become more labored. "I want you to promise me something."

I swallow hard as the tears continue to fall. "What is it?"

"I want you to play again."

"I don't know if I can," I admit. While I've long thought of picking my violin up again, I have no clue if the years of training I did are useful.

"You can," Gloria weakly argues back. Her breath rattles out of her and it's now that I realize she's sicker than my mom let on. "Play something easy and go from there. It's my final wish. I wish for you to play again."

~

I sit in the pew between my parents as the priest talks about life and living it to its fullest. Gloria passed away in her sleep a few days after I got to the hospital. She was surrounded by her family and mine. Well, I guess you could say we were all family.

In the days since she passed, I contacted Amelia and asked if she would help me learn *Ave Maria* on the violin. It was the quickest I had learned to play a piece of music through the tears that never stopped.

I have a speech prepared and when the priest gives me a nod, both of my parents squeeze my hands before I scoot out of the row and up to the podium.

Unfolding the speech, I look out into the crowd. I look at Gloria's family broken as they come to terms with the fact they lost a vital piece of their family.

Movement from the back of the church draws my attention and I see Adam looking every bit the man I fell in love with. Showing up when I didn't ask him to. Sending me his strength when I need it most.

"When I think of my childhood, I can't remember a time when that didn't include Gloria. My first day of school, every year, she would hand me toast and a piece of bacon. It was such a simple meal. But she knew my nerves of starting something new got to me. So she gave me comfort in whatever form she could." I close my eyes as I remember the painful moments. "Gloria was by my side for every moment. When my parents and I didn't see eye-to-eye, she gave me her strength. She was there when I fell in love. She was there when I graduated and when I performed in front of a packed auditorium. She was there when I suffered a loss."

I look back at my violin and bow sitting on a stand, waiting to be picked up. To let the music flow through the room with hopes that the notes will heal just a little.

"Before she passed, she told me her final wish was for me to play again. To be honest I haven't picked up my violin since I was eighteen as I put that part of my life behind me. But I could never say no to Gloria. So that's what I'm going to do for her. Play," I can't stop my voice from trembling or cracking as the tears that formed flow freely down my cheeks. "And I'm gonna say goodbye to one of my favorite people and my favorite part of my childhood."

Taking a breath, I walk over to my violin and I take center stage. Placing my violin on my shoulder and the bow in the ready position I take several deep breaths before I close my eyes and play.

I had long thought that when I stopped playing that my memorization skills would disappear with it. But that's not the case. Behind my closed eyes, I see every note. The crescendo, the decrescendo. The vibrato and trills. The runs and the long notes. I picture Gloria sitting and watching as I practice my piece for my recital. I see the smile and tears as I finish my piece flawlessly.

And when I finish this piece, there's nothing. No crowd cheering. No Gloria telling me I played beautifully. Just the sound of sniffles from the tears her family shed.

When the last note fades away, I open my eyes and place my violin back on the stand. Without another word or glance at the others, I clutch my speech and sit back between my parents.

More words are spoken about love and loss. The potential to make this loss mean something more than it being a loss.

The funeral ends with only immediate family allowed to head to the burial site. It hurt when my parents told me, but in the end, seeing the end to my childhood as Gloria is lowered into the ground may make me unrepairable.

We're walking out of the church when I spot Adam standing off to the side and I rush to him. Flinging my arms around his neck as the tears come.

His hand cradles my head with his other arm wrapping around my waist, holding me to him, and piecing me together. "You're okay, baby. I've got you."

"I can't believe you're here." I cry.

"Where you go, I go," Adam pulls back and looks me over. "I won't let you face the hard times on your own. You've got me."

Nodding my head, I wrap my arms around his waist. Nuzzling into his chest as I reality that he showed up when I needed him makes the love I have for him soar to the skies.

"Emily?" I hear behind me.

My body freezes as I remember my parents. Pulling back from Adam, I look up at him. "Ready to meet my parents?"

"Yeah, I'm ready." Adam places a kiss to the tip of my nose before I turn around and face my parents.

"Mom? Dad? I'd like you to meet Adam."

Adam

I drum my fingers on the steering wheel along to the beat of a Kendrick Lamar song. It's a Wednesday and Emily has been back home for a couple of weeks. Seeing her distraught over the loss of a person who was like a grandmother to her, was something I never thought I would have witnessed. Tack on me meeting her parents, which went smoothly, and she was exhausted.

"Mom? Dad? I'd like for you to meet Adam. Adam, these are my parents," Emily says as she introduces me to her parents.

"It's nice to meet you both," I offer as I hold my hand out for them to shake.

"Likewise. Honey, why don't we all go and get lunch?" Emily's Mom offers as we're still mingling in front of the church.

Emily slides her hand into mine as more of a reassurance that I'm here than for comfort. Or maybe it's for both. "Yeah. That sounds good."

We all walk towards the parking lot as Gloria's family has already left for the burial site. I pull my hand from Emily's and wrap my arm around her shoulder instead.

"Thank you for coming," she tells me as I steer us towards my rental car.

"I know you said not to. But baby, I don't want you to have to face the hard things alone."

When we get to my car, I open the door for her. But Emily turns before getting in. "I love you. I don't mean it in a surface-level way."

I duck my head so we're at eye-level and peck her on the lips. "I know what you mean."

She kisses me before ducking into the passenger seat.

"So where to?" I ask when I'm in the car.

"Our go-to has been this restaurant that has a garden terrace and looks over Central Park. They have really good food."

Putting the car in drive, I have her tell me which way to go. I've never been to New York and this isn't my ideal first time to want to come here. But I'm hoping these few days here with Emily will allow her and I to explore and be a real couple without the prying eyes or being terrified to show affection.

It takes us about thirty minutes to arrive at the restaurant. Emily was nervous being around Dylan, but I'm shaking in my suit at being around her parents. From what she told me, their relationship has been slowly building. But I can't separate the parents they are now from the parents they were when she was a kid.

"How did you two meet?" Emily's Dad, Mark, asks us.

"I went into his bar after the 'Meet the Teacher' event at school. Turns out we had a connection that wasn't known until he showed up for a parent-teacher conference."

"Oh? You're a dad?" Her Mom asks.

"Yes, ma'am. I have a son," I respond.

Emily's Mom's face lights up when she asks to see pictures of Dylan. I show her one of him on the first day of school and then one of the three of us at his baseball game a couple of weekends ago. Her Dad asks about my owning a restaurant and claims that they'll have to make a trip. Not just for my business, but for Emily as well.

After lunch, Emily insists we go for a walk in Central Park. I've never been so I enthusiastically agree.

"That went well," Emily states when we're well into the park.

I look down and see her face alive. "I was nervous, at first. But your parents are great."

"They've gotten better. I just don't think they knew how to be parents back then. Like what do two sought-after lawyers do with a kid? Once James died, I think having me put it into perspective. That could have been me who they were grieving after."

We find an empty bench to sit at and watch some guys play touch football.

"I'm glad you three are finding your way together," I admit and pull her into my side.

"Me too," she tells me and places a kiss on my jawline.

The rest of our time is spent playing tourist. Since Emily was so young when she lived here, she never got to explore the city the way others do. We went to the Morgan Library & Museum, walked around the West Village, and did a self-guided Sex & the City tour. We indulged in food from the food trucks, sweets until our stomachs cramped, and a wine tour to end off the weekend.

During one of the hardest periods of Emily's life, I fell

more in love with her. With her joy for life and the world around her. I fell in love with Emily Bailey.

~

I'M FINALLY SET to meet her friends this weekend. With us in New York for those few days, it set us back. But now that Emily is getting back to her happy self, our relationship has only gotten stronger.

My truck turns into the driveway and I pause when I see an unknown car. Thinking it's a rental for Jenny, I turn my truck off and get out. Only when I do, the driver exits too and my heart stops.

"Chelsea." Her name comes out like sand as I speak it for the first time in five years.

"Hi, Adam."

We silently stare at each other in my driveway. The cicadas singing in the background as the only noise to break the silence.

"What are you doing here?" I ask when the silence feels like it's close to suffocating me. All I wanted when I got home was to see Dylan and call Emily.

She takes a step forward but stops when I hold my hand up. "I miss you. And I miss Dylan."

"So? We've done just fine without you for the last six years."

"Adam, I made a mistake," Chelsea tries to plead with me.

My eyebrows hit my hairline. "You call serving me with divorce papers and signing your parental rights away a mistake?"

She looks away and I know what I said hits. But when

she looks back at me it's as if ice is running through my veins. "I want a chance to be what Dylan deserves."

"Well, I can give you the number for my lawyer and you can set up a meeting time. But you can't stay here."

"I want you back Adam. I never stopped loving you."

I cross my arms over my chest in an attempt to cover my clenched fists. "You're too late. Goodbye, Chelsea."

Turning my back on her, I rush into my house and lock the door.

Jenny peeks around. "Who was that?"

"Chelsea."

"I had no idea who she was. She just parked her car there and nothing."

I blow a breath out of my nose. "You didn't know. But she's not allowed in here. Under any circumstance."

"Of course."

I leave Jenny to get settled in the guest room while I head up and check in on Dylan. He's sprawled out in his bed with not a clue that a ghost from both of our past just tried to enter his world.

Softly closing his door, I walk down the carpeted hallway to my bedroom. When I shut the door, I lean back and let out an aggravated breath. I'll have to call my lawyer and see what she says. I may have nothing to worry about, but better safe than sorry.

Pulling out my phone, I see a text Emily sent over an hour ago. I debate responding or calling, but I'm learning that in the summer she's got a much different sleep schedule. So I call her instead.

"Hi," her soft voice over the phone instantly soothes me.

"Hi, baby."

I hear sheets rustling. "What's wrong?"

"I didn't want to tell you until I saw you. But Chelsea was waiting for me here when I got home."

"What?" The disbelief in Emily's question is evident.

"I know." My mind is still trying to make sense of if she was serious.

"You're planning to call your lawyer? I mean I don't think any lawyer would reinstate her rights. It's been six years. You've provided for and loved Dylan better than she ever could have." Emily reassures me with everything I already know.

Running my hand through my hair I walk into my bathroom and turn the water on for a shower to wash off the night from work and the shock from an unexpected visitor.

"You're an amazing dad, Adam. You put Dylan first. And that's more than I can say for her. Don't let her reappearance shake your foundation."

I let out a deep breath. "I won't. I promise I won't. Thank you."

"Always. Go shower. I'll see you later. I love you."

"I love you too, sunshine."

"Bye," she whispers before she ends the call.

I place my phone on my bathroom vanity, strip off my clothes, and get into the shower. The steaming hot water pounds down on my body instantly soothing my aching bones and pushing the last thirty minutes out of my mind.

I focus on Emily and her love and reassurance. I focus on Dylan and his goofy smile and never-ending energy. I think of the people in my life that would stand by me and attest to my ability with being an amazing father.

Letting her get to me could shake the very foundation that I've set in place. And that would break the promise that I gave to Emily.

Emily

Today's the day my world meets my other world. It took a while for us to get to this place. But I know my girls will love Adam when they meet him.

I pull into Adam's driveway and park next to his truck. He managed to get off the next couple of days. With him hiring another assistant general manager, his days and nights are a bit more flexible.

Taking my keys out of the ignition, I round to the back of my car and get my bag before walking up to the front door. I test the door handle and see it's unlocked, with a shake of my head, I push inside and turn the deadbolt.

"Adam? Why was your front door unlocked?" I shout when I close and lock the front door.

Dylan is at his friend's house for a sleepover. He's been there since early this afternoon apparently. God bless Sandra for hosting six rowdy little boys. So I decided with Dylan out, I would come over early. We've upped the days when I see Dylan. It was strange at first as Adam and I are already affectionately comfortable with one another. Dialing back the level of affection we show one another is hard for both of us. But Adam tells me if Dylan catches us, he'll have to get used to his Dad kissing his former teacher.

I dump my bags at the foot of the stairs and walk into the kitchen to see Adam tittering around in the fridge. A black tank top showcases his sculpted arms with the tattoos on his arm and the backward baseball cap makes me weak in the knees. Silently, I hop up onto the island and wait for him to turn around. And when he does, the smile that hits his face when he sees me is infectious.

"Hi, sunshine," he greets me and walks over to where I'm sitting. Placing the bag of corn on the cob on the island next to me, he wedges himself between my legs and leans forward to place a chaste kiss on my lips.

I drop my arms around his shoulders, and slide my hands under the neck of his shirt, taking him in. While his eyes aren't the bright forest green I love looking into when we're together, it doesn't make him any less handsome. But I fear knowing that Chelsea reappeared is weighing on him.

"Are you sure you're ready for today?"

"Yeah. I wanna meet your world." He reassures me.

I wrap my legs tighter around his waist and pull him closer to me. "I can't wait for them to meet my world."

"God I love you," Adam says, slamming his lips to mine.

My arms wrap around his shoulders and he wraps his arms around my waist. I squeal when he pulls me off the island and walks us to the couch. My legs lock at the base of his spine as I trail my lips down his neck.

Adam makes it to the couch and my legs go on either side of his hips when he sits. The dress I'm wearing flutters around us and leaves little barrier between him and I. His cock is already hard and I moan when I feel him brush my clit. I lift up a little before lowering onto him.

"How much time do we have?" Adam asks when he breaks the kiss and latches onto my collarbone.

Raising my arm, I look at the small watch on my wrist. "Plenty of time."

I slide back on his lap and unbutton and unzip his pants. Adam lifts as much as he can with me still on his thighs. His pants and boxer briefs slide down just enough to free him and he takes off his shirt, tossing it to the side. I trace my thumb over his slit. Rubbing the pre-cum that's leaked out.

"Don't play with me Em," Adam warns through clenched teeth.

Lifting an eyebrow I move off of him and pull my scrap of underwear off. Climbing back on the couch, I straddle his hips. Pumping him a few times, I rise up on my knees and rub the head of his cock through my opening, coating him in my arousal.

Adam places his hands on my waist, steadying me, as I slowly lower down on him. The full feeling is unmatched as I bottom out.

"God damn, baby. Your pussy is so tight. You feel so good wrapped around me."

I lift and swivel my hips, getting the most friction. Adam holds me still when I fully cover him and he moves forward, sliding his legs out before leaning back on the couch. The movement sends him impossibly deeper.

"Shit," I moan out when he feels bigger than before. My hands fall to the couch on either side of him.

"That feel good, baby?" He asks.

My hips move up and down his length. His hands on my hips help me keep rhythm. The sound of our skin slapping together, paired with our grunts and moans, fills the otherwise silent room. Adam lifts his hips in time with me and I feel my orgasm starting in my lower belly.

"Adam," I pant out. My voice gets higher pitch as my orgasm gets closer.

His hand comes between us and moves his thumb to my clit, still meeting my hips, rubbing tight circles and flicking the taught bud.

"Come on, Em. Come for me."

I flex my inner muscles and throw my head back when my orgasm hits me.

"That's it, baby," Adam praises.

My body laxes as I come down from my high. Adam peppers my face with kisses. Latching onto my neck with lips and teeth.

"Hold on tight," he warns before he slams his hips up into me, driving me higher again as he chases his release.

I flip his hat off, tugging on the strands of hair on the back of his head and expose his neck. I latch onto his neck, alternating between sucking, licking, and biting, moving to pull his earlobe between my teeth. My orgasm is building again, but I want Adam to come again.

"Come for me, baby. Fill me with your cum," I whisper into his ear and tunnel my tongue in his ear causing a whimper to fall from his mouth.

His grip on my hips gets impossibly harder as he ruts into me with quick motion until his body stills. I feel the warmth from his release filling me up as a second orgasm hits me. My name falls from his mouth in a whisper before he falls back into the cushion completely spent.

I place open-mouth kisses on his neck, jaw, chin, cheeks, and lips. My hips move slowly as I milk him dry.

Adam hugs me to him and buries his face in my neck.

We stay on the couch for way too long. But this, us,

soaking each other up as if we have all the time in the world is how we started.

~

ADAM FINISHES STIRRING the margarita pitcher when a knock on the door has us looking at each other like we got caught doing illegal things.

We weren't.

But having new people enter our world is terrifying.

"It's cool. It's going to be fine," I say nervously as I wipe my already dry hands on a dish towel and walk towards the door with Adam trailing behind me.

Adam wraps his arms around my shoulders as we walk step-in-step to the door. "Relax baby. It's going to be fun."

He kisses the back of my head and releases me to open the door. I didn't mention to Adam that Mason was tagging along so his intake of breath has me biting my tongue to keep from laughing.

"Hi, friends," I greet. "Come in," I motion to the side as I open the door wider. Adam holds his arm across my chest as my other world walks across the threshold.

"Nice place," Sarah is the first to break the gawking.

"Thank you," Adam says from behind me.

"Adam, this is Sarah," she waves her hand. "Jax," she holds her hand up. "And Kamryn and Mason."

Adam is still behind me after I introduce Mason to him. I stealthily pinch his arm and a startled yelp sounds.

"Sorry. It's nice to meet you. All of you. I've heard incredible things from Em."

"Well she's been incredibly tight-lipped about you," Kamryn says.

My body freezes at the tone she uses and I see Sarah shaking her head in disappointment.

"Kam!" Jax scolds her.

"Sorry."

We all stand in the foyer awkwardly.

"Does anyone want a drink?" Adam is the first to break the silence. He untangles himself from around me and places a kiss to the side of my head before he leads everyone to the kitchen leaving Kam and I.

It's never been this awkward between us. But standing in front of my best friend when she feels I've intentionally shut her out of this part of my life...well, I don't know how to navigate that.

"I'm sorry, Em."

I nod my head slowly as I gather more of my muddled thoughts. "Are you mad, Kam? That I didn't keep you up to date with this part of my life?"

"I think I'm more hurt that I kept you up-to-date with mine and Mason's reconnecting whereas you've been tightlipped."

"Kam, when have I ever been loose-lipped when it came to my love life? Even with James, I kept that close to me. I don't expect you to tell me everything that happens between you and Mason, so why do you expect that of me?"

I don't want this strained relationship between my best friend and I. We've gone thirteen years without fighting and without me being angry at her. Sure we had that period after losing James and Liam where we stopped talking. I needed that more than she did. But that time worked for us.

She pushes her hair out of her face and crosses her arms. "You're right. I watched you struggle after James and I just assumed that when you moved on you'd be outspoken about it."

"I get that. But my moving on is something that I needed to do without telling anyone else. It was something I needed before I announced it to the world."

"I just want you to be happy, Emmy."

I step forward and take her hands in mine. "I am. I'm so happy it's almost sickening. What I want is for you to get to know Adam. And when the time comes, Dylan as well."

"Love looks good on you." Kam acknowledges as she pulls me into a hug.

"Love looks good on you too, bestie."

"Now let's get a drink and hang out in the pool."

"Deal," I say as we walk into the kitchen arm-in-arm.

Conversation floats through the open doors. I get Kam and myself a glass, filling them up to the rim with margaritas and joining the group outside.

Walking to where Adam is standing talking with Mason, I sidle up next to him and wrap my arm around his waist. His own arm wraps around my shoulder as he hangs onto every word Mason says. It's adorable seeing him loosen up around Mason. When I first mentioned my connection to the quarterback I feared he would become obsessive. But so far he's managed to remain calm.

A splash of water hits my legs and I turn to see Sarah giving me a pointed look. Rolling my eyes at her, I disentangle myself from Adam and make my way to the pool. Handing her my drink, I whip off my dress and wade into the pool.

"You're not exactly subtle," I say pointedly to her.

Kam snorts as Sarah rolls her eyes. "Sweetie, when have you ever known that to be a trait of mine?"

"Fair point. So what do you think?" It's not that I need any of their approval, but it's nice to have it.

Sarah looks around me and blatantly checks out my

boyfriend. I splash her when she looks too long. Her smile is almost comical. "I can see why you fell for him. But there's something about him. I can't put my finger on it."

"It's the eyes," I sigh.

"The eyes," they all drone.

"How's work, Sarah?"

She takes a healthy sip of her drink.

"That good, huh?"

"We're doing damage control right now. One of the hockey players needs a PR makeover. So, because of me and my big mouth, I suggested a babysitter. And guess who has to do the babysitting?"

My mouth falls open. "You?"

"I sometimes hate my job."

"But you're the best publicist I've ever had," Mason interjects as he and Adam join us in the pool.

My mouth curves into a smile when I notice Sarah staring at Adam. I splash her again.

"What?" She asks innocently.

"Get your own single dad."

The laughter that spills out in the pool relaxes me. Adam pulls me into his arms as we wade in the pool.

This is what I always wanted. My worlds collide effortlessly as the summer sun beats down on us. The rest of the day passes by with more drinks and food Adam cooked on the grill. Music flows from the stereo he has connected outside and provides welcome background noise to an otherwise peaceful day.

As the sun begins to set, we get the firepit going along with the drinks that haven't stopped filling our cups.

"How's living together?" I ask Kam.

Kamryn and Mason are snuggled on a loveseat with her legs splayed over his.

"Cramped," Mason pipes up.

"Oh, hush. He's just mopey because he has to duck every time he comes downstairs."

"I have to agree with Mason," Sarah says.

"What!? It's a cozy house," Kam argues.

Mason snorts as he drinks from his beer. "Baby it's cozy for you, Lucy, and Poppy. But not for all four of us."

"Fine. Then find us a house for the four of us and I'll move in."

"Done." Mason accepts with a Cheshire cat-like grin.

"Do they do this often?" Adam asks low enough so only I can hear him.

"No," I say and roll my head toward him. "That's just Kam's personality coming out to shine."

Adam places a kiss on my nose, causing goosebumps to spread on my arms and legs. "Are you cold?" He asks when he sees me shiver.

"Nope."

He pulls me closer to his side and I see Sarah from across the fire with a soft smile on her face. I didn't want to rock the boat with Kam by telling her that Sarah knew about my steps with Adam first. Call it her being my oldest friend? But I needed Sarah's opinion more than I needed Kamryn's.

I fall more in love with him as he interacts with my friends. And I constantly get the thumbs up of approval from my girls and Mason.

But what I've come to learn is that when life is going too good, the other shoe is bound to drop.

Adam

I creep into Dylan's room with the hope that he's not already awake. With it being the fourth of July, I should be working. We have the big block party, but my team assured me that family comes first.

So here I am creeping into Dylan's room for his birthday.

When I'm close enough to his bed, I kneel on the side and gently shake him awake.

"Wake up, birthday boy." It takes a few more shakes and some raspberries to his neck for him to wake up.

The sleepy smile on his face makes everything worth it.

"It's my birthday!" Dylan exclaims and pops up out of bed.

"It is. What do you want to do today?"

He pouts his lips as he thinks about it. "The zoo."

"Today?"

"Yeah, Daddy. It's my day," he says, like I should know.

I ruffle his hair and stand up. My knees crack as I do and I let out a groan. "That it is. Do you want pancakes?"

He nods his head fast and then purses his lips.

"What's up, buddy?"

"Can Emily come to the zoo with us?"

My lips twitch and my heart warms. While we haven't been together all three of us. Dylan has been itching to spend time with Emily. "Yeah, buddy. She can come with us."

"Okay."

I lean down and kiss the top of his head and ruffle his hair before I head downstairs. I pull out the pancake mix and mixing bowls to get started on breakfast. When I have two cakes on the griddle, I call Emily.

"Hi, baby."

"Hi, sunshine. Do you have plans today?"

I hear a door close and a huff of laughter escape her mouth. "It's summer. That's my plan."

"Fair point." I cradle my phone between my ear and shoulder, flipping the pancakes when they're ready. "How would you feel about spending the day at the zoo with me and Dylan?"

"Really?"

"Yeah, baby. It's his birthday and he wants to go to the zoo. And he wants you to come along."

Emily blows out a breath and if I know her, she's holding back emotion. "Okay. Um, do you want me to meet you two there, or?"

"Don't be a goof. Dylan has requested pancakes and I'm extending the invite to you. If you haven't eaten yet."

"Does iced coffee count as a meal?" Emily deadpans.

"Absolutely not. Emily Marie, drive your cute butt over here and I will feed you."

"Yes, Daddy."

"Jesus Christ woman," I blow out a breath as I hear

laughter on the other end of the phone. "I'm gonna hang up. Bring a change of clothes and I'll see you soon."

"I love you." She sings songs into the phone.

"I love you, too."

With a laugh, I hang up and finish up the pancakes. On the other eye, I start up the bacon and eggs. Dylan might not eat all of it but I'm sure Emily and I can polish off the rest. The TV turning on signals that Dylan has emerged from his bedroom. Still dressed in his Iron Man pajamas, he sits and watches an episode of Transformers.

"Did you brush your teeth?"

A murmured 'yeah' comes from the living room. I have to accept that I didn't raise an early morning kid, even though it's almost nine in the morning. With the bacon sizzling and the eggs cooking I make work on my first cup of coffee of the day.

> Emily: Do I need to grab anything for the birthday boy and his daddy?

> Me: No and if you keep calling me that I'm withholding an orgasm for making me sprout a boner near my son.

> Emily: Promises, promises.

> Emily: Be there soon.

Ten minutes later my phone pings with a notification from the camera in the driveway. Knowing it's Emily, I make sure the eye on the stove is set to low and head to the door to meet her.

Her steps up the front stoop are timid. I try to see where she's coming from.

"Come here," I open my arms to her.

She walks into them easily. Her arms find their way around my waist and we just be. As a couple that's still finding solid ground. As a single dad who's dating his son's former teacher. But through the mud that's our new reality, we're just us.

"It's weird that I can spend so much time with you and still miss you when we're not together. That has to be a sign. Good or bad, I have no clue." Emily says while still wrapped around me like ivy.

I kiss the top of her head. "Well I know I've never felt like this. Don't laugh, okay?" I wait for her to nod before telling her, "You give me butterflies. Every time we're around one another. I sometimes have to pinch myself that you gave us a chance."

"I'm glad I did," she tells me.

"Daddy? Did you forget about the food?" Dylan yells from inside.

"Shit!" I start and rush back into the house with Emily's laughter following me.

"He doesn't always do this," I hear Dylan say as I quickly pull the half-burnt food off the stove.

I can still salvage the rest of the food. So I finish up breakfast while I feel the peanut gallery watching me.

"How old are you today?" Emily asks Dylan.

"I'm seven."

"No way. I loved being seven."

I turn and see them both sitting at the island and my heart warms.

"What did you do for your birthday?"

"Hmm," she muses as she tries to remember that far back. "I think my parents took me for ice cream. Since it was February and we were living in New York, it was too cold to do anything outside. But I claimed very early on that it was never too cold for ice cream."

I plate the rest of breakfast and put everything on the island. Dylan grabs more than what he can eat and Emily laughs when she sees how full his plate is.

"Can you eat all of that?" She asks him.

"Mm-hmm. I have to eat all my food so I can grow big and strong like my daddy."

Emily looks at me over the top of his head with a twinkle in her eyes. "Big and tall like your daddy, huh?"

Watch it, I mouth.

"Yeah and then I can get stronger and play baseball forever."

"I don't know about forever, buddy," I tell Dylan.

He shrugs and eats most of his food before he pushes away his plate. "When are we going to the zoo?"

"In a few hours. I need to clean up and you need to shower. Get off all of that syrup."

"Okay." Dylan says, slinking off his chair and heading upstairs.

Emily and I take our cleared plates and Dylan's half-eaten food to the sink. She rinses the dishes and I load them into the dishwasher.

"First meal done," I praise once everything is wiped down.

Emily leans with her back against the counter and I mirror her position on the opposite side.

"It does get easier," she claims. "My life is so much different now."

"How so?"

"I thought I'd be married and have a kid, maybe two, by now. Living in a house." She crosses the small distance, wrapping her arms around my waist and looks up at me. "You're not a consolation prize. I don't want you to think that. You are the prize. If it makes me a bad person for saying that I'm glad my life looks different, then so what."

I didn't think I was a consolation prize. But I'm glad she cleared that up. "I think you'd be a great mom. As much as I hate the way your past affected you I am glad that you ended up here."

~

I HOLD up my phone and take a picture of my two hearts while they watch the lions in the enclosure. We've been at the zoo for just over two hours. Most of which was spent running through the water sprinklers to hopefully cool off.

Summer has made itself known. There hasn't been a day when the temperature wasn't in the nineties. Maybe I should've insisted we do a children's museum instead. But then I wouldn't have seen the smile or heard the laughter spilling from my son's mouth. I wouldn't have seen the pure joy emanating from Emily at her first zoo experience. These are the moments that make being with them special.

"What's your favorite animal?" Dylan asks Emily.

The awkward band-aid has been ripped off. As soon as we entered the park, Dylan grabbed Emily's hand and toted her where he wanted to go.

"My favorite animals are squirrels and geese. But I also really like tigers. Maybe it has to do with *Aladdin* and how Jasmine had Rajah as her pet. I always thought that was cool."

"That would be really cool."

"What's your favorite animal?" Emily asks back.

"Sharks," Dylan claims proudly.

Emily blanches and I can't stop the bark of laughter from escaping.

"Why sharks?"

"Because they're so cool!" Dylan claims.

"I'll take your word for it," Emily hesitantly says.

The rest of the day is spent traipsing around the zoo until our feet hurt and Dylan is asleep on my shoulders. Emily makes me stop to take a picture of the three of us. And despite the dead weight of Dylan, my smile has never been more alive.

~

"He's still out," I announce when I walk into my bedroom. I close the door behind me and fall face-first on the bed next to Emily.

"I expected nothing less."

I feel movement on the bed as Emily moves closer to me. She straddles my back and the moan I let out has me glad the door is closed.

"Never stop that." I groan as she digs her thumbs into my lower back. I didn't realize how tight my back would get from carrying Dylan. He's a small kid, but man does he weigh a good amount.

"What do you two normally do for his birthday?" Her hands continue their magic on my back. Slowly I feel the muscles begin to loosen and I can finally breathe normally.

I flip through other birthdays of his and come up blank. "Now that you mention it, I can't remember. We always watch fireworks. Even though it's a holiday, Dyl still claims that the fireworks are a present for him. I usually cook on the grill and he has a cake. But I had no cake and no food prepared for the grill. I feel completely unprepared."

Emily slides off my back and lays next to me. "He had a

blast today. Don't think you need to go over the top for him."

"I know," I breathe out. "Sometimes I still feel like I'm failing."

"Adam, you are that little boy's hero. He worships the ground you walk on." Her hands slide through my hair and I love that she loves to do that. "What brought this on? Is it seeing Chelsea?"

"I thought I was fine after seeing her. You reassured me that I had nothing to worry about. But I can't stop the negativity and the crippling fear of what she said from rolling in."

"I'm with you. Every step of the way I am with you." Emily declares.

Emily

I slam my laptop shut with a huff. I've gone through several websites to figure out what to get Adam for his birthday. He's not materialistic and he doesn't collect knickknacks.

> Me: I need help!

Sarah: What's the problem?

Kam: I have bail money.

Jax: Need a getaway car?

> Me: I have no clue what to get Adam for his birthday.

Kam: Damn, I thought you'd need bail money.

> Me: You three are terrible.

Sarah: Come back! Does he like baseball?

> Me: Seriously?

Jax: Dumb question…

Sarah: I can get tickets for next week.

Me: Make it three tickets and you've got a deal.

Sarah: Done.

Me: Thank you. Love you!

With Adam's present sorted out, I stare at the case on my coffee table. A few days after I got home from New York, my parents had my violin shipped out to me. I'm doing my best to keep my promise to Gloria, despite the ache in my heart when I think about playing.

There has been a subtle urge to play again. It had been an urge for a while, but the funeral was what started it back up.

I take a deep breath and unzip the case. The polished wood and rosin-coated strings are like old friends greeting me home. I unstrap my violin from its holder and rest it in my lap like a guitar. I lightly strum the familiar strings with the sound filling my quiet apartment. My fingers get in position and the welcome tune of a Lana Del Rey song sounds.

I attach the chin rest to the underside of my violin. Plucking out the bow from the holder, I get into position and play.

My fingers are rusty, but after a few passes of the bow and my fingers moving on the strings, it's as if muscle memory is the motivator. I move from one song to the next. Playing from memory songs I hear on the radio and classical pieces I dabbled in when I was younger. By the time I open my eyes, I see the sun has started to set. Not quite ready to stop playing, I head out to my balcony and play the song I performed at my final recital.

It's like being taken down memory lane as I play a song I haven't thought of in almost ten years. My body moves to the music as I remember the long-forgotten music. As I play the final note, I hear a knock on my door.

Resting my violin in its case, I head to the door and check the peephole.

"Hi," I greet when I open the door, completely shocked by my visitor.

"You said it was okay to visit. So I took you up on that." Brandon claims as he stands on my welcome mat with, I'm guessing, Angie by his side.

I hold the door open wider for them to pass through. "I meant for you to call or text me first, ya goof."

"Pish, posh. I thought it'd be better to surprise you. I mean, it's summer. What else do you have going on?"

"Jerk," I say and walk into his open arms. "I missed you."

"Miss you too, squirt."

Brandon and I separate and I look over to Angie. "It's good to see you again," I tell her.

"You, too. I told Brandon we should have called before we even left the airport."

I look over at the culprit who's wearing a mischievous grin. "At least your other half is considerate of other people."

"That's why I keep her around," he says nonchalantly as Angie and I both scoff. "Were you playing when we knocked on the door?"

"Yeah," I say and walk around them towards the living room. "Keeping my promise to Gloria no matter how hard it is."

"I heard. I'm so sorry," Brandon says with no trace of humor.

"Thank you. And to respond to your earlier retort, I do have plans. Adam and Dylan were planning to come over for dinner. But I can cancel," I start and get my phone.

"No, don't."

"Again, I told you we should have called." Angie scolds him.

Brandon looks at her like he can't decide if he wants to kiss her, choke her, or maybe both. "Why not still have them come over?"

"Really?"

"Yeah. After the way you talked about them, I want to meet them both."

I flip my phone over in my hand before pulling up Adam's name.

"Hey, sunshine," he greets.

"Hi, baby. So listen, I have some friends that just got into town unexpectedly," I say the last word pointedly at Brandon. "I know the three of us were supposed to do dinner but any chance you want to add two more? If not, I told them I could cancel."

It's been harder balancing alone time with Adam now that Dylan knows about us. So I'm hoping he doesn't cancel. Do I see the three of us living in one house? Eventually, because going to bed and waking up with Adam is a dream of mine.

"Actually, my parents are in town. I'll drop Dylan off at their house and we can make it a double date."

"Are you sure?" I ask because I know how much he loves his time with Dylan.

"Yeah, baby. I'm sure. I'll head over to your place in about an hour," Adam tells me.

"Okay. I'll see you soon."

"Bye, baby."

"He said he's good to go. He's gonna drop Dylan off at his parents," I say as I face them.

"Okay."

"So how's it going with you two?" I ask them as I sit on my couch.

Brandon pulls Angie onto his lap and I smile when I see her squirming to get up. They're so comfortable with each other and I don't think it's any type of trauma bond that connects them. But a soul-deep, this is my person type of connection that connects them.

"We told our families," Brandon drops like it's no big deal.

I choke on my inhale and cough. "How did they take it?"

Angie runs her hand through Brandon's hair and an understanding look passes between them. "They weren't happy," she starts with a mournful tone to her voice. "They yelled, told us to break up, tried to disown me–us...but we stood our ground. And we moved in together in March."

"That's amazing news," I tell them. "Have you talked to your families since?"

"No," Angie admits with tears in her eyes. "Brandon's brothers have come around to us, so at least I have them. But his parents have basically shut him out and mine don't know how to act around me. So they stay away. It's like losing Liam all over again."

Brandon gently wipes her tears away and places a kiss on her temple. He whispers something in her ear that has her smiling as well as tears falling down her face. Luckily a knock on the door pulls me away from their private moment.

I check the peephole and see it's Adam on the other side.

"Hi, handsome," I greet when I open the door to him.

"Hi, baby," he greets and crowds me against the wall as the door closes behind him. "Do you have any idea how much I miss having you all to myself?"

My hands slide up his torso and tangle in the hair at the nape of his neck. I rise onto my tiptoes and hover my lips centimeters apart from his. When we're like this the rest of the world fades from existence. Adam erases the centimeter of space and our lips connect. His hands drift. One sliding into the back pocket of my ripped jeans and the other cradling the side of my face.

A throat clearing from the living room pauses our kiss. See? The rest of the world fades from existence.

I lower from my tiptoes and press a kiss to Adam's throat. "Come meet my friends." I take Adam's hand and drag him to the living room. "Brandon, Angie, this is Adam. Adam, this is Brandon and Angie."

"Hey, man, nice to meet you," Adam holds his hand out to Brandon who takes the offered hand. "Nice to meet you," Adam tells Angie and shakes her hand as well.

"So you two started dating in secret?" Adam is baffled.

"Mm-hmm," Angie starts. "He hated me at first. Or he hated what I represented. Until he didn't hate me at all."

"Now I can't imagine her not in my life," Brandon says.

"You are such a sap." I tease him and throw my balled up napkin at him.

Brandon sticks his tongue out at me which has Adam looking between the two of us with humor.

Dinner went well. Brandon and Angie were another piece of my world that Adam got to meet. Plus it was good to see them interact.

"We should head out," Brandon says and pushes back from the table.

"Where are you guys staying?"

Adam gets up and grabs everyone's dishes.

"The Rosemont Inn," Angie announces. "It's so pretty there."

"I'll have to check it out," I tell her and I mean it. "Have you decided if you'll let Kamryn know you're in town?"

Angie chews on her bottom lip and her hesitance is warranted. "I may ask you to be a buffer if I do meet up with her."

"I won't blame you if you do."

Brandon and Adam walk over to where we're standing. He slings his arm over her shoulder, anchoring her to him.

"Let me know if you two want any company while you're in town. I'm on summer break and have nothing but time."

I'll text you, Brandon mouths to me. "Will do," he says and leans over to hug me.

I turn and hug Angie then open the door. When they're down the stairs and out of sight I turn to Adam. "So, what did you think?"

He holds his hands out to me and walks backward. "I've liked all of the people in your life. Although I am amazed how you've managed to stay in Brandon's life after James."

"I almost didn't," I confess when we sit on the couch. Adam doesn't like that I'm not close enough to him, so he manhandles me to straddle his lap.

"It was too hard," he concludes.

"Yeah," I say and fiddle with the buttons on his plaid shirt. "It was too hard."

For a long while I felt I lost not only James but his entire family. We made great strides during Thanksgiving and I call his Mom monthly.

Adam rubs his hands up my thighs, bringing my attention to him. "I heard from my lawyer."

"You did? What's the next step?"

"Thankfully, Chelsea hasn't made any more moves. But we're looking to file a protective order. So fingers crossed that halts her steps."

"Do you think that'll stop her from trying to win you back?" I hate the insecurity that drips into my question. I may have grown up shy, but never insecure.

Adam twirls my hair around his finger and I watch as thoughts swirl through his mind. "I don't want to say no. Chelsea is more determined than anyone. But you have nothing to worry about."

"Okay," I tell him, even though deep down Dylan needs his Mom and Dad. "In other news, I figured out your birthday present."

"Please tell me it's us holed up in your apartment all day. Preferably naked," Adam's eyes grow wide and I'm almost tempted to make that a date.

"No. But remind me to make that a date of ours. How do you feel about you, me, and Dylan at a baseball game?"

"I say, I love you and I'm so lucky that you're mine," he says before pulling me forward and kissing me until I'm panting.

Little did I know that the moment where we spent wrapped up in each other would come with conditions. Conditions I was not ready to bend on. How hard can you love someone until you realize it hurts you more than it heals you?

Adam

"What do you mean she's filed to have her rights reinstated? She hasn't been around in six years." I shove my hands in my hair and tug. This is not the news I wanted after an incredible birthday week.

"She's making it out so she has a solid case. Adam, can you remember any time when she reached out to be a part of Dylan's life?"

I shake my head. "Never. She specifically said that being a Mom in a small city wasn't the life for her. And that being married to me wasn't for her either."

Hearing that your wife was unsatisfied in a marriage where all I did was dote on her, stung. I loved Chelsea as best as I could. I provided for her as best as I could. But in the end, this life was not the life that she wanted. So she took the first out.

"Adam, if this goes to court, I need you to be prepared for this to get dirty. Judges usually side with the mother. But in cases like this, since you've been his primary caregiver for the last six years, that's also in your favor."

I drop down in the chair in front of his desk. "If this goes to court, how long are we looking at?"

Max shuffles through his papers. "Between three months and two years."

"Two years? Max, she's already been out of our lives for six years."

"Adam, if the parents can reach an understanding, then the court would speed this along. But she also signed her rights away when you two divorced. So we have that red tape to cut through," Max tells me pointedly. "Look, let me do my job. In the meantime I need you to keep any and all records of if and when Chelsea comes around. Keep your head straight."

~

KEEP MY HEAD STRAIGHT. Like it's so easy to do. My ex-wife wants me back. My ex-wife wants to be a mother. My ex-wife is a total pain in my ass.

I pull into my driveway and slam my head against the headrest before heading inside. My parents are in town for a while and having them here while I was at the lawyers office was a weight off my chest. Dylan also requested that Emily come over while I was out and when I walk into the living room, I find them snuggled on the couch watching *Iron Man.*

Emily and my parents meet my eyes and they read the frustration. Her eyes flick upstairs, signaling to go up there. Nodding, I see her kiss the side of Dylan's head and untangle herself from his grasp. She loves him the way a mother should. Not with conditions. But she loves him because of me. And I couldn't have asked for a better partner than Emily.

I've just made it into my bedroom when Emily comes in and closes the door. I was already at Max's office when she got here and I'm finally taking her in. The navy blue dress she wears stops just above her knees with barely there straps. Her time spent with us at the pool and regular outside summer activities has given her a golden complexion. Emily's hair falls in loose waves down her back and sways with her steps as she moves into my space.

"How did it go?" She asks and rests her hands on my waist.

I clasp my hands at the small of her back and look into the eyes of the woman I love. "Max said if we go to court it could take a minimum of three months and a maximum of two years."

"What? But what judge would even decide to take this case further? She hasn't been around in years," Emily says what I've been saying since Chelsea decided to come back and spew her nonsense.

"That's what Max said. He's hopeful we don't go to court, but if we do, I want to prepare you. If I know Chelsea like I think I do, she'll stop at nothing to tear me down."

"What could she possibly do or say that would destroy your character?"

I bring my hand up and smooth the crinkle on her forehead. "She'll say I was a neglectful husband or that I trapped her into getting pregnant. God, it sounds asinine saying it out loud."

"Baby, your fears are warranted. You've created a life here, something with Dylan that she's now kicking herself in the ass for losing. Now she's trying to come back since she's in the mood to be a parent and that disrupts the life, the beautiful balance, you've created here with Dylan."

My arms wrap around Emily as I soak in her words. "You always know the right things to say."

"I spent a year listening to people's condolences. Those words were bound to regurgitate somehow."

"Stay the night," I tell her.

"Of course, I'll stay."

~

It's a rare night when Dylan doesn't have baseball practice. Selfishly I'm glad because I get him to myself. Well, split between myself, Emily, and my parents. Dylan loves having his grandparents around and they love that they can spoil him rotten.

We're in the backyard around the firepit when Dylan asks his grandparents if they can get some ice cream.

"I don't know, buddy. It's a little late," I chime in from across the firepit.

"Please, Daddy. I promise it won't keep me awake," he gives me his puppy dog eyes that has Emily laughing into my arm.

She's no help.

I look to my parents for an assist but they hide their smiles behind their drinks.

Also no help.

My head falls back and I look up at the stars. "One scoop. And I mean one scoop." I watch as Dylan jumps up from one of the outdoor sofas and runs inside. My parents get up as well and follow after him. "Thank you!"

"You're welcome, sweetheart," my mom calls out.

Emily is still laughing beside me.

"You were absolutely no help," I say as I try and fail to sound annoyed.

"But you caved so fast," she heaves out through fading laughter. Emily's laughter dies down as she looks into the fire. "What are you scared of?"

"Losing you," I tell her.

Emily sits up and makes sure to face me. "You're not going to lose me. Why would you say that?"

"Being at the hands of Chelsea, just waiting for her next move, has me terrified that the things she says or does will tear us apart and I don't want that."

"Is she that cruel? Or do you have that little faith that I'm not with you 100%? Because I meant what I said. I am with you every step of the way. No ex-wife is going to scare me away," Emily claims.

I press my lips to hers and swallow down her gasp of surprise. Emily meets my enthusiasm and moves over to straddle my lap. My hands fall to her hips and I roughly grind her over my cock pulling a moan from her.

"Move in with me—us," I blurt.

She pulls back. Lips swollen from our kiss, eyes half-lidded, and cheeks flushed. "What?"

"I know it's fast. But you're the only one I want. You're the only one I've wanted for the last year." Am I saying this because I'm scared? Probably.

"What's wrong with what we have now?"

Yeah, Adam. What is *wrong with what you two have now?* "I thought you'd want more. But just forget about it."

"Hey," she turns my face back towards her. "Don't do that. Don't dismiss me like that. Your emotions are all over the place. You can say that they're not, but they are. Do I see us living together? Baby, of course, I do. Since that night I crossed the line that's all I've thought about." Emily leans forward and our foreheads rest against the other. "But I don't want you saying or asking me things like this when your life is changing."

"So you're saying no."

"I'm saying not right now. Adam, I am in love with you. That still scares me. Moving to the next step with you scares me."

Am I knocked down by her rejection? Yes. If my mind wasn't so clouded with lawyers and Chelsea, would I have asked Emily at this moment? Probably not. I know we've moved at a steady pace since summer started and maybe I should have brought this up in a year. Did I set us back?

Emily's body relaxes into me and I realize she's fallen asleep. Carefully, I adjust her and get up with her still in my arms. The house is quiet when we come in from the backyard and I assume they're still at the ice cream shop. With each step up the stairs, my mind thinks back. I wish I could go back and wish I never asked her to move in. She knew why I asked. Hell, I knew why I asked.

I push open my bedroom door with my foot and softly close it, maneuvering to flick the lock and close us in for the night. Walking over to Emily's side of the bed, because yes she now has her own side, I pull back the comforter and sheets then set her on the edge of the bed. She manages to stay upright, so I unclasp her sandals and pull her dress up and off her body as well as the thin bra she decided to wear but is actually useless.

"Adam," she mumbles with her eyes still closed.

I kiss her on the forehead. "Lay back, baby."

Emily lays down, resting her head on the pillow and I pull the covers over her. I round the side of the bed and strip down to my boxer briefs and climb into bed, pulling Emily into me. Her breaths even out again and she links our hands together before releasing another sigh and falling back to sleep.

~

I wake up to Emily rubbing her fingertips up and down my torso. It's still dark outside and I doubt we were asleep for long. My left arm wraps around her and I press a kiss to her forehead.

"I'm sorry," she whispers as if she's afraid to wake the house.

"Whatever for?" I ask as I run my hand up and down her arm for my comfort more than hers.

"I don't like this weirdness between us. And I know that we'll have fights and not everything is going to be a cloudless sky, but you asking me to move in disarmed me."

"No, you were right. I let my emotions take over. I shouldn't have sprung that on you. So, I'm the one who's sorry."

She weaves her leg between mine and snuggles closer, releasing a huge sigh. "I love knowing I was right."

"Oh, did you now?" I ask and move my hands to tickle her. She tries to move away but my hands are magnetized to her body. I show no mercy as I straddle her body and continue my playful assault until she calls it.

"Mercy," Emily pants out and moves her hair back off her face. Her naked chest heaves and I can't keep my eyes off of her. The air changes from playful to heavy. "Take your boxers off," Emily commands.

I slide off the edge of the bed and do as she says. My cock springs free, bobbing and bouncing off my stomach. Mercy. I'm at her mercy.

"Now climb back up here," she orders.

I obey her order and climb back up on the bed. Emily places her hands on my hips and pulls me forward. Moving my body until I'm practically sitting on her chest. She slides down until my cock bumps her chin.

"Be a good boy and grab onto the headboard," she demands before taking me in her fist and licking at the pre-cum before sucking on my tip.

"Oh, fuck, Em," I choke out as one hand lands on the headboard and the other on the top of her head. She pulls me even closer so my cock slides to the back of her throat causing her to gag. "Shit, baby, I don't want to hurt you."

Emily pulls back and my cock slides from her warm mouth. "Fuck my face, Adam. If it's too much I'll tap you on your thigh."

I'm still hovering over her, not ready to make a move.

"Come on baby. Fuck my face and paint me with your cum." She drives her point home and holds my cock in one hand and licks from root to tip all the while holding eye contact.

"Are you sure?" I ask. We haven't done anything like this. And while we're both comfortable with sex, me on top is still new.

She rubs the head of my cock against her closed lips and it sends a shiver down my spine. "I'm positive," Emily says and opens her mouth.

I push my cock inside her mouth and Emily moans around my length. The sound sends a vibration to my balls. My thrusts are slow and steady as she sucks. Using her tongue to tease the underside of my shaft and flicking the head as I pull out. A line of spit mixed with cum strings from her mouth. It's the hottest thing I've seen and I almost come on the spot.

"If I'm gonna come, it's not going to be on your body," I

start as I move down the bed and pull her underwear down, tossing them to the floor.

"No? And where do you intend to come, Mr. Montgomery?" She raises her arms above her head and pushes her chest out. Taunting me. Teasing me.

"Jesus Christ, baby," I huff out and wedge myself between her spread legs. My arms cage her in and I line myself up at her opening. "To answer your question, inside of you." I respond as I slide into her pussy.

Emily moans, a bit too loudly, so I snuff out the sound and mesh my lips to hers. She wraps a leg high around my waist and I grab onto it, hooking it over my arm and sliding deeper as my thrusts never change their pace. Her hands roam over my body while her tongue tangles with mine.

"Adam," she pants out. Her pussy starts squeezing my cock as her orgasm gets closer.

I separate from her and kneel back on my heels, taking her with me. My arms hook under her legs and I hold her to me. "I want one more. You and me, coming together. Can you do that for me, baby?" I ask her and never once break this new pace as I bounce her on my cock.

"Yes. I wanna come with you," she says and hooks her arms around my neck.

"Good girl," I praise. At this new angle, I hit a spot that has Emily biting her bottom lip I fear she's going to break the skin.

Emily moves her hand between our bodies and strums her clit. I watch her fingers play with the little nub and my balls draw up when she clenches around me.

"Adam, I'm there, baby. I need to come."

I move her hand and rub her clit. I watch in fascination as a red flush covers her body. "Come for me, baby. I'm right there with you."

Her mouth opens with a silent scream as she falls over the edge. Watching her come is a thing of beauty and pulls my orgasm. My thrusts stutter as I work us both over and over. I fall on top of Emily, careful not to put too much of my weight on her.

"I love you," Emily tells me when she's finally caught her breath.

I slide my softening cock out of her and lay to the side. "I love you, too, angel."

She kisses my hand and slides out of the bed. I watch as she pulls on my discarded shirt and heads to the bathroom.

With her, I forget about the outside world. Emily comes out of the bathroom and I slide out of bed to do the same. Her eyes trail up and down my naked body and I make sure to exaggerate a stretch.

"My eyes are up here," I tease and swat her butt as I walk into the bathroom.

I clean up and walk back into the bedroom. Emily curls up to me and her body deflates. I think of how we started and how far we've come. We may have had a misunderstanding but we got through it. I just hope that with the custody, Chelsea, and my asking her to move in, we won't fall apart.

Emily

W hen it's summer break, I rarely check my teacher's email. But with a couple of weeks left of freedom, something niggled at me to do so.

Dear Ms. Bailey,

We hope you're having an amazing summer break!

Due to staffing issues, Bennett Elementary School would like to offer you a third grade teaching position for the start of the school year. Should you accept, please report to the main office August 27, 2021 to pick up your new curriculum.

Offer details, including salary, are mentioned in the agreement that is attached to this email. Please go through the agreement and sign it accordingly.

We look forward to your acceptance and would love to have you as part of our third grade teaching staff.

Best regards,

Marlena Stukes

Cincinnati School Board Director

· · ·

THIRD GRADE. That's a big step. Sure I would love to move up and teach older minds. But I love teaching the younger ones and shaping their minds.

I pick up my phone to call Adam but stop. Since the night he asked me to move in, things have been off for us. He's still as affectionate as ever. But I fear that my refusal put a small wall between us and that's the furthest from what I want. I want us to continue on this path that we've set up for our relationship. However, I've been questioning all of my steps since James died and I don't think I can go back to who I was then. Being with Adam has been a small bandaid on a larger issue that's me.

The walls of my apartment feel like they're closing in. I snatch my car keys off the counter and sprint out the door. I don't have a true destination in mind. But when I park down the street from Kamryn's office, I know she's who I need to talk to.

I follow the familiar steps and open the door to her office. It really is a beautiful space and in an incredible location. I take the elevator up to her floor and enter mild chaos. Music hums from the hidden speakers, the sound of sewing machines a familiar sound, and through the glass walls of the conference room I see Kam conducting a meeting. My best friend is a badass.

She must see movement out of the corner of her eye and her gaze lights up. I don't want to disturb her so I point in the direction of her office. I've always been envious of her office. With the view of downtown flanked by the baseball and football stadiums, I always wonder how she can get any work done.

The woosh of her office opening sends my focus to the door.

"This is a pleasant surprise," she greets and hugs me when she gets to her desk.

Her grip loosens but I continue to hug her tighter.

"What's wrong, Emmy?" I haven't heard that nickname in so long that it brings a wave of emotions over me.

"Adam asked me to move in with him," I tell her.

"What?" She asks and pulls away from me and this time I let her. "What did you say?"

I shrug and shake my head. "He's shaken up by his ex-wife coming back into town. She wants both Dylan and Adam back. Adam went to his lawyer to see what might happen," I explain and move to sit on her couch. "I think he asked me without thinking it through. That was our first misunderstanding and I thought we moved past it. But things have just been off for us."

"Do you see yourself living with him and Dylan?"

I send a grateful smile as she hands me a bottle of water but I make no move to open it. "I do see myself living with them and we've been non-stop for the last three months, which is the next logical step. But again, with his ex, I think he was more scared than anything."

"That's not all is it?"

I can never get anything past Kamryn. Her observational skills when it comes to the people in her life are sharp.

I shake my head. "I got an email offering me a third grade teaching spot. And it's so much change. The last time I dealt with so much change, I retreated. I lost half of myself and I finally got me back."

"Do you think this change is terrifying because it could mean security?"

"What do you mean?"

Kamryn adjusts her position on the couch and turns, fully facing me. "When you were dating James, there was this surety about you. I'm not even sure you recognized it. But I did. I saw how every move was made with confidence. You may have thought something over for a few seconds, but your decision was firm when you came to it. When you lost James, that surety and security about you, left. And even with you dating Adam, I don't think you ever got it back."

"So you're saying I need to find my own sense of surety and security before I can be sure and secure with Adam?"

"Emmy, I'm a failed psychology student. What do I know?" Kamryn jokes.

But something about what she's said hits harder than it needed to.

Kam starts shaking her head. "Emily, don't do something you'll regret."

My eyes fill with tears. "I think I have to."

"You can work through what you need to with Adam by your side."

"I don't know if I can," I say as the first tear slips down my face.

Kamryn scoots closer to me and hugs me to her side. The decision to let Adam, and subsequently Dylan, go is a painful choice that I have to make to find myself.

"I'm here whenever you need me," Kamryn comforts me with a kiss on my head.

~

I GOT HOME from Kamryn's office, drained. I paced in my living room, wearing a path in the area rug as I continued to war with myself. But ultimately, the healing side of me won out.

A knock on the door halts my movement. With a deep exhale, I walk to the door and open it to Adam.

"Hi, sunshine," he greets with none of the usual pep in his voice.

This week has been tough on him. Added with a girlfriend who rejected your move in question, I have no clue how he's coping.

"Hey. Come in," I tell him and open the door wider.

I close and lock the door then walk past him and sit on the couch. He sits next to me and I'm taken back to the morning he made me pancakes. We were so timid around each other, well I was timid around him. If only we could go back and slow our progress.

"I don't like this weirdness between us," Adam breaks the silence.

My gaze lifts to his and his features fall seeing the unshed tears in my eyes. "I don't either. But I don't know how we can get past it without it hanging over our heads."

"Baby, it's no—" he starts, but I cut him off.

"So you don't get the urge to ask me to move in every day? You don't get a little upset that I turned you down?"

"Well, of course I do. But that's normal for anyone who's been rejected."

"And can they move forward without the weirdness?"

His eyes fall to the floor and I know I've hit the mark. My heart is racing and I feel like I'm going to throw up.

"Emily, I know what you're about to do. Please, don't do this."

The unshed tears fall at hearing the pain in his voice. "Kamryn reminded me that when I was younger, I was so sure of myself. Every move I made was made with confidence. And along the way, I began to feel secure with who I surrounded myself with. After James, the confidence and security went away. Until I met you."

Adam meets my tearful gaze. His beautiful forest green eyes that I love looking into aren't as vibrant and I have myself to blame for that. "Are you saying you're not confident or secure being with me?"

"I'm saying that I need to be confident and secure with myself first. And to do that, I have to make it without you. Just for a little while." Those last words come out as a whisper. Because whether or not I find myself it'll have to be without Adam.

"There's nothing I can do to change your mind?"

I shake my head as more tears fall. "I need to focus on the changes that are happening to me. And you need to focus on Dylan."

He drops his head to the back of the couch. I wish, more than anything, that I could deal with changes like a normal person. But change has always made me run scared. I just hate that this change is making me run from Adam.

IN THE DAYS following Adam leaving my apartment, I've cleaned my apartment from top to bottom three times. I've also been non-stop crying but let's not talk about that.

A knock on the door stops me from scrubbing the shower in my guest bedroom. At least I think it's a knock on the door so I go back to cleaning. Until I hear it again. Standing up, I whip off my cleaning gloves and walk to the front door. The knock on the door starts again and with a huff, I open the door.

All of the annoyance leaves my body when I see who's

on the other side. "Mom? Dad? What are you two doing here?"

"Kamryn called us," my mom says as they step into my apartment. "Your best friend may still be a virtual stranger to us after all these years. But even through the phone, I can tell how much she loves you. And she told us that you might have broken up with Adam."

My eyes water as I stand in front of my parents like a scorned child. "And what? You two thought you could give your parental advice. I never got that from you before."

"And we will pay for that for the rest of our lives," my dad says and looks at me with concern. "Emily, why did you break up with Adam?"

"Because I couldn't handle it, okay?"

"Handle what, sweetheart?"

"Change! Okay? I can't handle change!" I yell as the tears fall down my face. "I never handled it well as a kid and I clearly can't handle it as an adult."

"What's changing, sweetheart?" My mom asks.

"Everything. Adam asked me to move in, he's about to be in a custody battle with his ex-wife, and I got a third grade teaching offer. All of those came one after the other and it was like my system went into shutdown mode."

My dad looks at me knowingly. "And you thought if you could eliminate two of those changes the third wouldn't be so bad."

My gaze falls to the floor and I nod like a child being punished.

"Emily, you are adaptable," my mom starts as she holds my face in her smooth hands. "And maybe that's on us for making that happen when you were a kid." She wipes away the tears that won't stop. "But running away from these changes won't make them go away. They'll still be there if you and Adam give it another shot."

"What if I screwed it up?"

"Honey, he flew all the way to New York when you told him not to. If you asked, I'm sure he would be waiting once the changes ironed themselves out."

My lips tremble as I remember the broken look on his face. "You didn't see his face."

"If it looks anywhere remotely close to what yours looks like I'm sure it'd be like looking in a mirror."

I can't even muster a smile. At that moment, I knew the decision I was making was a bad one. But at the time I was so sure it was the right one.

Adam

I've been an irritable asshole. My parents told me my words have consequences. I thought they were joking and used it as a scare tactic. Turns out they were right. Parents usually are.

Chelsea is still holding strong. We've tried mediation but that got us nowhere. Now we're waiting on a court date. So, yeah. Between Emily putting a pause, or a break, on us I've been an asshole. Maybe she was right to make that call. But she made the decision for me.

The only place I'm barely an asshole is at work. And I mean barely. I tend to stay in my office the majority of the time I'm there. But today I've decided to help out at the bar. It's not so busy for a Tuesday night, which isn't unusual. But it's summer.

Movement from the corner of my eye takes me in that direction. And the last person I expected to come into my place of work was Mason Brooks. I don't move from where I'm polishing a glass that's spotless. I know it's rude of me and I have a hunch I know what he's about to say.

He takes a seat in front of me and waits until he recognizes I'm not about to say anything. "You know I broke up with Kamryn in college?"

My eyes fly up to him above the glass to see his gaze firmly fixed on me. Other patrons have started whispering about the Bengals QB being in my restaurant. But still, he pays them no mind.

"I know. How could a couple so perfect have broken up?" Mason makes a joke.

I put the clean glass back and grab another, filling it up with ice water and placing it in front of him.

Mason huffs out a breath, his hands encircling the glass. "I had my reason for doing it. But it doesn't mean that decision didn't affect me."

"Why are you telling me this?"

"My fiancé came home from work frustrated with a decision her best friend was thinking of making. I couldn't see it at the time because I thought things just weren't working out. But then Rynny compared it to our break up."

"No offense," I start and pick up another glass to polish. "But our situations are nothing alike."

"You're right. They're nothing alike. But the pain is all the same."

I look at Mason and the haze from my heartache clears just a little. "I miss her more than anything. And maybe... maybe she was right to break us up. Maybe I should have prepared her for what's to come."

"Do you love her?"

"More than anything," I confess.

"Then hold onto that."

~

I GET HOME from work exhausted. Being angry does me no good. Missing Emily does me no good either. But being angry has also kept the fight for my son alive.

I see Jenny on the couch with her Kindle in hand. "How was he?"

"Good," she answers with a tight smile.

I fall on the far side of the couch with a bone-weary sigh.

Jenny stands up from the couch and heads toward the guest bedroom. "Adam?"

I turn my head towards her in a sign of acknowledgment.

"For what it's worth, I'm rooting for the both of you."

I let her words sit a little. Mason's words from earlier come back. To hold onto the love that I have for Emily in hopes that we can be better than the before.

"Goodnight, Jenny," I say after a few seconds from my spot on the couch.

"Night, Adam."

Jenny retreats to the guest room and I bask in the silence of my house. I get up and wander over to the bar and pour myself a double shot of whiskey before heading out to the backyard. Every spot out here is tainted with Emily's touch. In the few months we were together, we were wrapped up every chance we got.

Did we move too fast? Did I push her? No, that couldn't have been the case. She was all in as much as I was.

Dylan starts school tomorrow. I can't believe I'm about to have a second grader. I whip out my phone to text Emily but stop. She hasn't reached out and I need to respect that. I knock back the rest of my drink and head to bed.

~

My ALARM GOES off way too early. The pounding in my head from the whiskey does nothing to help either.

Throwing my feet over the side of the bed, I blindly walk to the bathroom to take care of business. I throw on a pair of jeans with a long-sleeved henley and push the sleeves up to my elbows. I'm walking downstairs to the tune of the morning news along with Dylan and Jenny talking animatedly.

"Morning, buddy. Excited for your first day?" I ask and kiss him on the top of the head before heading to pour myself a cup of coffee.

"Yeah. But what if I don't know anyone in my class?"

I take a healthy sip of the strong bean water and sit next to Dylan. "I'm sure you'll know plenty of kids in your class. Sandra said Jackson is supposed to be in your class."

"Oh, yeah," Dylan says like he forgot. Which, to be fair, he probably did forget.

"You're good to take him to school?" Jenny asks while she puts her books in her backpack.

"Yeah, all good. Get to class."

"Okay. Bye, Dylan. Have a great first day. I want to hear all about it when you get home."

"Bye," he says around a mouthful of cereal.

I look at my little boy who has no idea of the changes that have happened. He thinks Emily got another job because that's what I told him when she stopped coming over. The lying hurts. The hurting hurts.

The time on the clock reveals it's time to go. And I think I'm more nervous than Dylan.

"Time to go kiddo. Go get your shoes on," I order as I put his bowl in the sink and pack up his lunchbox.

"Here's your shoes, Daddy." Dylan drops my boots with a thud by my barstool.

I smirk as I walk to them and slide them on. "Thanks, buddy."

Three minutes later we are out of the house with the windows down and the music playing a radio classic. Dylan chitter-chatters over the music like he hasn't spoken in a year in the backseat. I don't respond because he's always chattering away. We pull into the backed-up school drop-off line and my heart is in my throat. I have no clue if Emily does drop-offs because we never talked about that part of her life.

I'm an idiot.

My hands sweat and I grip the steering wheel tighter as we inch closer to the entrance. Our truck and two others are the next bunch for drop-offs. When we get to the front of the line, I see her. My gaze hones in on her like a laser beam. As soon as I stop the truck Dylan opens the door to leave.

"Hey, mister!" I call out and tap my cheek for a kiss before he hops out of my truck.

Dylan pecks my cheek with a slobbery kiss and I'm a bad father if I say that my focus has been on Emily the entire time. Does she think about me?

She gives Dylan a warm smile when he walks over to her. I never thought I'd be jealous of my kid. But I am.

I wait for her to look back up and when she does, I give her a small smile and a wave before I'm driving away from the school.

Stupid. Stupid. Stupid.

I check my email while at a stoplight and see an email from Max. Reading the contents of the email, I get to the end and see a date.

"December?!" I screech when he answers the phone.

"I did my best to avoid going to court. But Adam, she's

making a good enough case," Max tries his best to calm me over the phone.

"She's not even thinking about Dylan and how this could affect him," I say as I throw my head back against the headrest. "So what next?"

If Chelsea *were* thinking about Dylan, which I know she's not, then maybe I could excuse her actions. But I can't.

"CPS will come and do an interview and they'll inspect Dylan's home life."

I grind my back teeth so hard they might crack. "Who's getting interviewed?"

"You and Dylan."

"He's just a kid, Max," I say as I swallow around the ball of emotions clogging my throat.

"I know Adam. I hate that this is happening to you. The court has assigned a social worker to your case. It's standard for cases like this."

Max explains what's to happen next, but I black it out. December. We go to court in December. It's then that I'll let a judge listen to whatever lies Chelsea spews. I won't let her take my son. She may have birthed him. But I was the one to love and care for him unconditionally. He's mine. And he always will be mine.

Emily

Two months. It's been two months without Adam. Oh, I've seen him every morning for school drop-off. And every single day my heart aches with the need to be with him. To run my hands through his shoulder-length hair. To stare into those forest green eyes that are identical to his son's. To trace the tattoos that cover his body.

I miss him more than words can explain.

In these two months without him, I finally started seeing a therapist. It was long overdue and the girls told me exactly that.

The sessions have been painful. We went back to the beginning. Back to the root of my issues. My parents, their abandonment and neglect during my childhood. We talk about James and how, because my parents weren't around, I developed an attachment style relationship with him. Did I confuse attention with love? No. I loved James. No one can dispute that.

I'm packing up my things at the end of the day when Melissa stops by.

"Hey, stranger," she greets me when she's at my door.

"Ugh, I miss having my classroom across from yours." I tell her as I go to hug her.

"Ditto. So how's life?"

I move back to my desk and blow out a breath. "It's going. How are you and your beau?"

"We're good. We finally set a wedding date."

"That's incredible," I tell my friend with a forced smile.

"Thanks. Tell me how you're really doing."

"Like I wanna cry every second of every day. But I can't," I say as emotion takes over and clogs my throat.

Melissa looks at me the way a mother would comfort a child. "Is there any way you could fix it?"

"Maybe," I whisper.

I GET HOME from work an hour later with a large pepperoni pizza and a bottle of wine tucked firmly in my grasp. I'm walking up the stairs when I see my girls waiting for me in front of my door with two more pizza boxes and a bottle of tequila.

"What are you three doing here?"

"Getting you out of your funk," Kam declares.

They move aside when I hold up my keys to unlock the door. We all meander inside and head towards the kitchen.

"I'm not in a funk," I argue back when I set the food down.

"You're so in a funk!" The three of them yell.

I turn and dump my bags on the chair in the living room and turn towards my girls. "I don't know what I feel."

"You're me in college," Kamryn says and pours us all chilled shots of tequila ignoring the wine I bought.

Sarah claps her hands which makes me jump. "That's who you remind me of."

I move to the kitchen and pick up a shot glass, downing the tequila with barely a wince. Kamryn eyes me warily and I motion for another shot.

"So, I'm in a funk," I admit after my second shot.

"We know, sweetie. That's why we're here."

I bend over to take my heels off. Anything to keep my hands busy. "I miss Adam. But I'm still working on myself and I heard that he has his court hearing in December. How selfish would I be if I just waltzed back into his life after turning it inside out?"

Jax gathers the boxes of pizza and places them on my dining table. The greasy, delicious smell of pizza beckons me, and I wander to the table and sit. I pick up and chew a slice while the girls take their seats.

"Did you know Mason went to visit Adam at his restaurant?"

"No. When?" I ask Kam.

She puts her half-bitten slice of pizza back in the box and dusts her hands off. "About a week after you two broke up. Mason said he was cold towards him. Which I didn't think was possible with the way he fawned over him when they first met. But what Mason could tell was that he's miserable without you."

I stare into the box of pizza hoping it'll give me my answer. The traitorous slices give me nothing.

"I don't even know if he'd want to hear from me," I whine. I know that's far from the truth. But I keep seeing his look of defeat that day when I called us off. I vowed to never be the person to put that look on anyone's face. Yet I did with the man I'm head-over-heels in love with.

"Oh, she figured it out," someone chimes.

My gaze is unfocused as I think of the steps that are five in front of me instead of the one I need to get to first. "I need to go to his restaurant."

"Atta, girl," Sarah says from next to me. "Jax put the pizza in the fridge. We're going to help Emily get her man back."

~

WE GET to Monty's and I tell Sarah to park her car next to Adam's truck. We get out of her car and the girls walk forward but my feet won't move.

"Em?"

"I'm nervous. And this also feels like a full circle moment for him and me," I say and pace in the parking lot.

Kamryn rounds back to me and loops her arm through mine. "I know it's hard."

"Easy for you to say. You're wearing the ring," I note as I look down at the rock on her finger. Mason finally proposed to Kamryn in the house he bought for them a couple of months ago. We all knew it was coming. We just weren't sure of when.

"I am. And you could too," she pleads. By her side, I didn't realize we were walking until we stopped at the entrance. From here I can't make out a crowd. And I'm assuming that since it's October that it's not busy. "Em, life is easier when you have someone in your corner. Helping you fight the bad days and cheering you on through the good days. We both know it's not easy, but Adam loves you. He wouldn't be the one if he didn't let you remember James in a healthy way. He wouldn't be the one if he didn't love you, and he does."

I turn to look at Kam and I see Sarah and Jax waiting for

my next move. I untangle myself from Kam and stand in front of the door.

With a deep breath, I open the door and look for the man who still owns my heart. I wait for my eyes to adjust to the dim lighting and then I see him. Standing behind the bar like he was just a year ago. Only this time it's utter confusion on his face.

"Hi," I greet him and the mostly empty restaurant.

Adam says nothing, but his eyes say everything. *I miss you. I love you. Why did you push me away?*

"Okay," I murmur and move a step closer to where he's at. "I got scared. I hate change. And so much change was happening that I needed to find my footing on the ground before I ultimately destroyed everything in my path. To do that, I needed less in my life."

His eyebrows fly to his hairline and I'm realizing how that sounded.

"No, Adam," I plead and walk closer to the bar. "You are more. You are the more in my life." I wait and see for my words to process. And when I see that they have I continue. "I've been seeing a therapist. We dug deep. It was painful. But it really does go back to my parents. And how I developed an attachment style relationship with James and I didn't want that to carry over to you. To us. So I needed to re-evaluate my life before you and I could finally ride off into the sunset. I love you. I am in love with you. I see the future with you and Dylan. I see more kids—our kids. Adam, I love you. And if I need to go through change like a butterfly, then I'd rather do it with you."

I finish my speech out of breath. I glance around and see I've gathered the attention of those in the bar. And I wait. Wait for Adam to acknowledge all that I've said. Wait for Adam to move from behind the bar. I wait. Now I know what rejection feels like. So with as much dignity as I have left, I send him a half-smile, tap on the bar, and walk out the door.

The girls are waiting on pins and needles when I come out and I just shrug. I'm about to open my mouth to tell them what didn't happen when I hear the door open behind me.

"Emily!" Adam shouts as he runs towards me.

"Adam, I don't really feel like reliving–" I'm cut off when he kisses me; a breath-stealing, heart-stopping, earth-shattering kiss. Our lips meld together and all of the tension flows out of my body. He teases my lips with his tongue and I open to him, gladly. His tongue dances with mine and I feel like I can't get close enough to him. My hands slide into the back pockets of his jeans and I hold him to me. No inch of space threatens to separate us.

The girls whooping behind us disrupt us from our reunion.

"I'm sorry," I tell him when our lips are no longer mashed together. "If it's any consolation I was an absolute mess."

"That does make me feel slightly better. But all is forgiven, baby," Adam drops his forehead to mine. "Just promise if you run, you take me and Dylan with you."

"Deal."

Throats clearing behind me has our attention pulled to our friends. Adam wraps his arms around my shoulders and rests his head on top of mine.

"So since we delivered her here, do we get a drink?" Sarah asks.

Adam

Irritable asshole who? That was me. And I have some people to apologize to. But first I need to take Emily home. Seeing her in the passenger seat of my truck brings a sense of peace that I didn't know existed until she wasn't there.

"What are you thinking?" Emily asks when we're at a stop light.

I rest my head back on the headrest and angle my head towards her. "How I like having you back in my passenger seat."

She grabs my hand that's resting on the center console and links our fingers together. "I like it too," she says shyly.

"Don't get shy on me." I tell her.

"You don't like me shy?"

"I like you mine." I admit and she turns her head towards the window, but I don't miss her cheeks lifting with a smile.

The drive back to her place is comfortable. And one I missed these past two months. As much as I hate to admit it, this time apart was necessary. It hurt like hell to not be with

Emily, but I needed it to get all of my ducks in a row regarding the custody case.

I flip the turn signal and turn into Emily's neighborhood. I do love this area for her. But I still want her to move in with me. That's not something that'll stop niggling in the back of my mind. I pull into the parking lot and park next to her car. And I get deja vu all over again. This flashback specifically from the morning I made her pancakes.

"How's everything going with custody?" Em asks from next to me. She takes off her seatbelt and rests against the door.

"About as good as can be expected. CPS came out last week which sent me into a freakout. Thankfully my parents came back into town."

"That's good," Emily says but hesitates. "And Chelsea? Any word on her?"

"She's petitioning to get her parental rights reinstated." Saying it aloud makes me as angry as when Max told me she filed.

Emily huffs out a heavy exhale. "I'll have no faith in the justice system if any judge reinstates her rights. Claiming you want to be a mother doesn't erase the fact that she left. She willingly left you and Dylan."

I turn to Emily. "I love that you're so passionate about this."

"I'm passionate about parents wanting their kids," she claims.

"I know you are."

"What does Dylan know?" Emily asks and moves forward to lean on the center console.

"Not much. I'm doing my best to shield him from the worst."

"That's what makes you an incredible father."

"Thanks, baby," I say and lean forward to kiss her on the forehead. My stomach droops with butterflies. Yes, men get butterflies. "So what do we do now?"

"Well, first I need to alert the school that I'm dating a student's father. And then we take it slow until your court date."

I loop a tendril of her hair around my finger. The silky smooth fibers slip through my fingers. "And then what?"

"I'm putting the ball in your court," Emily tells me with a smile.

"So if I ask you to move in again, are you going to say no?"

"Ask me again in two months," she volleys back and leans forward, sealing our lips together. My hand slides into the hair at the nape of her neck and I hold her there as I claim her mouth for the second time tonight. Emily is putty in my hands as my tongue slides between her lips. The moan she lets out when our tongues dance is still one of my favorite sounds from her.

My other hand travels down her torso and my thumb finds her pointed nipple threatening to be touched through her shirt. I apply pressure with my thumb and swallow down Emily's gasp. I almost come in my pants when she sucks my bottom lip between her teeth.

I fly back from her because this is not how I want our reunion to be. "Okay, that's enough."

"You started it," she says. Her eyes are wild and her lips are swollen from my assault.

"I know. And now I'm stopping it."

"Ever the gentleman," she states as she bends and gets her purse.

"Stay the night this weekend."

She leans forward and pecks my lips. "Yes."

~

IT'S BEEN three days since Emily knocked me on my ass and came back into my life. When I got home from dropping her off, Jenny assumed something good happened based on the smile that wouldn't leave my face.

Now I'm picking Dylan up from school which is rare as he chooses to ride the bus. I'm standing at the front of my truck waiting for him to appear. The bell ringing from the school sounds and my heart races. Is Emily on pick-up duty? This really is something we should discuss. Because getting even a small glimpse of her in her element is such a mind trip.

The school doors open and surprisingly, he's the first one out. His backpack flops against his back as he runs to my truck.

"Did you run out of class, buddy?" I ask him.

"No."

"Okay," I say and move to open his door for him. I take his backpack and let him climb up. Popping his bag in the middle seat, I close the door and round the truck. As soon as I open the door, I see Emily standing there with kids swarming around her as they walk to their parents' cars. She wears a long skirt with a cream sweater tucked into the front and what Jenny calls "booties" on her feet. If I could take her picture without looking like a creep I would, so I send her a wink instead and get a bashful smile out of her. Emily sends a small, last-minute wave as I pull away from the curb and head to the house.

"Hey, Dylan?" I ask when we're almost home and look at him in the rearview mirror.

"Yeah, Daddy?"

I focus back on the road. "How would you feel about Ms. Emily coming over tonight?"

"Is she your girlfriend again?" His question floors me.

"What do you know about girlfriends?"

"Well," he begins and this should be interesting. "A kid in my class has a girlfriend but she got mad at him until he brought her a piece of chocolate and said they're boyfriend-girlfriend again."

I cover my laugh with a snort. "Well, that's not exactly how it worked for us. But, yes, Emily is my girlfriend again. Are you okay with that?"

"She makes you happy. And you haven't been happy in a while."

Well, damn. They say kids are intuitive, but they never say how intuitive until you have a kid of your own.

"When did you get so smart?" I ask, not expecting a response.

"Since I turned seven," he responds with a toothless smile.

Shaking my head and trying not to laugh, I take the turn into our neighborhood. An unfamiliar car is parked by the mailbox. It's not unusual, but with Chelsea sniffing around my senses are on overload. I continue on and pull into the driveway, checking the rearview mirror every other second until I'm parked.

"How about pizza tonight?" I ask Dylan.

"Can we watch the new Marvel movie too?"

I think about which one he hasn't seen and figure it's safe enough for him to watch. "Sure. But when I say plug your ears, you plug your ears. Got it?"

"Got it, Daddy."

"Okay. Get your stuff and let's head inside." I park and

turn the truck off, then wait for Dylan to meet me around the front of the truck. Footsteps that aren't Dylan's sound behind me and I turn to face Chelsea.

"Daddy, who is that?" Dylan asks when he's next to me.

"No one buddy." I tell him and hand him my keys. "Go inside and start your homework. I'll be there in a minute."

I watch Dylan walk up to the door and head inside the house. I subtly move so I'm blocking the front door. "What are you doing here, Chelsea?"

"He's beautiful," she claims.

"Again, what are you doing here?"

Emily picks the perfect time to pull into my driveway. I should've texted her to come at a later time.

Chelsea looks at Emily's approaching car and turns back to me. "It seems I've been replaced."

"Replacing means something was there to begin with. I won't ask my question again."

"I talked to my lawyer and I'm dropping my petition to reinstate my parental rights. Your lawyer already knows so you should be getting an email from him soon. It was a mistake to come here and threaten the world you've created. And to try and win you back." She turns her head and looks at Emily still sitting in her car. "It seems you have everything you need here."

"Not that I really care, but why change your mind? Do you know the hell I've been through?" To see she's just giving up after the strain it put on my relationship.

"And I'm sorry for that. You've given him a life. You've loved him the way a parent should. As much as I wish I was, I'm not capable of that," she admits what I knew from the beginning.

I look towards Emily and see she's waiting for a sign that

I need her. I'll always need her. But this right here is what I need to do alone.

"Goodbye, Chelsea. Hope you have a nice life," I tell her. I mean that and hope she never comes back.

"Goodbye, Adam," she says and I see the finality in her expression.

Chelsea turns and walks back down to the driveway entrance. And a sense of relief has me breathing like I'm free. Free from the fear of Dylan being taken away from me. Free to finally live my life with two of the people I love most in the world.

Emily finally gets out of her car with her bags hanging off her shoulder. "Are you okay, baby?"

I pull her to me and wrap my arms around her as I look over the face I've memorized and could draw from memory. "Yeah, baby. I'm okay." I kiss her on the forehead and take her bags from her. And really, I am okay. Chelsea eradicating herself for good means I can move forward and not stress wondering if she'll return.

Emily and I walk up the front steps and into the house. The TV blaring greets us and I knew I should have stipulated that Dylan could watch TV after he does his homework. We take our shoes off and line them along the wall and I drop her bags off at the foot of the stairs.

"Dyl, did you start your homework?" I call out as we walk down the hall towards the living room.

"Stern, Daddy," Emily whispers and I smack her on the butt as I pass her.

I see Dylan scramble off the couch and head to the kitchen table. "What did I tell you? Homework first and then TV."

"Sorry, Daddy," he says and attempts to throw his puppy dog eyes at me. I lift an eyebrow to show I'm unaffected. His expression lifts when Emily pops out from behind me. "Ms. Emily," he gushes and runs to her.

She meets his enthusiasm and pulls him into her arms. "I missed you, buddy."

"Are you and Daddy, boyfriend and girlfriend again?"

"We are," she claims.

"Good. Because Daddy was grouchy without you here."

"Way to sell me out, dude," I feign offense and move to tickle him.

"Hey, no tickling him," Emily scolds me. She puts Dylan down and kisses the top of his head. "Go do your homework and let me know if you need help."

I stand and watch their interaction with a full heart. How much Dylan loves Emily is a thing of beauty and I'm hopeful to see more interactions like this in the future.

"Plug your ears, Dylan," I tell him. Okay, this movie was a bad choice for little ears. I look over and see Emily plug his ears. Yes, the little snake stole my woman. The smirk Em threw my way when Dylan cuddled up next to her made me want to ground him.

But this is good. Their getting along is what I was nervous about the most. It helped that we all had a summer together.

The movie nears the end and I look over at Dylan asleep in Emily's arms. I roll off the couch and move towards her, bending down to pick him up and carry him upstairs. My steps are sure and Dylan doesn't wake once. Luckily, I had him take a bath before we turned on the movie so I lay him down in his bed and tuck him in. With a kiss on his forehead, I back out of his room and shut the door.

I walk down the hallway with the intention of heading back downstairs. But I see the light peek from under my closed bedroom door and know my girl is in there. I open the door to my room and see Emily with her feet up on the couch in front of the window, scrolling on her phone.

"Move in with us," I say as I sit down on the couch.

"Baby, I told you to ask me again in two months."

I take her hands in mine and pull her up onto my lap as her legs go on either side of my hips. "What difference does two months make? Besides, now that Chelsea has given up, neither of us have that added stress or fear hanging over our heads."

Her hands trail up my chest and I can't stop the shiver that works its way through me. "Why are you really asking me? I mean I know I expected this to pop up maybe next year. But why now?"

"Because I want to make a life together," I start and clarify when her eyebrows raise. "Not in the baby sense, although that too," I say as I lock my hands around her waist. "I want this life with you. I want movie nights, date nights, long days at the ballpark with Dylan, and lazy days in bed. I want to watch from the kitchen as you serenade the world with your violin. You told me to find yourself that you needed to make it without me for a little while. And I'm glad that time worked for us. But, baby, I can't make it without you. I don't want to. So move in with us and make us a family."

Emily leans forward and presses her lips to mine. Her tongue licks at my lips and I willingly open, moaning into her mouth as our tongues collide. "If you ask me to move in, you're also asking for Biscuit to break your no-pet rule."

"You two are a packaged deal. Wait, are you saying yes?"

She nods her head in quick succession. "Yes, I'll move in with you."

I capture her lips in mine and carry us over to the bed where neither of us comes up for air for the rest of the night.

Emily
Five Months Later

My phone dings with a text from Brandon. I open it and squeal when I see a picture of him and Angie with matching wedding bands. I exit my car and walk towards Adam's restaurant.

"You can't just spring a picture like that on someone," I say when he picks up the phone.

"Yeah, well if you'd answer my phone calls you'd know that we got married last month."

I stop outside of Monty's. "Shut up!"

Brandon's chuckle comes through the phone. "I know. We'll tell you all about it when we're up there next week."

"Oh, thank you for letting me know this time," I deadpan.

"Angie made me."

"I'm sure she did. Well I'm about to walk into Adam's restaurant but I'll see you next week."

"Okay. Bye, Em," he says.

I put my phone in my back pocket with a smile and open the door with a screech. The lights are off, but in their place are flameless candles, rose petals, and *Lana Del Rey* crooning softly over the speakers.

"Adam," I breathe out.

"I planned to do this at home, but this is where we began," he says from behind me.

I turn around and see him down on one knee. Dressed in jeans and a flannel like that day at the parent-teacher conference, but this time he's holding a ring box.

"A year ago you wiped the line away. A year ago, you decided to give this single dad a chance. I feel like I've given you plenty of speeches in our time together. But this one ends with a crucial question. Will you marry me?" He asks and opens up the ring box.

"Yes," I tell him as if I would say anything else.

Adam slides the ring on my finger and I don't even know how it looks on my finger because all I see is him.

"She said yes!" Adam cheers and our friends and family pour out from the kitchen and the patio.

Now I can't stop the tears from falling. "You did this for us?"

"No, baby," Adam tells me and wraps me in his arms. "I did this for you. Because you deserve to be celebrated every single day."

I rise up on my tiptoes and murmur, "I love you," against his lips before sealing our new future together.

Epilogue

Emily - Three Years Later

Gurgling and little legs kicking from the bassinet signals that my little girl is awake.

"James Rose, what are you doing awake?" I coo as I bend over carefully to pick her up. I settle into the glider that's in our bedroom and feed my baby girl.

When we found out I was pregnant with a girl, I asked Adam if he ever thought of girl names. His response was that he never thought he'd have a daughter and that I should be the one to name her. So I chose James. Named after one of the most impactful people to ever come into my life. Adam looked at me and said James Rose and that was that. Our little girl had her name.

Some would say Adam and I moved fast. But I think we moved at just the right pace. Soon after we got engaged we went right into wedding planning. But after a month of putting off the actual planning, we decided on an intimate backyard wedding. And in the early winter afternoon,

Adam and I exchanged vows in front of our family and closest friends.

How did Dylan take us getting married? He was over-joyed and immediately moved into calling me mom. Of course, I cried when he first called me that. And when Adam asked if I wanted to adopt Dylan as my own, I cried for a week straight.

My heart is full of love with my three heartbeats. I wouldn't have it any other way.

~

Adam - Two Years Later

I am one lucky son of a gun. I have an incredible wife, who only gets more breathtaking as the years go by. A lively son, who is, God help me, about to go into high school. Dylan still loves his *Marvel* and *Transformers* marathons with Emily. I have a vivacious little girl who has me wrapped around her little finger. James is about as mobile as one can get at two years old. She inherited her mother's delicate nose, but the eyes are all Montgomery much to my wife's dismay. Emily claims our eyes are her weakness so we make sure to use them on her as much as possible.

Me: Dylan is spending the night at Jackson's house.

Me: And your parents took James for the weekend.

Emily: Are you saying what I think you're saying?

> Me: First solo date night in three years. Get home soon, baby.

> Emily: Leaving the grocery store now.

My wife gets home fifteen minutes later to a glass of wine with a heavy pour and steaks cooking on the grill.

"Are you recreating our date from all those years ago?" Emily asks as she wraps her arm around my waist.

"If I say I am, are you going to tease me?"

"Not in the slightest," she tells me and goes to sit at the table.

The food finishes just minutes later and we eat in comfortable silence. It's a welcome silence without the kids rushing us to finish our food.

Emily pushes her almost empty plate away and sips down more wine. Something is niggling at the back of her mind. I can tell.

"What's on your mind, baby?"

"I want another baby," she blurts out.

That is not what I thought she was going to say. I mean, I'm in my mid-forties, so it's not impossible. "Are you sure?"

"Yeah," she starts. "Just one more. If it happens, it happens. I know I've said our family is complete, but lately, I've felt like we're missing a piece."

I nod my head subtly. "Okay."

"Okay?"

"Yes, baby. I've felt the same but didn't want to push you on the topic."

"You mean we could've been already trying for another baby?" She asks incredulously. Emily scoots back from the table and walks over to my side. Her hands weave through my shoulder-length hair and she tugs, angling my head back. "You are something else, Mr. Montgomery."

Shivers work through my body when she calls me that. My hand drifts up between her legs and under her dress. "This the game you wanna play?"

Her mouth parts when my fingers ghost over her pussy and the warmth from her heat has me biting down on my back teeth. "Is the game where you get me pregnant?"

"No games, baby."

Our lips hover in front of the others. I swallow down her pants as I continue teasing her. Emily lets out a groan of frustration and I hold back a smirk. She grabs my hand and pulls me inside with her. I willingly let her drag me upstairs. As soon as we're in our room she closes the door and slams me up against it, fusing her mouth to mine.

"No games, my ass," she starts as she lifts my shirt up my torso and tosses it behind her. "You, Adam Joseph Montgomery, are a liar. Now, our kids are gone for the weekend and I haven't had an uninterrupted night of sex with my husband in a very long time."

Emily backs away and unzips her dress, letting the fabric pool around her feet and leaving her in nothing but a dark blue lace set. I step towards her but she stops me with a finger.

"Pants off," she orders.

I do her bidding because I'm desperate to be inside my wife. At the same time, she reaches behind her and unclasps her bra. Letting the straps loosen off her shoulders before she's bare to me.

I take a step towards her and don't stop until I'm right in front of her. Her pointed nipples graze my chest with every deep inhale. My hand sinks into her hair and I tip her head back, forcing her to meet my gaze. "On the bed and spread your legs."

She does as I say and crawls on the bed. Laying back she

spreads her legs in invitation. I round the bed so I'm standing in the middle with an unobstructed view and crawl up after her.

My hands trail up her legs and grip the waistband of her panties, drawing them down her legs and tossing them to the floor. I settle between her and grab her legs, holding them up and apart. My painfully hard cock bobs against my stomach and I see her pussy glistening with her arousal.

"Don't tease me, baby," Emily heaves out.

"Me?" I question as I line up at her entrance and slide into her pussy with a groan. "Never."

Emily reaches for me and I slide even deeper inside of her. I slow my pace as I make love to my wife. She's been my other half for almost a decade. We've made this home I built with Dylan impenetrable. We've filled this home with more life and love than I ever thought possible.

Later that night, with Emily asleep on my chest and the night sky the backdrop to our world, I look down at the woman who waltzed into my bar completely heartbroken. And I look at her now, as my wife and mother to our beautiful kids.

"Make it without you?" I scoff quietly and pull Emily closer. She tightens her hold on me and I press a kiss to her head. "Baby, my world begins and ends with you."

Acknowledgments

For those of you who were in my DMs wanting Emily to get her HEA, I hope it was worth it. I loved diving into these characters. The breaking and healing is what this series is about.

Thank you to my cover designer, Kimberly, you continue to knock it out of the park. I know this is only the second cover between the two of us but your talent is insane. Thank you for bringing this book to life and for your incredible friendship.

Thank you to my alpha readers, Kalie, Mia, Sammie, and Caitlin; you four were instrumental in me getting this book right.

Thank you to my beta readers, Kaitlyn, Kendra, Miriam, and Tiffani; thank you for your feedback and help in letting me know what did and did not work.

To my ARC Team: I can't express how much I adore you all and your excitement for this book.

Thank you to Jess at TrulyYours PR for handling my ARCs. You made this release a breeze.

To you, the reader, thank you for taking a chance on an indie author's second book. If you would be so kind to leave a review on Amazon, it would be much appreciated.

To paraphrase what Taylor Swift said, "This story isn't mine anymore."

About the Author

Elleese Black is a thirty-something millennial. With a degree in Psychology she took her love of the subject to diving into fictional characters. She grew up reading romance books with swoon and tears, fortunately they all end with a happily ever after.

When she's not writing or working, she's a cat mom to two zany black cats, taking a CycleBar class, reading when she shouldn't, or doom scrolling until the wee hours of the night.

Elleese loves to hear from readers. So send her a DM on Instagram (@elleeseblack.author), she'll love it.

Newsletter

Also by Elleese Black

The Night We Met

Make It Without You

Book 3 - TBA

Book 4 - TBA

9 798991 773508